Copyright 2021 for David Owain Hughes

Cover design by Red Cape Graphic Design

Second Edition Published 2021 by Red Cape Publishing

The characters and events in this book are fictitious. Any similarities to real persons, living or dead, is coincidental and not intended by the author.

South by Southwest Wales

Book One

David Owain Hughes

Chapter 1

Samson was sat at the bar, hunched over his whisky on the rocks. Old Bushmills was his favourite brand and the Jazz Hole was the only joint in town that served it, which just happened to be his kind of place in the ever-modernising 1940s Chicago.

He frequented the Hole most evenings, where he burned his pay and listened to the new talent. Hell, if he could afford to live at the small club then he would; but the only room for rent was the bottom of a whisky bottle, which he could barely afford anyway.

Samson was nursing his eighth whisky and was down to his last yard in beer tokens. With his bills paid, the rest of his mazuma was his to do with as he pleased.

Business was bad for washed-up private eyes like Samson. Work had all but dried up. For the last two years, he'd struggled to find jobs just to keep his business afloat.

"Back five years, things had been golden, punk," he slurred, turning to the young buck sitting next to him. Through glazed eyes, Samson took in the man's fancy attire: black slacks, crisp white Oxford shirt with rolled up sleeves and braces, two-tone black and white shoes.

"Excuse me?"

"I was cracking the huge cases and sending the big bad wolves to the caboose when I was your age, pal. Drug dealers, pushers, mules, pimps, rapists, muggers, carjackers, killers... You name the trader, and chances are ole' Samson here put 'em in the big house."

"Are you talking to *me*?" he asked Samson.

Samson shifted his gaze toward the mirror that hung behind the bar. "Best goddamn decade of my life..." he slurred, holding up his drink as though to toast to his reflection. "Here's to the best gumshoe this rat hole for a city has ever seen!"

"Drunken fool!" the younger man said, putting his money on the counter and getting up to leave.

Samson snorted, downed the fiery contents, and then placed his glass on the bar. After straightening his fedora and tie, he called the barman over.

"Steve, can I get another, please?"

Samson liked Steve. Sure, the man was a bit of a palooka, but he was a salt-of-the-Earth kind of guy.

He'd fit perfectly into a Raymond Chandler novel... Samson thought, eyeing the large, brutish-looking barman. Just over Steve's shoulder, Samson saw a skinny black male musician onstage assembling a saxophone. *I've not seen his mug around here before. The kid must be new. I hope he's as good as his ice-cool swagger holds him out to be.*

Steve shook his head. "Think maybe you've had enough, Valentine. How abouts you pack it in and go home for the evening?" When he said so, it held weight—Steve owned the place, after all.

Valentine, Samson groused. *Always with the Valentine.*

Not once could Samson recall the moustachioed barman referring to him by his first name.

"I just want to hear the kid play, Steve. You know how I like to listen to the new talent. Come on, give a guy a break."

Steve sighed as he stopped in front of Samson and put his hands on the bar. "Why do you keep coming in here, Valentine? You know you can't afford to plough through my whisky the way you do."

"How do you know I'm not close to cracking the big one, wise guy?"

"Sorry, I forgot I was talking to the *real* Sam Spade." Both men smiled, Steve laughed. "Next you'll be hauling me in for selling liquor during prohibition…"

"You know, sarcasm isn't your strongest suit, pal. I'd stick to the day job and can the humour altogether; you haven't got the face or charm for it. Besides, prohibition went out seven years ago."

"Ah, shut your *yap*, Valentine!" He turned to grab the Old Bushmills off the shelf behind him and uncapped it. "Yap?" he said to himself. "Now you've got me talking like you, Valentine." After filling Samson's glass, he replaced the bottle. "This one's free."

"There—"

Steve waved his hand. "You're a good customer, Val. The odd one or two on the house ain't goin' to cripple me, but you really should consider leaving the socialising alone."

"Duly noted, Steve. Now, would you be so kind

as to remove yourself from my sight? You're spoiling the view." Samson took a sip from his drink and indicated the musician with a stiff nod.

Steve smiled, whipped the towel off his shoulder and headed down to the other end of the bar where a pack of suits were waiting to be served.

Samson removed his tin of cigarillos and lighter from the pocket of his trench coat and lit one. As he blew the first thin trails of smoke from his mouth, the sax player started. The lights dimmed.

The soft, melancholic sounds danced inside Samson's head as he took another drag on his thin cigar. He reached for his whisky and downed a mouthful; all the while his gaze never leaving the young performer.

Such talent...

When the song came to an end, Samson pounded the rest of his drink and gave a standing ovation.

"Steve!" he shouted over the applause. "Another, please."

With his tumbler now full, Samson settled on his barstool to watch the rest of the performance, not caring that it was now almost three in the morning.

The sax's ghostly sounds turned his blood cold—the hairs at the back of his neck stood on end.

This kid's good; he's going places, he thought, slugging back his whisky and calling for top-ups.

***

The music came to an end at four and Samson found he was one of a few customers left in the musty Jazz Hole, which wasn't uncommon. Usually, he was last out of the door.

On shaking legs that barely supported his large frame, Samson stood and exhaled loudly—the whisky had drowned his brain. His vision wavered, a fog rolled down over his eyes.

"*Time*, people!" Steve bellowed, ringing a bell mounted on the wall behind the bar. In the brass, the word *Titanic* had been inscribed. Steve liked to tell naïve barflies how the clanger had been retrieved from the infamous ship's wreck.

"He definitely needs to leave the joking there," Samson muttered, patting himself down to locate the key to his flat.

"That means you *too*, Valentine—my sofa's off limits these days. You know that."

"Yeah, so you keep saying," Samson said, letting out a series of wild hiccups as he walked towards the door, fearing his pins would collapse beneath him like a house of cards.

"Mind your step, Val. I'll see you tomorrow evening," Steve called.

"Not if I see you first, pilgrim!" Samson said, grabbing a hold of the brass door handle and pulling it towards him.

"I really do wish you'd knock it off with the Americanisms, not to mention the fedora and trench coat—this is *not* 1940s Chicago!"

"Uhmm-ugh!" Samson grumbled incoherently, walking out into the late summer night. A stiff breeze tousled his hair and flapped the lapels of his battleship grey coat.

The ugly sounds of the city engulfed him, playing out in a neon haze: loud, pounding disco music, drunken teens shouting and baiting each other into fights, distant sirens, the rush of traffic, backfires, thumps, bangs and screams.

He knew muggings, sex crimes and drug pushing were going on all around him in the city—they had always been there, but things were never so bad as they were now.

At one time, Samson had taken pride in helping to keep the streets clean. Once, he'd have been proud to call Cardiff his home, but not these days.

Cardiff? he thought. *No, Chicago!* He looked up at the modern skyscrapers that loomed over him like demonic idols. All of a sudden, the city didn't seem right. He was confused, disoriented, and turned back to look at the jazz club, with its 40s décor.

"What the...?" he mouthed, turning to walk down the street. A newspaper blew towards him, which he bent over to snag. His eyes sought out the date: "Tenth of the fifth, two-thousand-and-one." The name of the rag: *Cardiff Metro News*.

Too much to drink, boyo.

He shook his head and shuffled towards home.

Crime was rampant. The police were overrun and didn't have the time, energy or patience for the help of Samson and his lot. The private eyes had been squeezed out. Besides, most of the cops were on the gangsters' payroll.

Serpico never takes a bribe! he thought, and belched. *Where does Steve get off on telling me to can the Americanisms and my dress sense?*

He swayed as he ambled along the street and had to catch himself against the corner of a building to keep from falling over. The air was noxious here. It, along with his heavy intoxication, set his stomach whirling.

I could never give up the fedora and coat. It's who I am. It's my identity. When the bad guys see me coming, they run for their hideouts, but their getaway cars just ain't fast enough for good ole' boy Sam Valentine.

"Hey, freak—go back to *Casablanca*!" someone yelled.

Samson ignored the comment. He was far too drunk to fight or give a damn what people thought of him. At least, that was what he told himself. Drunk or not, the words stung a bit. He raised the lapels of his coat and lowered his hat over his face.

Samson was a relic. Worse—a dinosaur. At least people kept relics and cared for them in places like museums. Dinosaurs were dead. Nowadays, there was as much a need in Cardiff for private eyes as there was for dinosaurs, which was to say, there may once have been a purpose for their existence but when that became obsolete, so did they. Sure, dinosaurs were kept in museums too, but as oddities of the past, and not something most people looked back upon and wished still existed today.

A noise caught his attention as he approached the street corner. He stopped and snapped his head to the left—a couple were rutting like wild animals in the doorway of a pub that had closed its doors for the night.

Her skirt was bunched around her hips, her knickers at her ankles. One high-heeled shoe had come free and lay on its side close to the gutter.

"Fuck me harder!" she squealed between sharp intakes of breath.

Samson caught a flash of her bouncing breasts before looking at the man. The fella, a skinny runt who was half hidden by the shadows, whispered into her ear before yanking on her hair. Her head snatched back and she yelped with delight.

Whore.

Samson was about to say something to them, when he noticed a wino sleeping on the floor close by. A needle jutted from the vein in his filthy arm. An empty bottle of Mother's Ruin lay by his side, and the crotch of his khaki shorts was piss-soaked.

A hint of excrement clung to the air.

"Bloody hell!" Samson uttered, moving on. *Things used to be classy around here. Broads were elegant, especially city ones—they had real pride. The younger generation don't give a damn.*

Further down the street he turned a blind eye to a group of hoods dealing drugs, thinking he saw a roscoe being handed over. The thugs stared him down as he approached. They weren't going to take his shit, not that he was in any shape to start any. Sure, he was tough, but not enough to take on six bruisers, and certainly not while piss drunk.

Not even the thugs are like they used to be, he lamented. *At one time, they had a bit more respect for authority. The new, younger breed of gangster will stab you without thinking twice, let alone tell you to fuck off.* For the next twenty minutes he swayed and staggered through the streets until he reached his home: Queen's Street Flats, a tower block comprised of ten apartments, a reception area and four lifts, three of which weren't working.

When he got to the main entrance, Samson noticed some men, a woman and a few youths seeking shelter in the doorway with their sleeping bags and cardboard boxes. The place stank of shit and weed.

"Disgusting!" he burped. "Come on, move along. Officer of the law coming through, people," he told them.

"Piss off, Valentine—you're a washed-up hack!" one of the homeless said from the shadows.

The others sniggered.

Three years ago he would have done something about them and their lip, but he felt too old, tired, out of shape and disheartened to bother. The city was a rotting cesspool, and he was just one man.

Instead, he charged by, heat coming to his cheeks. When he eventually passed inside, he walked over to the one working lift and called it. It didn't come.

"Jesus!" He slammed his fist against the aluminium doors. "Stuff this." He walked to the stairs and climbed to the third floor and his flat.

***

He wheezed and panted his way to his door and leaned against the wall until his racing heart settled.

Black spots danced before his vision.

"I need to slow up with the drinking." He closed his eyes as tight as he could and pinched the bridge of his nose between his thumb and forefinger.

Samson took a couple of deep breaths and reopened his eyes.

Something caught his attention.

"Huh?"

He saw a white piece of paper protruding from his letterbox—an envelope, covered in bloody handprints.

He looked both ways to see if anyone else stood in the hallway, then slipped on a pair of leather gloves and snatched the letter from the box. His heart rate kicked up a few notches when he saw the writing among the blood spatters.

Comply or die, snitch!

Chapter 2

His key scraped against the door's lock. Sweat burst across his forehead.

"Come on, come on!" Samson muttered, desperately trying to fire the Yale home. Hearing a door slam closed somewhere in the building nearly sent him into a panic. He snatched a glance over his shoulder. A floorboard creaked.

A light above him winked out.

His key slipped into the lock.

Without hesitating, he turned it, disengaging the bolts. Samson pushed the door inwards with such force that the handle slipped from his grasp and it slammed against the inside wall.

"Shit!"

He dived through the door, slamming it closed behind him and engaging the locks and security chain. Samson looked down at the blood-stained envelope in his shaking paw. "I need a drink," he said, removing his gloves.

He placed the letter on his sideboard and walked through his box-sized flat, passing through the sparsely furnished living room and into the equally bare kitchen. Even though he lived alone, he kept the place as clean and tidy as he could, and made a point of painting his pad every summer.

Damn place could do with a broad's touch, mind, he thought.

Samson reached for the bread bin. He flipped it

open, revealing a half-guzzled bottle of Glenfiddich. He grabbed a tumbler out of the cupboard from above the breakfast bench and poured himself a double-double. The firewater came level with the glass's rim.

"Better!" He slammed the near empty tumbler down, his eyes drifting up as he stared into the living room. From where he stood, Samson could see the letter. "Got to be some kind of mistake; people can't go around threatening me—I'm Johnny law!"

His hands started to relax. The tremble in his legs subsided.

"Got to be a mistake, it's just got to be. People only come to me for the mundane jobs. Nothing serious. Okay, so the last one was pretty well-paid, but it was nothing heavy, and it certainly wouldn't have invoked such a threat... Maybe it's a lover I caught cheating? Nah, I wouldn't think so."

Samson picked up his glass and swallowed the dregs in one swift guzzle. Some of the whisky drizzled down the sides of his mouth and chin. He wiped it away with his free hand.

After thumping the tumbler back down on the table, he stood and glared at the bloody envelope. Then he pulled his eyes from it and looked at the almost dry bottle of whisky. He needed another. Badly.

"That stuff will put ya in your grave, Sam!" Angie, his late second wife prattled within his skull.

Oh, the irony! he thought. *She's the one who's six feet under. Fancy losing two wives to cancer;*

just how unlucky can a guy be, right? I'm pretty sure I'm damned. He smiled, but it was soon wiped away.

The envelope.

The *blood-spattered* envelope.

It gnawed at him.

Open it, damn it! You used to live for this shit, said one part of him.

Yeah, but I've lost my mettle, said the other.

"You can blame that on the drink, Samson!" his wife nagged. *"It's eroded your brain and turned you into a timid little dreamer. Where's that bad guy bashing bruiser I fell in love with gone?"*

Sorry, Angie. I've been nothing but a disappointment. What must you think of me? he thought, looking about his kitchen.

He straightened and curled his large paws into fists.

A fire swelled in his guts.

He thumped the table hard, sending the tumbler airborne. It rattled to a standstill.

"I ain't going to be a failure any longer. I'm taking my dignity back."

Samson snatched the letter off the sideboard and steadied his breathing before ripping it open. Inside was a folded piece of paper, smeared with blood.

He plucked the paper out, not caring about getting his prints on it, and unfolded it—something hit the floor. Samson looked down and saw two severed fingers on the carpet; there was a gold wedding band on one of the stubby, hairy digits. He noticed the nails had been removed.

Torture.

The word bounced around inside his skull until it hit home.

Vomit raced up his throat, but he bit it back down.

"Jesus H. *Christ!*" He held his liquid meals together and read, hoping the message would offer answers.

If you're reading this, then you're well aware that your petty little friend is no more. I hope you like the gift I've included for you. If you don't want to end up the same way as that no good, lying piece of shit, then I suggest you get your arse to Cardiff Central station by 02:00 a.m. tomorrow morning—there's a package of mine coming in on the Carmarthenshire train.

Don't be late. Or I'll start cutting some of your ***bits off, and I won't begin with your fingers.***

Kindest,
XRay

"XRay?" Samson thought out loud. "That nickname doesn't ring a bell." He tapped his chin and rolled his eyes skyward. "Package, what package? And what friend? I don't *have* any."

He looked down at the severed fingers, and then bent to retrieve them. "I definitely need another drink now."

* * *

The bottle shook in his hand.

"*Leave the whisky where it is, Samson!*" Angie

was back.

"I can't," he argued, scooping up the tumbler to fill it.

"*What would Sam Spade think of you?*" she jabbed.

"Get out of my head, *Angie*! You've been dead five years, for Christ's sake."

"*I didn't stop loving you when you became a penniless drunk because you were a good man, Samson. Be* him *again.*"

"Easier said than done." He took a slug. "Who the hell is XRay?" Samson stalked back into the living room and saw a number nine written on the back of the envelope.

"Nine? I'm *six*." He opened his door and looked up at the plastic number affixed there. It showed nine. "Impossible." He reached out and touched it. A screw had slipped out, causing it to slide down, turning the six into a nine.

"Well, bloody hell," he huffed, a laugh escaping him as he slapped a hand to his knee. "What a fool I am." Samson was about to close the door when he heard a thump from above.

His living room light shook on its thick white cord.

Goose pimples climbed his arms and the blood froze in his veins. The little hairs at the back of his neck stood on end. His heart galloped.

Crap! It came from number nine. One way or another, I have to go up there. This doesn't belong to me, he thought, looking at the letter. He'd managed to stuff the fingers back into what was left of the envelope.

Samson grabbed his keys from the sideboard, left his flat, and closed the door behind him as quietly as he could.

The light on the landing was still out.

He released the breath he'd been holding.

"Get a grip on yourself, man," he told himself in the shadowy hallway. From below, he heard people coming and going—someone cursed about having to use the stairs, as the 'cunting lifts are out again'.

"Got any crack, man?" Samson heard a man ask as the main door to the building opened and then slammed shut. A gust of wind tore up the stairwell, sending a shiver through him.

"I wish someone would move those tramps along."

"*Why don't* you *do it, stud?*" Angie asked.

"Go away."

He proceeded towards the stairs leading to flat nine. By the time he reached the foot of the staircase, silence had fallen like a pall within the building.

Samson started climbing, wishing he'd picked up something hefty from inside his flat to defend himself.

The stairway was dark. He took the stairs slowly, moving up one step at a time. The lack of light didn't bother him so much as the thought that someone might be lurking in the shadows—such as the person who'd delivered him the unwanted mail. His ears pricked at the faintest sound.

There's nobody there, he told himself. *Nine. Who*

lives there? The new guy, right? The one people call 'Vampire', because he's never seen in daylight. By keeping the cogs in his mind turning, Samson kept from spooking himself. *XRay, Vampire—what a crazy world we live in these days.*

When he reached the top step, he looked around the corner to his right, followed by a glance to the left. Nothing. The hallway was deserted. Moonlight, mixed with the neon blazing from the apartment block's sign, poured through the skylight and side windows, illuminating flats seven and eight in a milky-purple hue.

Flat nine was at the far end of the hall. The door was tucked into the corner, out of sight.

He stood for a moment, waiting, listening. A TV or a radio blared from behind one of the doors.

Here goes nothing.

Samson stepped onto the landing and walked past flat number eight. When he got to nine, he stood in front of it and raised his hand to knock. Instead, he froze and looked down at his feet. Light seeped out from beneath the door.

Someone was home.

I'm about to spoil this poor mug's evening! Samson gave the wood three hard thumps, and then stood back. *What if the stoolpigeon comes at me with a knife, possibly a roscoe?*

He pushed his fears aside and gave the door a few more welts.

It won't come to that.

When there was no answer, Samson stepped forward and put his ear to the wood. A cat meowed, a radio played soft blues by Muddy Waters.

What's this palooka's real name?

Samson looked down at the flat's buzzer. Underneath the button to activate the chime he saw the name *Johnson* etched on a thin piece of paper behind the Perspex that kept it in place.

Vampire Johnson? He almost laughed at that one, which scared him. *Jesus, I thought my sense of humour was returning.*

"Johnson? Are you in there?" Samson gave the door more knocks. It creaked open on its hinges—whoever was here had left it ajar. *He left it off the latch? If that's the case, he can't have gone too far.*

A musty smell emanated from inside, causing Samson's nose to wrinkle.

"Johnson? This is Samson Valentine. I live in flat six. I have mail for you."

Nothing, besides the cat and Muddy.

"It was delivered to me by accident. I'm coming in."

At times like this, Samson wished he owned a gun.

Then I could pump some lead if things got hairy.

Often, he would imagine himself in a shootout on a mist-covered shipping dock, or caught in a gunfight down a smog-filled alley.

Yeah, I used to live for this madness.

"Johnson?" He feared his yelling would bring someone running.

As he walked past the radio, he switched it off and a new sound met his ears.

A faint creak.

"Who's there?" Samson shouted. "Answer me, goddamn it, or I'll start spraying lead!"

Nothing. Just a persistent groan from a distance and the cat's cries.

Samson walked into the kitchen, immediately colliding with the corpse that dangled from the ceiling. Johnson's neck was stretched by the crude hangman's noose fashioned from knotted tea towels.

His tongue lolled from between purple lips. His face had lost its colour, leaving behind an ashen tone. He was fully clothed, but shoeless. Tucked between the buttons of his shirt was a crumpled piece of paper.

With a trembling hand, Samson stepped forward and plucked the note from its home. Opening it, he read aloud.

To whoever finds this, I'm sorry. I couldn't go on. The underworld knows I'm a dirty fucking grass—they know I live in the pockets of the police. If I didn't do myself in, then they would have done it for me. One thing I will ask of you is that you warn my family. Get them out of town. When XRay and his backers come for me, they'll also go for my family. I know I wasn't a good man and that I'm a coward, but my loved ones don't deserve to die. Please, help!

Vampire.

A wave of nausea washed over him.

The ole' guts ain't what they used to be. Not that I'm used to seeing such sights, he thought. After steadying himself, a smile flicked across his mouth, but died instantly. He reached for his cigarillos and lighter from his pocket, lit one and stared up at the bloated face of the low-level foot soldier.

"I can't believe this son of a gun actually went by the nickname Vampire."

Now, I can either turn this over to the boys in blue, or I can get out there to the apple and start sniffing around, he thought, looking out the kitchen window at the neon jungle before him. *Maybe I can find out what type of business this here Vampire got himself mixed up in. Perhaps pinch Mr. XRay while I'm at it.*

"*A return to glory, Sam...*" Angie nagged.

As he turned to leave, he noticed the pro skirt dead on Vampire's sofa.

He knew her face well. Too well, in fact. The hooker had been a steady singer at the Hole a few years back, until she fell from grace and got mixed up with the wrong crowd.

Samson had tried to help her. He had given her his bed on many an occasion—not for her to practice her secondary career, but only because it was the gentlemanly thing to do. The right thing to do. She was so young, she could have passed for his daughter.

"Stevie!" he cried, shaking his head. Her thin, almost bony corpse was covered in dried blood. Her blonde hair was a red mess; a thatch of horror. Her make-up was smeared. Her lips covered in foam and vomit, suggesting an overdose.

Why the blood?

"What the hell did he do to her, Vampire?"

And then he noticed her delicate throat. It had been sliced open.

Samson stood, scrunched up the suicide note and stalked towards the door, his mind made up.

"Some hop-head's going to pay for this, and the local body collector may want to start organising Chicago overcoats," he said, rubbing the day-old stubble that mottled his chin.

Did he have it in him? He didn't know, but he had to try.

He slammed the door as he went, leaving the dead to their big sleep.

Chapter 3

Angie wouldn't shut up.

She hadn't been this active in a long time. He blamed it on sobriety, and planned to change that between now and having to go to the train station tomorrow morning.

I should have kept drinking when I got back from the Hole, he thought as he sat in his worn-out easy chair. He had a fresh glass of whisky in one hand, a cigarillo in the other, an ashtray sat on his crotch. A new bottle of Glenfiddich, which he'd dug out from its hiding place in the bedroom cupboard, stood by the side of his chair.

Soft jazz played on his gramophone.

He sat in the dark, curtains closed to a sliver. The early morning sunrise shone into his flat.

Samson tipped his head back, expelling smoke into the air above him. Between the two vices and the soothing sound of Nina Simone, he felt detached from his body.

His eyes locked onto the ceiling. He could see Stevie's young, pretty face up there, beyond the boards and carpet. "The dark terrified her," he muttered, taking a solid gulp of whisky, followed by a hearty drag on his cigar. "Should have kept drinking, Samson; this ugly, violent world just ain't fit for your kind to walk any longer—only the young and strong can move about in this hell."

Nina was replaced by Miles Davis.

Samson reread the suicide note, along with the letter he'd received with the detached fingers.

"How could they make the mistake of delivering to the wrong door? Okay, so the whole number thing threw them, but still! Surely XRay's hatchetmen know where one of their own lives?" he wondered aloud. "Doesn't make sense."

"They're going to mistake you *for Vampire!"* Angie said.

"I know, muffin. I know." Tears formed in his eyes. "Why did you have to leave me, babe?" He swallowed the rest of his whisky and poured another. "Knock it off!" He slapped his face. "She's dead. Keep chasing ghosts, and you'll wind up in the nuthouse."

"Keep pounding whisky and you'll end up in the boneyard!"

He ignored her and looked at the letters, which lay in a pile on the arm of his chair.

"Not much can be gleaned from them. The only thing I can do is go to the train station, get the package, and go from there."

With the next whisky spent, he decided against another.

Best get my head down. I need to be up in a few hours, and I think I'll mosey on over to the docks and see if I can find out about Stevie's involvement with Vampire.

He rose from his chair, headed to the bedroom. He turned the gramophone off as he went. *I always did wonder where Stevie disappeared to. We were so close.*

"The daughter we could never have, Sam."

Samson stripped out of his suit and placed his fedora on the hat stand. He flopped onto his bed, his head spinning.

First Angie, now Stevie.

"Don't forget Claire."

Claire, wife number one.

His mind drifted and his eyes closed, but sleep didn't come easy: his dreams were a swirling mess.

***

The blare of mid-afternoon work traffic stirred him and Samson awoke with a start. He sat bolt upright.

"What, where?!" he gasped in the darkness of his room—a blackout roller blind covered his window, shutting out the sun. Sweat rolled down his face and out-of-shape body. "Nightmares," he muttered, running a hand through his shaggy hair, followed by a rub of his unkempt chin.

He pushed himself off the bed and made his way into the living room for a whisky, taking it to the bathroom with him.

"Ugh, you look like something the cat dragged in, Val." Samson ripped his gaze away from the bathroom mirror and took a piss. It came out in a hot, angry stream. All he could smell was whisky. Once finished, he washed his hands and downed the firewater in one gulp.

He poured another.

Samson drank as he dressed and then headed out

the door with both letters stuffed into the breast pocket of his coat. As he made his way down the staircase, he donned his fedora and tie.

"Best I call in that mess upstairs—I don't want the good ole' boys thinking I'm withholding too much information."

When he stepped outside, the glaring sun hurt his eyes and made his brain ache, but it didn't stop him. He walked into the middle of the street and tried to flag a taxi.

A clattering sound from above caused him to look up. Samson saw trains moving in opposite directions. "That's the best piece of engineering the great city of Chicago could have brought in." Smoke engulfed him, causing him to cough and fan his face with his hat.

"Taxi!" a man yelled next to him.

Samson noticed the chap was well-dressed, with a copy of that day's *Chicago Defender* tucked under his arm. Samson didn't care much for that newspaper—he preferred the *South Town Star*, which had a better quality of journalism, as far as he was concerned.

A Yellow Cab Company taxi screeched to a halt in front of them. Samson had to jump back or else risk losing his toes to the cab's tyres. The cab was off again once the businessman had clambered inside.

"Don't mind the rest of us, palooka!" Samson raised his fist and shook it.

"Get in, chap," someone said.

"Huh?" Samson looked over his shoulder and

saw a Checker Taxi parked beside him.

"I said get in—meter's running. I ain't got all day."

Sam did as he was instructed. Before he could speak, the cabby cut in.

"Huh, of all the taxis in all the towns in all the world, you step into mine."

Samson gave the driver a hard stare. "Docks," he said, dryly.

"Jesus, pal—did a whisky-head crawl up your arse and die? You reek."

"Step on it!" Samson snapped. "I ain't paying you to gab, palooka."

The cabby didn't answer, just laughed and shook his head. As the taxi pulled from the curb, Samson noticed a gang of youths loitering outside his apartment block.

"Bloody wasters," he muttered.

He turned in his seat and looked at them through the back window. They were unloading bottles of cheap cider out of shopping bags. Before the taxi disappeared around a corner, Samson had enough time to see them pass a bag of drugs and a few bottles of pills between themselves.

"In broad daylight, too! They have no shame."

The boys in blue won't do a damn thing about it, either. They won't even move them along. Nobody cares—I'm the last of the good guys. A lone ranger among a land full of injuns, he thought.

***

The cabby didn't speak much, and brushed off Samson's conversation about the great cab wars that broke out in the city a few years back. The man didn't seem to know what he was talking about.

Some professional, he'd thought, and kept his mouth shut from that point on. He'd spent the rest of the journey looking out of the windows at people queuing at the big department stores—the Marshall Field and Co., and the Carson Pirie Scott's. He'd marvelled at the refined, sophisticated ladies in their pretty late afternoon dresses, furs and big hats.

Ten minutes later, the taxi pulled up at the docks. Samson paid the driver and got out.

"Thanks," Samson muttered, his lips around a cigarillo as he flicked his lighter.

The sun was starting to set behind the docked ships, casting them in a red-orange hue. Waves could be heard crashing against the port's walls, along with dock workers laughing and talking, as they hauled cargo up, down and off the ships.

Samson looked around as he drew on his cigar. He wasn't sure who he was searching for, or where he or she might be found. The place had changed dramatically in the past twelve months. It wasn't an area he frequented, but he knew the pro skirts hung around here.

"Maybe I'm too early," he said, looking at his watch. It was a lick after seven.

He made his way along the dockyard and stopped to speak with a worker. "Hey, excuse me, friend."

The large, chequered-shirt wearing man turned

and stared at Samson. "Who are you? You can't be here!" he said, shoving his clipboard into Samson's chest.

"Relax, pal. I'm with the law."

The man looked bewildered. "The law?"

"Yeah, and I'm down here investigating a murder. Mind telling me where I can find the skirts?"

"Skirts? Law? You're talking in riddles, mate."

"The skirts, the pros—you know. *Whores*, man. The whores."

"Not here, matey! They've not worked the dockyards in almost two years." He turned and pointed behind him. "They hang around over there these days. Call it the Magic Roundabout, they do."

Samson looked over the man's shoulder. There was no roundabout. The man had pointed toward a stretch of road that led into the city. His head spun. The place didn't look the same. Disorientation crashed down onto Samson's addled mind.

"Did you hear me, lawman?" the worker sniggered.

Samson saw the words *Cardiff Shipping* stencilled on the crates and ships around him.

"Where—where am I?" he mumbled.

"Hey man, are you feeling okay?"

Samson shook his head. "I mean, what time?"

The guy looked at his watch. "Usually around nine, I'd say. Most of us have gone home by then, and that's when the weirdos come out to play. Until then, they hide and whisper in the shadows. Now, if you'll excuse me, I've got to get these crates unloaded." He indicated a stack of large boxes on the back of a wagon.

Samson nodded, dragged on his cigar and walked towards the road the man had pointed to. As he sauntered on, he noticed the graffiti splashed across most of the walls, buildings, bins, cargo containers, and everything else the street gangs saw fit to tag. A word that kept appearing amongst the brightly drawn gang stamps was XRay.

"Who the hell is this person, a Messiah? The second coming? Bloody flunkies and their codenames!"

* * *

It was a shade past seven-thirty when Samson reached his destination. Already there was a lone lady on the street corner. Samson eyed her for a second, just to make sure she was what he thought she appeared to be. She wore a short skirt that almost revealed her knickers, thigh-high boots, a glossy blouse and a petite fur jacket. Her pink bra was visible through her top's flimsy fabric.

He walked in her direction.

A car pulled to the curb in front of her. She bent over and talked to the driver through the open passenger window.

Best step on it, Valentine. We can't lose her and risk being stuck around here for another hour or so.

"Miss?" he called, seeing her grab the car's door handle. "Miss!" Samson raised his voice, finally getting her attention.

She looked over her shoulder, confusion plain on her face.

"Can I have a quick word, please?"

"Who are you?" She looked him up and down.

"Valentine. Samson Valentine—I'm a private investigator working out of Chi—Cardiff. I have a few questions I'd like to ask."

"Can't you see I'm working here?" she huffed.

"Are you coming?" the driver asked, thumping the steering wheel.

"Hang on," she told him. "What's this about?"

"If we could go somewhere—"

"I'm not going anywhere until you tell me what's going on. Also, I want to see some ID."

Smart girl, he thought. *I like her moxie.*

"Fuck this!" The driver put his car into drive and sped off.

"Great. You've just cost me a job, dickhead!" She jabbed a finger at Samson's face.

He ignored her and handed over his ID. "I'm investigating the death of Stevie Oaks. I believe she worked these docks?"

"Why are you poking your nose into her death? Shouldn't the real police be handling it?"

"So you knew she'd been killed? How?"

"News travels fast around these parts."

"You don't seem too upset about it. I was a close friend of Stevie's, before she wound up getting murdered by some lowlife. Now, you can either tell me what you know, or I'll pinch you for street walking."

"Huh, I know a bit about police work. You can't

just arrest me, arsehole! You don't have the power—"

"Maybe," he cut her off, "but I sure as hell *can* take you in, missy—I can make a citizen's arrest, see."

The colour slowly drained from her face. "Look, I don't know much, okay? I have a daughter at home who needs her mother. I need to hook."

"I'm not interested in you. I'm interested in the string-puller, the person in charge. Do you know who killed her?"

The skirt shuffled her feet. Her eyes made rapid, twitchy movements. Sweat beaded her brow. "I can't say too much," she whispered. "He has people everywhere."

"Who has people everywhere?" He grabbed her by the shoulders. "XRay?"

She gave a slight nod of her head.

"He works you gals?"

"No. That'd be Magic Mike. He can be found at the Railroad Café. It's just down the road. He *might* be willing to tell you more, if you can lean on him. Please, don't tell him we spoke, or I'm likely to end up like our mutual friend," she said, pushing past him to walk off.

There were more questions he wanted to ask, but didn't want to push too much, just in case it did get her nailed. "Miss?"

"What?" she turned on him, stomping her foot.

"Your name?"

"Roxie, why?"

"I might be back,"

Arms crossed, she rolled her eyes. "Great, can't wait."

With that, Roxie wiggled her fine arse into the dying light, leaving Samson to stand alone beneath a streetlamp that drenched him in an orange glow.

"Magic Mike?" he muttered, rubbing his chin. He lit a fresh cigarillo and made his way towards the Railroad Café.

* * *

The joint was a real piece of work, he mused, which was to say, it wasn't a real café at all.

Sure, the exterior had all the hallmarks of a greasy spoon: menu boards clung to the walls on either side of the front door, which had *Railroad Cafe* stencilled across the glass and windows. Someone had even taken the time to place quaint tables and chairs outside, complete with tiny flowerpots and chequered tablecloths.

Who the hell are they kiddin'? Samson thought, approaching the front door. *From a mile off, anyone can tell it's a whorehouse, even a drunken, washed up bozo like me.* He looked up at the top windows and saw some girls displaying their goods.

Before he could enter, a huge black man walked out to greet him. He was draped in gold: rings, chains, watches…

"Who's you, blood?" the bouncer snarled.

Samson stood back. He'd always considered himself a big bloke, but the beast who stood before him cast a shadow over Samson.

"Magic Mike?" Samson asked.

"Who's asking, fool? Speak up."

Samson reached for his wallet, provoking Magic Mike to produce a flick-knife from his oversized jacket. "Slowly, player," Mike said, shoving the blade under Samson's nose.

"I was just going for my wallet, friend. No need to be so hot-headed. Here," he said, handing Mike his ID.

"You a pig?"

"Not quite, but I do work in the field of law. I'm here to ask—"

"Says you a private investigator."

"Did you know Stevie Oaks?"

"Yo man, get the fuck outta here, before I set the dogs on your arse!" Mike said, brandishing his knife at Samson.

"Did you?" Samson shouted.

"Dat whore got wha' she deserved!"

Samson narrowed his eyes. "Thanks." He clenched his teeth. A flash of electricity sparked through his guts, and a chunk of his former self clicked back into place.

"Wha' for?"

"For the information. It was all I needed to know."

"*Do it!*" Angie yelled.

In a swift, precise movement, Samson knocked the flick knife to one side with one hand, whilst hopping into the air to give the side of Mike's bull-like neck a chop with his other.

"Ugh!" the bigger man groaned, bending over.

Samson powered upward with a knee, catching Mike square in the jaw. He heard Magic's back crack as he was forced upright. With all his strength, Samson shoved his opponent in the chest, hurling him backward and through the front window of the café.

The glass rained down in silver droplets, reminding him of spent shells.

Mike's whores scattered like rabbits out of a hutch.

Not stopping to see if the man was injured or not, Samson headed out onto the main street.

"I think he's dead!" he heard a girl screech.

Stopping to light another cigarillo, a grin pulled across Samson's face.

Talk about a dead end! Hopefully I'll have more luck tonight at the train station as I work my way up this greasy pole.

Chapter 4

Had that been him back there with Mike? Where had the burst of violence come from? He'd seen red at the man's blasé attitude, and an image of Stevie's lifeless body with her slit throat had filled his vision.

After leaving the café, Samson had spent time walking around in a daze, thinking he should have gone back and arrested Mike, *if* he was still breathing.

What if the skirts call the good ole' boys and give them my description? No, they won't do that—there's too much risk involved: they wouldn't want the cops sniffing around the place and finding Mike's, or indeed XRay's, dirty secrets. No, they'll deal with me internally—so to speak—if they wish to do so. However, I need to do things by the book.

Samson decided not to flag a taxi back to the rotten apple; instead, he hoofed it there. When he finally got back into the city he planned to go home, but thought better of it when he realised it was only nine-thirty, and the door to the Hole had opened half an hour ago.

He needed a drink; to disappear down the rabbit hole for a few hours.

As he neared the club, Samson spotted the young man he'd been talking to the previous night. He was standing by the entrance smoking a cigarette. Something about him was wrong. He was wearing boots, jeans and a leather jacket, and the words inscribed on his T-shirt made no sense.

"The Sex Pistols...?"

"Oh, Christ! Not you again," said the young man, shaking his head.

Samson paid him no heed and walked into the Jazz Hole. Just beyond the entrance, he stood and immersed himself in the fine décor of 40s Chicago. At the piano sat Sam—not really his name, he knew—playing to a crowded bar of men in fashionable suits and hats with firm brims. They were eyeing up a party of dames in glitzy dresses, furs and equally impressive headwear. Everyone smoked fine cigarettes and sipped from Steve's most prestigious flutes, suggesting the liquid contained within them was potent and expensive.

On stage was a choice canary. She was a pip with good gams. Her gold dress hugged her hourglass shape, ending at mid-thigh.

Samson thought he was going to have to roll his tongue back into his mouth.

"Who's the muffin?" he asked Steve, flicking his head to indicate the jazz singer.

"Name's Melanie Blues. How apt, right?" Steve smiled. "Whisky?"

"Please." Samson removed his fedora and placed it on the bar. "What happened to the pipe-gobbler?"

"The *what*?" Steve took a tumbler from the rack behind him and started to fill it.

"The sax player."

"Oh, right. Meh, I tried to book him but he

wasn't interested."

"Shame," Samson tutted.

"What the hell happened to you? You look like *shit*, Val!"

"Long story, Steve." Samson slugged the offered whisky. "'Nother, please."

Steve obliged. "Want me to run you a tab?"

"You mean I've cleared the previous one?"

"Yep, two weeks ago. Don't you remember? You paid in full from your last paycheque."

"Vaguely," Samson admitted. "You hear of a fella by the name of Vampire or XRay?"

"Can't say I have. Why?"

"I had a run-in with one of their goons earlier, after I found out he was pushing a couple of pro skirts around, so I pushed *him* around. I gave him a few lefts and a right."

"Skirts? You mean hookers?" Steve asked.

Sam nodded. "Remember Stevie Oaks? She used to sing here."

"Aye, I do."

"I found her and her squeeze dead last night in the flat above mine. I think this XRay bloke has something to do with it. Anyway, I have a hot tip to follow up on this evening."

"Jesus, Sam. Sounds deep! Are you sure you're in good enough shape for such heroics? Ain't you getting on a bit to be acting like John Wayne?"

Samson couldn't hear Steve, because he was looking through the man. He swallowed his second whisky and asked for a third, followed by a fourth. When the fifth was poured, he settled on a barstool.

"Plenty of fight left in this old dog. And if you'd seen how I took down ole' Mikey Roundabout and his four goons, then you'd know better than to ask that."

"Just be careful. It's not like it used to be out there, Sam, and I can't have my best customer whacked."

"I need to get to the bottom of it, Steve. It's personal. I knew Stevie well. When she hit rock bottom, she came to me for help."

"Why you?"

"I used to work with her dad. He was on the force and used to leak information my way. It was thanks to him that I managed to make such a name for myself when I first started out as a gumshoe." Then he said, more to himself, "Where in the hell did it all go wrong?"

After downing his fifth drink he asked for another.

Steve filled the glass.

"Waiter!" a man called from the bar's end.

"Got to go, Val. Speak later."

Samson shrugged and turned to listen to the canary. *For a white woman, she sounds a lot like Nina Simone,* he thought, lighting a cigarillo. Much as he wanted to, he found he couldn't concentrate on her singing. Thoughts of Stevie and what those goons did to her invaded his mind.

If Roxie knew about Stevie, then did she know about the hit before it happened? Could she have prevented it? Maybe Magic Mike has a big mouth and boasted about it to his girls? He might've wanted to instill fear. Keep them in check. Samson walked over to the payphone that clung to a wall close to the stage and lifted the receiver. He then thumbed the nine three times.

"I want to report a murder." He spoke fast, giving the address and relevant information. Samson hung up.

He returned to his stool and drained his drink.

Best make that my last. I'll need a clear head for tonight.

Samson took a fleeting glance at the canary and left. "See you soon, Steve," he called over the noise. The barman didn't hear him.

He headed outside.

Night had fully descended over the apple, bringing out the foul creatures that stalked the shadows. For a moment, Samson stood in the doorway breathing. A strong waft of burgers, chips, kebabs and other greasy foods washed over him—the stench clogged his nostrils and knotted his guts.

"You've not eaten in thirty-six hours, Sam..."

Welcome back, Angie, he thought, making his way towards the street that boasted multiple takeaways.

***

After grabbing a bite to eat, Samson took a slow walk home through the filth that dragged his hometown from respectable to despicable.

It wasn't just the rowdy nightclubs run by unscrupulous owners who pumped drug money into their businesses, but the homeless, the druggies, the dealers, the pushers, the pimps, the hookers, the hoodlums, the gangs and the uncouth youth who liked to rock the Kasbah in darkened doorways.

The garbage control the streets.

There wasn't a copper in sight.

The city had been lost to the criminal syndicates.

Maybe XRay's behind it all, he thought, stuffing a few lukewarm chips into his mouth.

A loud gathering of whoops, cheers and wolf whistles erupted from his left. Samson stopped and turned.

"Well, this is new. More sin. Great. Just what we need," he sneered whilst looking at the gaudy neon lights of the strip joint. The psychedelic signs promised 'Live Nudes', 'Clean Girls' and 'Good Beer'—it reeked of corruption.

"What have women become?" Samson tutted.

"If you're not coming in, get the fuck away from the door!" a man built like a silverback snapped at Samson. His tight black suit and dark shades were a dead giveaway as to what the knucklehead's profession was.

"Not my kind of place, boob," Samson said, putting more chips into his mouth. Before the bouncer could reply, Samson walked away.

***

Police officers were already swarming his apartment block by the time Samson arrived, reminding him of worker ants as they scuttled in, out and around the building.

"Can I get through?" he asked one of the officers guarding the cordon.

"Do you live here?" the copper asked, turning and giving him a hard, cold stare.

"Yes."

"Sorry, but you can't go in, sir—it's a crime scene."

"I'm with—" Samson was about to explain who he was, when someone interrupted.

"It is okay, let him through."

Samson ducked beneath the police line and shook hands with the man who'd granted him access. "It's been a while, Davies. *Still* a D.I.?"

Davies nodded. "I'll make chief one day."

"Oh, I'm sure," Samson smiled. *I wonder if the palooka can detect my sarcasm? From the look on his face, I doubt it. He couldn't police his way out of a soggy bag.*

"Were you here last night?"

"Not until mid-morning, no—I was at the Hole."

"Still drinking Steve's watered-down whisky, huh?" Davies had a wry smile on his face.

"Yeah, but if I drink enough of it, it does the trick. Can't complain. What's happened?"

"At the moment it's looking like a murder-suicide."

"Oh…?" Samson scratched his head.

"Did you know the fella who lived above you? He went by the name 'Vampire'?"

"Can't say I do. He dead up there?"

"We found the bastard strung up in his kitchen.

Suicide."

"And the murder?"

"It seems the piece of shit butchered a local whore before doing himself in."

"Bloody hell. And right above me, too!" Samson let his jaw sag. "Any chance I can get to my flat?"

"Can't see why not. You working on anything at the moment?"

"No." Samson walked towards the apartment block.

"Well, I know how you like to keep your ear to the ground; to try and get information off the vine. If you do hear something on the streets, be sure to inform us, Samson."

"You got it, *chief!*" he said, and thought, *Ya palooka.*

Davies's mouth opened, about to say something, but Samson didn't give him the opportunity. He ducked beneath a second police line and opened the door to the building. He noticed the homeless had gone. *They'll be back—a foul stench never truly goes away, no matter how many windows you open.*

Police packed the lobby as he breezed through and walked to the staircase. Even though he couldn't see them, he knew the good ole' boys were staring at him.

God, they hate me. What I stand for. To hell with 'em. I'm the night crusader. No. I am the night! he thought.

***

Samson was puffing for air when he reached his flat, but he didn't stop to catch his breath when he noticed his door standing ajar, exposing the blackness beyond.

He took a deep, shaky breath, and then ambled towards his apartment. The darkness flowed towards him and snatched his air away like a cool blade slipped between the ribs. A shiver cut a path down his spine.

Is it possible I left it off the latch, thinking I'd closed it?

"*They're on to you*," Angie's voice exploded at the back of his mind.

"No, too soon, surely?" he muttered. "Would the girls have given me away? No, I doubt it—they would have seen me as a saviour. Maybe. If not, then Mike. He *must* be still alive. *Shit!*"

He nudged the door open with his foot. It groaned as it eased backwards and tapped against the interior wall.

"If anyone's in there, you best beat it! I'm packing heat, jug heads."

Silence.

"Come on, I'm warning you! Amscray, now, or I'll come in spitting lead."

He flicked a switch and the room burst into light.

Everything seemed in place. Nothing disturbed.

"I *must* have left the door open. That'll teach me for rushing. Stupid, stupid."

Samson laughed nervously as he closed the door, engaged the deadbolt and then headed for his gramophone. After switching it on he removed his hat and coat, then slackened his tie, before flopping into his chair. The clock above the TV told him it was almost eleven.

"Time enough for some shut eye," he muttered.

Once he'd kicked off his shoes, he got back up to fetch his alarm clock from his bedroom. He set it for one. Samson turned the lights off and dropped into his seat once again.

**

A shrill sound drilled its way through Samson's whisky-soaked skull, his eyes fluttered in a lazy fashion. He felt groggy and annoyed.

He reached out and thumped his alarm clock, sending it to the floor with a dull thud.

The noise continued.

Samson's eyes shot open.

"The *phone*!" he blurted, springing from his seat. In the light that filtered through his windows, courtesy of the moon and a few streetlights, Samson was able to snatch a glimpse at the wall cock.

00:45.

"Who the—*Hello*!" His grip on the phone's receiver tightened. "Who *is* this? Do you know the hour?"

"Valentine?" asked a smooth as silk voice.

"*Yeah*?" His jaw clicked.

"Samson Valentine?"

"Look muffin, I'm about thirty seconds from—"

"I've been staring at your number for hours. If I'd known how sexy you sounded, I would have called sooner."

"Who the hell is this?"

"Violet. Violet Barnes. *Mrs.*"

"Well, *Mrs.* Barnes, what are you doing on my wire at this hour?"

"*It's a ruse!*" Angie said. He ignored her.

"I'm told you're one of the best *dicks* in town, Mr. Valentine?"

He smiled. Her playful approach was starting to win him over. "Try the *only* dick in town. What can I do you for?"

"I'm looking for a man of your talents."

"Don't tell me, you have suspicions about your fella?" he smiled.

"I fear he's plotting my murder with a mutual friend. Can you help me?"

Before answering, he thought about the station. He had to be there—he *needed* to find out why Stevie had lost her life. "I'm kind of in the middle of—"

"How does fifty-thou in cold hard cash sound?"

His silence spoke volumes.

"I see I have your attention," she said after a beat.

"I guess this is why your husband is fixing to make you brown bread, Mrs. Barnes."

"Brown bread? Dead? See, you are good!"

A laugh escaped him, which sounded creepy within his flat. "I like your moxie, kid."

"Does that mean you'll help, Valentine?"

"I have something to take care of this evening, but I can be at your place tomorrow afternoon. Let me take your number and address, please."

She gave him what he wanted. "I'll see you tomorrow."

"Sure, Mrs. Barnes."

"Violet, please."

"Violet. I might run a little late, but don't give up on me."

"Okay, Valentine."

"By the way, how did you come by my—"

She hung up. Dead air hissed down his ear. He set the receiver back into its carriage.

In the dimness of the light, he looked at her address and then stuffed it into the top pocket of his shirt.

"Things just keep getting better," he chirped, turning towards the bathroom.

The water was cold on his cheeks, which helped clear the whisky-mist that had formed behind his eyes. After patting his face dry with a towel, and brushing his hair and teeth, Samson headed back to the living room where he grabbed his coat and hat.

As he closed the door to his flat, he checked his watch: one-fifteen.

Samson had no time to dawdle. He scuttled down the corridor and took the steps two at a time.

When he got outside, he noticed the homeless were back.

"Looks like it's another episode of *Z Cars*, boys!" one of them said. The others laughed.

He ignored them and disappeared into the neon-lit concrete hell before him.

Chapter 5

When he arrived at the train station it was one-thirty, and the place was lit up like a Christmas tree.

Not surprising, he thought. *It's a city that never sleeps, much like NYC—it's always on the move.* It had been a long time since he'd visited this part of Chicago, let alone the transport depot itself. *The last time I was here, I was just a pup. Turn of the century, maybe? It was around the time they'd started laying these tracks. God, I remember it like it was yesterday.*

The usual rabble were hanging around outside the station entrance—hooded flunkies, a couple of homeless booze hounds, needle-heads, glue-sniffers, flashers and your average, low-key palookas who were spraying bus stops and shop shutters.

A group of youths were using a homeless man's duffle bag for a football; meanwhile, their idiotic broads drank cheap cider from the sidelines and yelled, swore, and egged their boyfriends on.

Samson ignored them.

I have a date with destiny—let the good ole' boys sort this lot out, he thought, entering the train station.

"Give me back my bag, you son of a bitch!" he heard the old man say. "Got my whole life in that sack you pricks are using as a toy. Hey, mister!" he called to Samson. "Give me a hand here!"

"You wan' it, come get it, ya old *cunt*!" one of

the thugs yelled.

"Yeah, what are you waiting for, gramps?" a second hoodlum chirped.

Samson quickened his pace, remembering why he didn't visit this part of the city any longer.

Looking over his shoulder, he saw the homeless guy wrestling with one of the lads that held his bundle. From behind, a muffin blindsided the codger with a bottle to the side of his head, sending him to the ground.

The rest of the gang piled around him like vultures.

Circling him.

Jeering at him.

Some of the lads whipped their dicks out and pissed on him, before laying into him with boots and fists.

Samson felt like a coward. He *could* have stopped it, and would have a few years back, when he hadn't been so cynical and hardened by the loss of two wives and a job he loved. Well, the job he was still clinging to. Just.

He flipped his lapels up and moved into the station.

"You put Magic Mike down."

Don't start, Angie. Now's not the time.

"What was so different with him?"

He ignored her, shifting his attention to the information boards, which hung from the ceiling. Samson found the section he was looking for. His train, which was coming in from Haverfordwest, was due on platform one at exactly two a.m.

Samson looked at his watch.

01:40.

Plenty of time to kill, he thought, looking about the foyer as he dragged on his cigarillo. *It's creepy quiet here tonight. The bad guys are plotting. Trouble is brewing.* He narrowed his eyes. *Well, they don't scare me.*

Samson walked to the windows and looked out into the city. The thugs had moved on. The homeless man was getting up and brushing himself off. He was shouting something, and shaking his fist in the air, but Samson couldn't make head nor tail of it.

Glad he's okay. Again, not a good cop in sight.

One of the doors at the far end of the train station breezed open, allowing litter to blow in along with two salty-looking fellas dressed as though they were up to no good. Samson had seen plenty of their kind before.

They wore trench coats, good suits and trilby hats. Both men had their hands buried in their pockets.

A chopper squad, Samson thought. *Probably got Tommy guns tucked up inside their coats.*

A chill scurried up his back. He pulled his coat tighter around him and decided to make his way to platform one.

Let's see if the palookas follow.

He didn't have to wait long to know their intentions. He heard their footfalls *click-clack* behind him, their pace slightly quicker than his.

Another couple of XRay's hatchet-men, I fear.

Well, let 'em try something. I dare *them.*

When he got to the foot of the stairs that led to platform one, Samson risked a quick look behind him before dashing up the steps. The two goons were headed his way all right, but they'd slowed their approach.

After reaching the platform, Samson found the coffee hut was open. He shuffled over to it and ordered a cup of tea.

By now, the well-dressed bozos were on the platform with him.

It was ten to the hour.

A train rushed past Samson's back, kicking up rubbish from off the lines, along with a gust of wind that almost bowled him over. He spotted a woman sleeping rough on a bench a few feet away—she was covered in newspapers.

"This city is going to wrack and ruin," he muttered, blowing on his drink. He'd positioned himself to face a vending machine, so he could see the mobsters' reflections in the glass.

A bit early to be catching a train, boys? Even for a couple of suits.

"*Keep your eye on 'em, Sam!*" Angie warned.

When the thugs started conversing and laughing among themselves, Samson thought he might have got it wrong, now that they now appeared harmless. Samson started pacing as he waited for the late-night train.

Let's see what happens.

If the two he suspected were indeed thugs, then they'd be looking for Vampire, and not him. To them, he was just another faceless Joe. He was safe, for now.

Why send thugs? Did XRay not trust Vampire to do as he was told? Did they know he was dead? If they do, then they've probably come to pick up the package, and if that's the case, I may as well go home. Disappear back into the night.

He felt cheated.

It was fun whilst it lasted... Hang on; if these are XRay's goons, then they'd also be connected to Mike! The thought made his skin crawl. *If the girls sold me out, then they might know I'm the man who harmed him.* Samson took a nervous glance at them—the men appeared to be paying him no attention. *No, they're here purely for the package—they would have done me over for Mike by now.*

Samson took a sip of tea and winced as his lips blistered.

"What the hell!" he groaned. "Did she make this with lava?"

About to give up and head home, Samson saw train lights in the distance.

I could take a look and see what happens—it would slake my curiosity.

"*Careful, Sam,*" Angie warned.

Cool your engines, gal.

"*Why waste your time? You have the Barnes woman and a healthy pay day to look forward to. You don't have to risk your neck for this.*"

"Quiet, Angie. Please!"

The train was close. Samson could hear it clacking along the rails. Its whistle blew, splitting the still night air.

The suits made a move, and one of them gave him a quick once-over. Samson played dumb, acting as though he hadn't noticed. Then the tannoy boomed overhead, announcing the arrival of the late-night train.

Thirty seconds later, the train pulled to a stop, its brakes squealing. Smoke engulfed the platform. When the doors opened, the suited men parted ways. One went to the left, the other, to the right.

Samson was piggy-in-the-middle and blew on his tea, still making it look as though he was none the wiser—not that either was paying him any heed.

I have them fooled.

He stood before an open door just as a fat conductor walked out.

"Getting on, mate?" His Yorkshire accent threw Samson.

"Waiting for a friend." He tried his tea again. "*Jesus*! How hot do they have to boil the water?"

"Yeah, same at every station," the conductor said with a smile.

Samson ignored him.

From behind the conductor came another man who pushed his way past.

"*Hey*! An 'excuse me' would have been nice."

"You Vampire?" the young, unkempt man asked. His eyes flitted side to side beneath his sweat-covered brow. "I have your boss's package."

A mere kid, Samson thought. Without a second thought, the gumshoe stuck his hand out to receive the small, square box. "This is for Mr. XRay, right?"

"Yeah, of course. Oh, *shit*!"

"What?" Samson asked, looking up and seeing what the boy was staring at. One of the suited thugs was moving swiftly in their direction. He was removing a hand from his coat. "Shit, *knife*!"

Before Samson could turn to make a run for it, the boy was shoved from the carriage by the second goon, who yelled at them. "*Freeze*!" He pointed a bean shooter at them.

In a flash, Samson threw his scalding tea into the man's face.

"*Argh*!" the hatchet-man screamed, losing his footing and falling from the train. As he staggered about blind, he fell between the carriages and onto the track.

Samson heard bones break.

"Run, kid! *Now*!"

Before Samson could reach a hand out to the fallen goon to help him, the guard blew his whistle and the doors slammed shut. The train started to pull away, and the man who'd fallen onto the tracks began screaming afresh as he was dragged to his death.

The second jug head was now running towards them "*Stop*!" he yelled.

But he was too large and sluggish to catch up with Samson, who held the package under his arm as he hotfooted it down the steps to the foyer and then out the exit.

Samson ran until he was out of breath. By then, he was well clear of the station.

I definitely need to leave the whisky where it is, he thought, wheezing.

"*Those bloody cigars, too!*" Angie chirped.

I don't need a ruddy lecture, babe.

Once he'd caught his wind again, Samson pushed off the wall and continued along at slow pace. As he went, he glanced over his shoulder—the second goon appeared to have given up the chase. He paused for a moment to eyeball the package.

It was wrapped in brown paper, with no markings.

He shook it, but it made no sound, as though it were solid on the inside.

He put it to his nose, but could not detect any peculiar scents.

Open it already! his mind nagged.

No, not yet, the other part of him answered. *Got to get back to the safety of my flat.*

Samson kept looking behind him to make sure he wasn't being tailed. The streets were empty, apart from the odd person walking among the shadows like a ghost.

He needed to move. In a few hours or so, the place would be jumping.

He sauntered into an all-night coffee shop and decided to rest there. He settled into one of the booths with a wide-angle view of the dining floor, so he could watch the activity in the diner. Soft piano music played over the speakers; the inviting aroma of greasy food filled his nostrils.

"Pot of coffee, please," he said to the pretty young waitress who gave him a welcoming look.

Old enough to be your daddy, muffin, he thought.

"We have a special on our pies this evening. Would you like some?"

"What flavours do you have?"

"Well, let's see... We have apple, cherry, mixed berry, rhubarb, elderberry..."

"*Elderberry?*" he said, drumming his fingers on the tabletop. "How unusual. I'll have a slice of that, please."

"Got it."

As he was about to pluck the package from under his coat, thinking he was alone, the young girl spoke again.

"A bit cold and late to be out roaming the streets, isn't it?"

He looked up at her and sought out her nametag. Alice.

"Don't you think this is a dangerous job for a young lady?" he asked her.

She smiled, and then giggled. "Not at all. My dad works the kitchen and my mum is upstairs. Plus, I'm like, nineteen."

"Oh, I see. A family-run venture."

"Are you homeless?"

"Do I *look* homeless?" he asked. *Who's the snoop here?* he thought. "Any chance of that coffee, Alice? A guy is pretty cold."

She smiled again, wider this time, which exposed her gapped teeth. He found it endearing. "Of course, sorry. Once I start yapping, there's no stopping me. One of these days my dad's going to kill me."

And then she was gone, back behind the counter

and through a door at the rear of the shop.

The package was well taped down, with no perceptible edges or weak spots. Samson picked up one of the knives at the table and tried to saw through some of the tape, but the blade was too dull.

"Here you go," Alice said, "one pot of coffee and a slice of elderberry pie." She placed his food down in front of him. "Anything else I can get you?"

"No thanks, Alice. You've been a delight." He winked, putting the package to one side. *It'll have to wait,* he thought, eyeing the huge, doorstop wedge of pie he'd been given. "You think I need feeding up?" He picked up the fork that had come with the pie. "Any chance of some cream?"

"Sure." She darted off, making him giggle.

"What a sweet little muffin." He cut off a piece of pie and forked it into his mouth. It tasted nice, the temperature just right.

The package burned a hole at the back of his mind, but he tried to forget about it.

I need this. His feet ached from the running and his heart was only now just starting to settle down. *Who were those goons? Well, one of them won't be doing much talking* ever *again.*

"Here's your cream, sir."

"Please, call me Sam," he answered her. "I might be back for more of this delicious pie, so we may as well get on first name terms."

"Okay, *Sam.*"

"Thanks," he said, taking the small pot from her and pouring the contents over what was left of the pie.

When she was gone, he went back to his musing.

I'm in deep. The mule didn't have a damned clue, and he's going back to his people to tell them he's offloaded the parcel to the right person.

"*Shit!*" He spat crumbs. Samson put his fork aside and drank a mouthful of coffee. "I need to try—"

When he looked up, coffee almost dribbled out of his sagging mouth.

Goon number two was standing outside the coffee shop. He had his face pressed to the glass.

Slowly, Samson stood.

The thug lumbered through the door like a squat ogre, his eyes fixed on Samson. "You have something that belongs to my boss. I want it. Give it to me now or I'm going to have to take it from you, and it won't be pretty, pal."

Samson took a step towards the counter.

The hatchet-man put his hand in his pocket and brought out his knife. "Now, what's it to be?"

"Wait," Samson said, removing his wallet. He placed a tenner on the counter. "We can't do this in here, it's a family joint."

"I don't give a flying—"

A police siren outside caused the bozo to turn and look.

Samson took his chance. He ran into the kitchen, snatched a frying pan off the wall and yelled his apologies to Alice as he went whizzing by on his way to the restaurant's back door. "I'll bring it back, *promise!*"

The door opened onto a back alley. After a swift

look about, Samson dashed to the left, knowing exactly where he was. He heard the door to the coffee shop crash against the wall behind him, and he looked back. The goon was on his trail.

"Get back here!"

"Like hell," Samson muttered between ragged breaths. His heart sank as he closed on a gated fence. In his youth, he might have cleared it easy, but the extra pounds Samson had put on of late all but convinced him there was no going over that door. The only way past was through.

He threw his weight into his shoulder and rammed the door. The rotted wood gave easily and he charged through without breaking stride.

Not too far down the side street, Samson felt his legs start to give. The slow burn that had begun in his calves would not be ignored. He didn't have it in him to keep running much longer.

He needed to end this, and fast.

I can't lead him back to my flat.

When Samson rounded the next corner, he spun to give his back to the wall and pressed himself against it. His fingers tightened around the handle of the frying pan as he focused on the goon's approaching footfalls.

This was it—he'd get one chance, one lucky swing, and if it didn't connect, it'd be all over. His heart felt like it was going to pound its way out his ribcage.

Come on, come on, you bastard...

When he saw the man's shadow approach on the floor, he held his breath and primed his arm for a swing.

One, two...

On three Samson let loose with the frying pan, sending it airborne in a wide arc that caught nothing but air. The pan hit the wall behind him with a solid *clang!* and the shock of the sudden impact numbed his arm to his shoulder.

"You thought I was *that* stupid?" the palooka jeered as he drove a fist into Samson's exposed gut, knocking the wind out of him.

Samson staggered, then righted himself for another swing of the pan that failed to strike home. The thug gave him a one-two to the chest, then the kidney, that sent Samson tottering against the wall for support.

The parcel fell from inside his coat, slid along the floor and into the darkness.

The goon rushed for it.

Big mistake!

Samson steadied himself and clobbered the thick-set man across the base of his skull.

"He'll live," Samson muttered, scooping the package up into his arms. He hesitated only so long as to take the goon's knife and wallet, then made a hasty retreat from the alley. He'd want to run an I.D. check on him later, but at the moment, escape was paramount.

Escape, and a drink and good smoke when he got home.

***

The sun was already starting to rise by the time he reached his flat. He helped himself to a nightcap and collapsed into his chair with the parcel in his lap.

Sleep came quickly enough.

Chapter 6

Samson woke up screaming. He leapt out of his chair, sending the package airborne. It crashed to the ground and skittered away from him.

"What—what—where?" he gasped. He looked out the window and saw the sun setting behind the buildings opposite. Soon the streets would be filled with the filthy, night-crawling criminals. "Jesus, how long have I been out?" He stepped over to the mantelpiece and looked down at his watch—six p.m. "Christ, I've not slept like that in an age."

He blinked a few times and put a hand to his chin. A few days' worth of stubble had formed there. Samson moved into the kitchen and immediately his eyes fell on the empty bottle of whisky that stood next to the toaster.

I don't remember... And then it hit him—he'd got up in the middle of the night and slugged the stuff. *No wonder I was out for so long. Ugh, I need a shower and a shave.*

***

After stripping out of his clothes, he bundled the lot and threw it in the washing machine. He then took a straight razor to his stubble before jumping in the shower. He felt as though he hadn't had hot water on his skin in days, which sounded about right, as Samson had lived most of his life out on the streets. His nest was more of a pit stop than a home, a place he could go to for a sleep, piss, shite or for something to eat.

It was HQ. A base.

Ever since work had dried up and Angie died, Samson spent less time here than at the Jazz Hole, the shack he called home.

There's a point, he thought, stepping out of the shower and grabbing a towel. *I bet Steve's been wondering where I've got to. Maybe I should go down there and have a few later this evening.* Then he remembered the package.

Samson wrapped the towel around his waist and walked into the kitchen. Instead of going for a cup and teabag, he went to the cupboard and pulled out a fresh bottle of whisky. It was the last.

Sod it!

He took it into the living room along with a glass.

"*I thought you'd started turning a new leaf, Sam,*" Angie said.

Little steps, doll face. Little steps. He picked the package up off the floor and collapsed into his chair with his whisky and glass on the table at his side. His smokes sat comfortably within reach.

"Good, because I wasn't getting back up to fetch them," he said, grinning as he poured himself a large glass of firewater.

He turned the parcel in his hands, looking to see where it could be torn open. Not finding a weak spot, he took to it with his teeth and chewed at a corner until it was soggy enough to rip open.

The small box came apart in his bear-like hands, revealing a shiny object with rough edges. "What is it?" he mouthed, pulling at the packaging some more. Soon enough, he was staring at the biggest diamond he'd ever seen. The shine that radiated off it was almost blinding.

"*Phew!*" he whistled. "Must be worth a bomb."

Out of the box a note fluttered to his lap. Samson picked it up and read it aloud. "Once collected, please deposit to Big O at the Green Baize Pool Hall."

There was no sign off. No number. Nothing that would identify the sender.

And then what the goon had said to him on the platform echoed in his mind.

"Was he referring to XRay when he mentioned his boss? I'm starting to think no, that he and thug number one are working for someone else, someone who's had this stolen from them by XRay's lot." He lobbed the stone in the air as he thought. "It makes sense, because they had no idea who I was. Interesting."

He looked at his watch.

21:22.

I need to deliver this and find out more, he thought. *If XRay's lot don't know Vampire's dead by now, which is unlikely, given it's been hours since I did the pickup, then they soon will.*

Then, as though someone had been reading his mind, he heard a faint ringing.

He squinted and pricked his ears.

"Is that coming from upstairs?"

Slowly, he got out of the chair and opened his door. The ringing was now clear. After the thirtieth or fortieth ring, it stopped and started again. The unanswered call sounded angry.

Samson left his door open and went to the window. When he got there, he looked down at the opposite street corner.

Someone stood at the payphone, the receiver pressed between his ear and his shoulder.

Samson kept his eyes trained on the person at the payphone and counted the rings. When the person on the street hung up, the phone upstairs went dead.

So, they don't know about you Vamp! Fancy the package mule making such a mistake. Idiot. He wanted to laugh, but knew they'd soon cotton on to the fact that someone else made the collection.

The phone started ringing again.

The person was still at the payphone. Close by was a car with its engine running.

There might be another nearby, casing the joint. He continued to muse as he stared out the window at the lurking hatchet-men. *You'd think word would have hit the streets about Vampire by now... Why aren't they coming up here in search of him? They must be itching to get their hands on the stone.*

It occurred to him that, whoever Vampire worked for, his employer had already deemed him disposable. Even if he had made it to Big O with the stone, they still would have turned his lights out. He'd be dead either way.

He stepped away from the window, closed his door, killed the lights and retrieved the note from where he'd dropped it on the table.

Big O? Name sounds familiar, he thought, turning the little card over in his hand.

Without thinking any more about it, he went to his bedroom to dress and pour himself another whisky. The phone continued to ring even as he left his flat, and he felt tempted to answer it.

"No, I'm in enough trouble as it is. I'd be a prize palooka to go up there and answer that call." Just as he was about to close his door, Samson's phone started to jangle, stopping him dead in his tracks.

He turned and pushed his door wide.

"This is getting weird…" He walked into his flat and snatched the receiver out of its cradle. "Hello?"

"Sam."

He knew the voice but couldn't place it.

"Are you in the habit of standing up wealthy, attractive women?"

"Oh, *damn*! Violet."

"That's right, Mr. Valentine. I've been waiting for your call. I appreciate you are a busy man, but…"

She didn't sound angry, just hurt, which wasn't a surprise because she was a woman with a target on her head.

"I'm sorry," Samson went on. "Your offer totally slipped my mind, doll. I'm just heading out the door on a job, but it shouldn't take me too long. Can I call you later this evening?"

"Shouldn't be a problem. My husband has informed me that he will be out of town on business for the next couple of weeks. Although, I know exactly what he's up to."

"If you know, then it's the boys in blue you need, *not* a private eye."

"Maybe, but I *could* be wrong. Besides, I doubt they can protect me as well as you can."

"I—" he started, but she cut him off.

"No, I doubt it. Besides, I need to make absolutely sure, Mr. Valentine. I'll see you later. Try and call before coming."

The line went dead.

Where did I put her address? he mused. *My shirt*, the thought occurred to him, and his eyes grew wide with panic. *The washing machine!*

***

After recovering Violet's information and picking up the package he'd taped back together, Samson left his flat for the second time. His destination: the seedy pool hall run by Big O in the heart of the city. If he was going to get to the bottom of this mess and make some arrests, then he needed more to go on.

His trek through the city's main shopping avenue, Queen's Street, added time to his journey, but he didn't care. After the night he'd had so far, Samson didn't trust walking the back streets or less populated areas of the city.

He didn't trust the shadows.

The parks were also no-go areas—the city's gangs controlled them. Even the police refused to patrol them. Samson didn't fancy getting bushwhacked by an XRay hatchet-man or japped by one of his rivals.

They're still looking for Vampire, remember? he thought, wolfing down a pasty he'd picked up at an all-night bakery. *However, after this little meeting with Big O, who's probably another low-level thug for XRay, then they're going to be alert to me. Good.*

The high street was bustling. It was late. Past ten. The people walking out and about were nightshift workers, deadheads, tramps and drunks—most of the high-end troublemakers stuck to the back alleys, under bridges or any dark spot they could find.

Then again, some were barefaced enough to do their thing in the main street. Samson had seen plenty of it over the years he'd worked the city. Druggies had no problem shooting up in front of shoppers, some of whom were mothers with their children or babies in prams. He'd even seen homeless people rutting, shitting and pissing in the town centre in broad daylight, not to mention an abundance of drunken violence.

A cesspool.

He felt the weight of the package in his coat's pocket and smiled.

"*Taking the job offer from the Barnes woman is probably for the best, Sam,*" Angie said. "*Get out of the area for a few days. Disappear, especially after making the drop.*"

One step ahead of you, babe. He stopped, stuffing the last of his pasty into his mouth, dusting the crumbs off his clean shirt and waistcoat before moving on.

When he was a few buildings away from the Green Baize, he heard hard rock music playing and the sound of pool balls clacking. Standing outside, he took in the one-eyed building: it was in need of a plaster and paint job. Raucous laughter poured from within. A neon eight ball flickered on and off above the front windows. The pool hall's sign had seen better days—the first O in Pool was missing, along with one L in Hall.

Before entering, Samson lit a cigarillo.

Back in the day, long before the whores, thugs and bent coppers ran Chicago, this had been a respectable billiards hall, he thought. He'd known the guy who'd ran it. Peter Ibbs. *Poor fella's long gone. Heart attack.*

The Green Baize was now a notorious hotbed for gang members, flunkies, bikers, crooks, prostitutes and any other mean bastard who dared cross its threshold—it was a pirate ship that had run aground.

He had major reservations about entering, especially dressed the way he was.

Had there not been whisky swishing around inside his guts, then Samson probably would have moved on. He was feeling brave, much like he had felt with Mike. His former self was emerging.

"But why allow the drunks to hurt that poor homeless man? You never did answer me..."

Like I said, Angie—baby steps.

The trembling in his hands had stopped.

He stubbed his cigarillo out on the wall and walked through the doors into a toxic cloud.

Samson could smell marijuana and harder drugs in the air, alongside the odours of stale sex, cigar smoke and musty ale. The joint itself looked decayed; the walls were rotten. Plaster covered the floors.

Samson walked down a long, dark corridor leading into the viper's pit. He pushed open the main bar's door and it creaked like the rigging of an old ship. All eyes in the pool hall locked on him. The club went quiet, save for the clacking of pool balls.

Samson gulped. It felt as though he was trying to swallow razorblades.

He held it together and braced himself. "I'm looking for Big O," his voice boomed, sounding confident.

A couple of patched bikers at the bar turned to face him. He'd heard of their gang—the Boas; a colourful bunch with an impressive rap sheet.

The long-haired one of the pair spoke, managing to sound pleasant and somewhat friendly. "He's changing a couple of barrels, mate."

"Yeah," his pal choked out, who sounded as though he smoked sixty a day. "He'll be back shortly."

Samson could hear the tar bubbling in the palooka's chest. He released a clutched breath and looked about him—the men had gone back to shooting pool, laughing and talking amongst themselves.

"You may want to go 'round the other side," Long Hair said. "To the lounge. He'll be there before 'e comes back 'ere."

"Thanks," Samson said, walking through the throng of bikers. He noticed one was wearing an eye-patch. Another had a scar running from the bridge of his nose to his throat.

What a pretty lot.

He didn't let them rattle him. Considering he'd let the booze take control of him, Samson was impressed with how well he was handling himself. He was also thankful for his size, which was a deterrent to any of these palookas starting trouble. Still, he smiled and nodded as he went.

Some of them grunted under their breath, but he ignored them.

When he got to the opposite end of the bar he saw another door that led to the lounge. There was a commotion coming from beyond it.

Slowly, Samson placed one of his big, scuffed paws to the brass push plate and shoved.

The door opened.

Inside, there was a woman groaning, a second gasping.

Somewhere within the room, a guy spoke.

"That's it, bitches—get it the fuck on!"

When Samson rounded the corner, he saw where the noise was coming from: on a pool table in front of him lay a naked, large-breasted broad who was covered in white powder.

Cocaine, Samson guessed.

The second woman, who wore thigh-high boots, stockings, and a suspender belt with nothing on top, was kneeling on the table. Her face was buried between the other woman's legs as she made gratuitous sounds of sucking and licking, much like a child would whilst eating a delicious ice-lolly.

Samson felt repulsed.

The oaf he'd heard was bent over the cocaine-covered muffin. His nose was buried between her cartoonishly-sized breasts; his hands moulded them whilst his fingers tweaked her nipples.

She writhed.

"Excuse me," Samson called out, "don't mean to interrupt the party, but I'm here on business."

The kneeling girl turned to face him—she had cocaine residue plastered across her mouth, chin and cheeks. A little spot of it dusted her nose. On closer inspection, Samson could see her mouth was wet from the other girl's juices.

His stomach flip-flopped.

Lying Girl didn't move, apart from her legs, which appeared to be trembling.

"Who the *fuck* are you? A fucking pig *cunt*?!" the man bellowed, straightening. "I don't know you. I don't know your mug. That mug don't belong in *my* club!"

Samson took a step back. The guy was big—not Magic Mike big, but he was pushing six-feet in stature. His goatee was completely white, his head bald and gleaming. He wore thin glasses and a T-shirt with its sleeves completely missing. Written on his shirt above the drawing of a naked devil girl were the words '*Pussy, Pills and Pipes—the Devil's Tools of Trade*'.

When he took a few steps forward, Samson

heard the sound of chains rattling, which drew his attention to the decorative ones hanging from his side. He also had one around his neck with a huge padlock on it.

The khaki, knee-length shorts he wore exposed his heavily tattooed calves. As he got closer, Samson saw the guy had one blue eye and one green.

"I asked who the *fuck* you are, old man!"

Old? I'm only forty-five, Samson thought. "Cool your engines, friend. I'm here with a package for Mr. XRay, your boss? It came in on the train last nigh—"

"That was Vampire's pick up, honky."

"You are Big O, right?"

"Yeah, but you ain't Vamp." Big O detoured towards a table and plucked a baseball bat from beneath it. The wood glinted in the light, revealing the words Kansas City T-Bones etched across its surface. "And I certainly didn't invite you to my little snow party here, so- again, who the *fuck* are you? Best you start talking, or you're going to spend the next year picking up your fucking teeth from off my floor."

"Easy, friend," Samson said, reaching into his trench coat.

The girls fidgeted and screeched, possibly thinking Samson was pulling a gun. They hotfooted it into the shadows and beyond.

"Nice and cool, pal," Big O said, jabbing the bat in Samson's direction.

Samson produced the package. "Catch!" he said,

tossing it to Big O. "Your boss's, I believe?"

"How did you come by this? Who are you, and where's Vampire?"

"First, I want information."

Big O burst out laughing, his mouth opening wide to expose multiple gold teeth. "Not a fucking chance." He advanced with the bat held out in front of him. "Now, *you* start talking."

Samson reached into his coat pocket again. "Hold it right there or I'll brighten this joint with Chicago lightning!"

"You're *packing*?"

"Think I'd come into a jungle like this without a roscoe? You're nuts."

"You're fucking dead."

"Start talking or I'll fill you full of lead," Samson warned. "Where can I find XRay?"

"Man, you're crazy—he's a ghost."

"You're about as much help as Magic Mike."

"*You* busted up Mike?!"

"The punk's still alive? He had it coming. Now, spill," Samson said, thrusting his hand against the lining of his pocket.

"Don't shoot!" Big O said, throwing the bat to one side.

Samson picked it up. "Well, where can I find him?"

"His main hangout is Ziggy's."

"That ramshackle arcade?"

"Yeah, either there or the Queen's Casino."

"On St. Mary's street?"

Big O nodded.

"Thanks." Samson moved towards the exit. "If you're lying, I'll be coming back with the boys in blue and shutting this place down."

"Tell me who you are!" Big O yelled as Samson approached the door.

"Valentine, kid. Sam Valentine." He smiled and left the Green Baize Pool Hall with the bat tucked inside his coat. *It may come in handy,* he thought.

***

Back outside and breathing in the fresh air, he lit a cigarillo and decided to take a stroll down to Ziggy's Slots to see if he could weed out XRay.

The night was young, and Samson was on the prowl.

I'll find out why you paid the ultimate price, Stevie. You just wait and see if I don't.

For the first time in years, Samson felt like a giant, like he could take on the city and win.

Fresh anger started to boil in his guts.

Chapter 7

If Big O's Green Baize Pool Hall is a one-eyed joint, then Ziggy's Slots is a blind beggar wearing soiled slacks, Samson thought, dragging on his cigarillo.

He stood across the street, casing the joint. His mission: to see who was coming, going, and hanging around the place. There didn't appear to be any muscle on the door, which he was thankful for.

It's not much of an HQ for a criminal warlord, suggesting Big O was lying. Maybe I should try the casino?

"*You might as well have a gander now that you're here*," Angie said.

He nodded, continuing to stare at *Ziggy's Slots*. He chewed on the end of his smoke.

The building was comprised of two storeys, with the upper windows bricked over. The lower ones were alive with blinking bulbs and filthy neon lights, which drowned the pavement in a psychedelic glow.

Like Big O's sign, some of the letters were missing from this establishment's name. Those that remained were written across the grimy windows and arched over the doorway. From where Samson stood, he had a clear view of most of the slot machines and the proprietor's booth, where notes could be exchanged for coins to play the one-armed bandits.

I'm sure Big O has called ahead to warn them of my arrival. They're probably waiting for me at the casino, too. The slugger hidden beneath his coat felt good. *Well, I'd hate to disappoint them.*

Samson stalked across the street, making sure the bat was fully concealed. Once inside, he found the rat hole devoid of customers—and yet the noise coming from the machines was deafening.

Undeterred, he moved towards the booth and found it empty.

"Where is everyone?" He turned in a circle, and that was when he saw the door towards the rear. Stencilled into it was the word: Manager. "Got ya."

He went for the door, slinging the bat out of his coat for a good two-handed grip, and threw himself against it with his heel in the lead. The door whipped open, its knob smashing into the wall behind.

There were two men inside. One sat behind the desk with the office phone in his hand—*Ziggy*, he presumed—while the other was a fat bozo with a crooked nose and chin. *The muscle*, Samson thought.

The heavy moved to get up. Samson brought the bat crashing down on the man's head, sending him to the ground with a groan.

"*You*, put the phone down!" Samson demanded. "Are you Ziggy?"

Ziggy nodded and dropped the receiver. He wore aviators and a jumper that looked as though his grandmother had knitted it.

"Please, don't hurt me," he whimpered.

"Where's XRay?" Samson demanded. "It's time he took a short walk to the caboose for killing Stevie."

"What? *Who*?"

"A young skirt."

"That two-bit whore?"

Samson walked to the desk and put his bat through the phone. "The hell you say, sap?"

"Nothing. I don't know anyone or anything! Please, I just work here."

"As a foot soldier for XRay, right? Well, where in the hell is he? Speak, damn you."

"I don't know—I'm telling you the truth."

"Is that right?" asked Samson, his tone deceptively cool. Then he choked up on the bat and swung for the fences. Ziggy fell backward onto his arse as the bat swept his desktop clean. Picture frames, a pocket calculator, a desktop planner—all this went airborne and slammed into the far wall, where it streaked down and collected in a broken heap of unrecognizable junk.

"Jesus, stop it! Are you crazy?" Ziggy screamed, cowering. "You do know he owns this place. He'll have your guts for fish food!"

"Crazy? Probably. I haven't had my whisky fix. I'm going to ask you once more." Samson grabbed the scrawny man's hand and held it down on his desk. "If you don't tell me what I want to know, I'll bust it, so talk. Where is he?"

"Please…"

The bat whistled through the air and met the desktop with a slam and the crunch of broken fingers.

"Aaaugh!" he cried, instant tears streaming down his cheeks. His eyeballs rolled backward in their sockets. Samson though the man was going to pass out.

"Tell me!" Samson yelled, shaking him. "Or so help me God, I will pulverize your mitt beyond use!"

"The—the casino!" Ziggy screamed in Samson's face. "You, fucking bastard! I'll make sure you— this is police brutality, *pig*."

Samson let Ziggy's hand go. Ziggy made to stand up and Samson clubbed him in the face, knocking him backwards and into his chair.

"Lights out, palooka," he said, looking down at Ziggy's smashed and bleeding nose. "If I find out you're lying, I'll be back!"

***

Two minutes later he was outside Ziggy's and heading across town to the casino. The bat was hidden, once again, beneath his coat. His hands were shaking.

Where has the old Samson come from suddenly? I've not experienced that brutal, don't-take-no-crap attitude side in some time.

"The booze, Sam—it's wearing off. You've been taking it easier the last couple of nights. It's unearthing the old you. The man I fell in love with," Angie responded.

Yeah, but that Sam was a wild fool; that's why he

lost his job on the force.

"Yeah, but that Sam got stuff sorted; he was a man's man."

He looked at his hands. They were spattered with blood. *I can't do this. I spent years trying to forget this Sam. Drink— I need a drink.*

"No, you don't. Cleanse your system. Get back to being that shoot-from-the-hip guy, lover."

I don't think I can be him. My confidence, the lack of work and drink... It's taken its toll. Angie, I miss you.

"I know, lover, but I'm here—always will be."

I need you in my arms, muffin. Badly. I'm confused all the time.

***

When Samson got to the centre of town, he ran across a young saxophonist playing soft blues. His carry case was open, exposing the pittance he'd made thus far. Samson recognised the lad as being the one who'd played at the Jazz Hole a few nights ago.

The young musician had not seen Samson, who stood close by in the shadows. And while Samson didn't have time to waste, it was never a waste of time when it came to listening to good jazz.

He looks different. Modern—this is 40s Chicago, right? Samson looked about him. He didn't recognise the city, it was new. *Where were the overhead trains? The chequered and yellow cabs? The old wooden hotdog carts?*

His head began to spin.

Everything was big, bright and loud.

Samson recognised the song being played. *Hotel California*. Never had he heard it performed in such a way.

Night-time city life shuffled on around them, and they could have been the last two on Earth at that moment.

When the song came to an end, Samson stepped from behind the lamppost he'd been leaning against and threw a few coins into the lad's saxophone case.

"You've got a good sound, kid," Samson said, tipping his fedora and moving on.

"*Thanks!*" the musician said.

"No problem, kid. No problem," Samson muttered, popping a cigarillo into his gob. "Just keep doing what you're doing."

***

After walking a further ten minutes, Samson was standing outside the Queen's Casino. Just setting eyes upon the place gave him a sinking feeling that Big O might have lied to him. The establishment was boarded up. A throng of homeless hid in the darkened doorways, and others roamed around inside, behind some of the broken windows. Yet another group stood outside, huddled around a fire they'd started in a steel drum.

He heard them whispering.

They were talking. Laughing at him.

"What's the big idea?" he snapped. "Or is there

another Queen's Casino?" He didn't know. Couldn't remember. Samson was out of touch with the fast-developing city around him. "It's a goddamn ruse!"

He looked up at the top windows, fearing an ambush.

Chicago typewriters! his mind screamed on seeing six well-dressed mobsters pointing Tommy guns down at him. *They'll riddle me full of holes.* As he was about to dive for cover, one of them yelled down at him.

"Get out of here, cop! Your kind ain't welcome."

"Yeah, or we'll make Swiss cheese out of ya!" a second gangster said.

"Don't shoot," Samson pleaded. "There's civilians down here."

"Best get stepping, 'en," the first voice said again. "XRay don't feel like meetin' tonight."

Samson walked away, his arms in the air. *A goddamn ruse, alright.*

When he was far enough back the chopper squad vanished from the windows.

"You feeling okay, fella?" someone asked.

Samson saw it was one of the homeless. A couple of the others were sniggering. He scratched his head. "Yeah, fine..."

He looked up at the building once more. There was nobody there. Most of the letters on the front were missing. Only the Q and S remained. Puzzled, he approached one of the exposed windows and poked his head inside. The joint stank of dead animals.

"What the hell's he doin'?" a man called out.

"No fucking idea, Dave."

"Piss off, copper!" a woman jeered.

"There were men up at those windows. Six of them—they had machine guns!" Samson said, telling no one in particular. "They were about to mow us down, but I scared 'em off. I'll come back with reinforcements."

"Fire claimed this place years ago," one of the homeless replied. "It belongs to us now, piggy-wiggy, and us alone; ain't anybody else here, ya freak."

They laughed.

One oinked.

Another snorted.

"Go away!" another called out.

Samson didn't need telling twice.

Maybe Steve can shed some light on a few things, he thought, turning to leave for the Jazz Hole. The anger that had built in his guts was turning to absolute bewilderment and fear.

Samson was thirsty and tired. He needed to sit down and think things through, to get his head clear. *I imagined those men?* As he rounded the corner, he took one last look at the casino, seeing the mobsters once more at the window looking down at him.

***

By the time he got to the Jazz Hole, it was past midnight. The joint was dead, apart from a few barflies. There was a fella on stage drenched in azure lighting playing a harmonica.

"Hey Steve, the usual," said Samson.

The barman looked up from his paper—there were tears in his eyes. "Seems like an age since I saw you last."

"Something wrong, friend?"

Steve shook his head. Without saying a word, he poured Samson his drink and placed it on the bar. Their eyes met. "They're looking for you, Sam. Word's out and they think you wasted Vampire."

"*What*? Who?" Steve averted his eyes. "*Who*?" Samson demanded.

"You know who, and they want *it* back." Steve slammed the whisky bottle down on its shelf. "They're willing to forget about Vampire and Mike."

Samson leaned over the bar and grabbed Steve by his shirt. He pulled him close until their noses touched. "What are you talking about, palooka?"

Steve smacked Samson's hands away and fell back against the shelves. "What the hell's wrong with you?"

The music stopped.

The Jazz Hole fell into silence.

"Tell me what you know, damn it!"

"I was trying to, until you went batshit crazy on me." Steve's jaw tensed, and then he addressed his punters. "It's okay, everyone—go back to what you were doing."

The musician started back up.

"XRay," Steve said in hushed tones. "His thugs are looking for you. You never told me you hurt

Magic Mike—he's in the hospital."

"I told you the last time I was in here, didn't I? When was that? Last night? Night before? I did come in, didn't I?"

"Sam, knock it off with the 40s lingo, yeah? It's getting boring. People laugh at you…"

Samson took a step back. He must have looked every bit as wounded as he felt.

"Sorry, I didn't mean to sound so harsh," Steve went on. "Anyway, you haven't been in here in a couple of nights—I had no idea about Mike or that Vampire chap. You killed him?"

"No! Well, I hurt Mike but I didn't kill—hang on, you know Mike?" Samson took a slug of whisky and asked for another.

"Yes. I knew him. Well, *of* him. He's one of XRay's key figures, and controls the docks, works the whores and runs a protection racket over the businesses around the area. You've crippled some serious muscle! Word is you've pissed off XRay. Big time."

Samson smiled and downed his second whisky. "Another," he said, tapping his glass, "and that's what they get for hurting my friend."

"What friend?"

"Stevie—" he started, but stopped himself. *I must have imagined that whole conversation I thought I'd had with Steve,* he thought, and then told the barman of Stevie and Vampire, and how he'd found them.

"Okay, so you've been dragged into something that's way over your head," Steve said.

Samson nodded.

"Just give them what they want—you can end this, Sam, tonight! At first they'd thought it was that clown...er...erm—"

"Vampire?" Samson offered.

"Yeah, that's right. They thought he'd stolen the package and was running amok hurting XRay's men."

Samson slugged the third drink.

Steve automatically poured another.

"Seems you paid a visit to that pool shark Big O and spilled your guts?"

"I may have let slip who I was—where's the Queen's Casino?"

"The place doesn't operate any longer."

"So, it *was* just a ruse." Samson didn't mention the men he'd seen at the window. *It must have been the shadows playing tricks on me. Nah, my presence spooked 'em. Probably ran back sobbing to big bad XRay.*

"Anyway, XRay sent some of his thugs here. I'm not sure how they got the information on your hangout, but they've probably got your home address, too. They just want the package back, Sam—the one you *pretended* to give Big O."

"They can wait. I have important business to take care of first—a job that offers some serious cabbage, Steve." He straightened his crooked fedora, slammed the rest of his drink, and stuck a twenty on the bar. "I'll be back in a day or two."

"You don't understand. They said they'd return and torch my bar, Sam!"

Filthy bozos. "Did they tell you what they wanted me to do?"

"They gave me a number. Call them the moment you get in." Steve handed Samson a piece of paper.

"Thanks."

"Make sure you call them, Sam. *Please.* I can't lose this place."

"It's under control." Samson walked out into the night. It was raining, but it didn't bother him—it felt nice and cool against his flushed face.

The thought of XRay and his goons leaning on Steve didn't sit well with Samson. The fire in his belly started to rekindle as he walked in the now pelting rain.

No way am I going to let a couple of two-bit thugs push me or my friend around!

***

When he arrived back at his apartment block, Samson was happy to see the homeless had dispersed, because the way he was feeling, he was worried he would have laid into them.

The whisky was no longer deadening him. For the first time in a long while he could think straight, and the whisky shakes were starting to settle down.

He entered the empty foyer and walked to the stairs, taking them two at a time, wanting to be in his easy chair with a whisky in his hand and music playing in his darkened living room.

Samson reached his floor and realised something was wrong. He was uneasy—butterflies fluttered in his guts. As he walked along the landing towards his door, he saw it was fully open, with light coming from inside.

He stopped. *I definitely closed my door this time, and turned my lights off.*

From within, his phone started ringing. *Violet*! Swallowing his fear, he walked inside. The place had been turned upside down: mirrors lay shattered on the ground; drawers had been pulled from cupboards with their contents scattered about like confetti; all his furniture had been toppled, along with his kitchen table and chairs.

"*Bastards*!"

As he waded through the mess to the phone to answer it, it stopped ringing. Samson then picked up the receiver, dialled Violet's number and proceeded to tell her that he couldn't make it tonight but would be with her tomorrow for sure. After hanging up, Samson rang the number Steve had given him.

"Hello?" The voice was low, calm.

"XRay? This is Valentine. I have what you want. There's—"

"No. Now, listen. I'm not going to repeat myself. You have until midnight, Saturday, to bring what's ours to the dock. Don't be late."

The line went dead.

"Damn it!" Samson slammed the phone down, tempted to call back, but instead, he grabbed the near-empty bottle of whisky, played his gramophone, righted his chair and collapsed into it after killing the lights. For all he cared right now, the whole world could go to hell in a hand basket.

Chapter 8

Samson opened his eyes to the sound of a big band playing inside his head. His throat was bone dry and sore from snoring.

"*Ugh*...! he groaned, stretching, inadvertently brushing the whisky bottle off his gut. It hit the floor and rolled towards the door, the dregs within sloshing, slowing its getaway.

The events from last night came flooding back.

Someone broke in here and rummaged around in search of the stone—Violet! *I can't keep her waiting longer, damn it—her life could be in danger.*

Samson got to his feet and checked the time. It was seven p.m. "Hell's bells, I need to get moving." He looked at himself in the mirror above the mantelpiece. "Damn, I look like death warmed over. I need to sort myself—I can't go to her looking like this."

Samson dialled her number. It rang a dozen times before he gave up. His heart raced. *Why isn't she answering? Did they tap my phone? Have they got to her, too? Bastards.*

Samson tried again.

Nothing.

After the fourth attempt he gave up.

She could be in the shower, or out shopping—anything! Put it out of your mind and get ready to go over there.

As he headed into his bedroom to undress for a

shower, he knelt by the mat next to his bed and pulled up the loose floorboard hidden beneath it: XRay's diamond was concealed there.

A smile spread across his face.

With the board and mat replaced, Samson made his way into the bathroom to shave and shower before returning to his bedroom to dress and pack a small bag: two shirts, fresh tie, clean trousers, socks and pants—he needed to make sure he had enough gear in his car in case he was out of town longer than expected.

"Remember, you've got to be at the docks by midnight, Saturday."

"Yes, I know, Angie, and if I'm not done with the Barnes woman by then, I'll come back here and settle my business with XRay first."

"Good, because you wouldn't want Steve to suffer…"

"Angie, *please*!" He zipped his bag up with a hard yank and took it into the living room, grabbed his car keys from the fruit bowl and left, making sure his door was locked.

***

Violet Barnes lived in Newport, the next city over.

He was worried about her, mainly because his calls went unanswered. His stomach was in knots.

I might find her dead, he thought. *What if the husband returned and executed his plan? But maybe her silence is down to XRay and his goons? No, I'm over-thinking things. She's fine. Safe. They gave me until midnight, Saturday. Then again, who could trust a palooka who broke the law for a living?*

Samson tried to put things to the back of his mind as he drove.

Hope she's got good whisky.

***

The motorway was fairly quiet. His run to Newport was unhampered, smooth.

When he found Violet's street, King's Head Avenue, he whistled as he turned onto it. Samson wound his window down and slowed the car's pace. The place reeked of wealth. *They're not houses, but mini, unaffordable mansions; with whitewashed walls and gleaming picket fences,* he thought, eyeing the homes.

On the driveways of each home, expensive cars were parked in their twos. Threes, in some cases. The public street might as well have been paved in gold from how ritzy the neighbourhood looked.

He followed the street until he came to a set of gates. The top of the house beyond peeked out from above the tops of manicured hedges and an imposing perimeter wall.

"How am I supposed to get up there…?" he let his words trail off on spotting an intercom attached to one of the concrete pillars supporting the gate. Samson rolled his car up to it and pressed the button.

As he waited for a response, he looked up and

saw the cameras looking down at him.

"Not sure if you can hear me, but I'm Samson Valentine—I'm here on business."

He tried the buzzer again, holding the button down a bit longer than before.

Samson glanced up with a pleading look and a jerk of his shoulders, as if to say 'what am I supposed to do now, sit here and rot?' And that's when he heard the gates click and groan as they slowly drew inwards.

"Well, that's a relief," he muttered, putting the car in gear. *The husband didn't come home early after all...*

His car rolled up the driveway. On either side of the narrow strip of road were bushes and trees. Leaves fluttered from gnarled limbs; they scattered across his bonnet and nestled in between the wipers.

"Place is a goddamn palace." When he arrived at the end of the path, he spotted a multitude of sports cars parked on the gravel around a couple of huge fountains. To his left, Samson made out stables in the dying light, along with huge lawns and a tennis court.

He whistled again.

When he exited his car, he felt as though he was spending thousands just by standing there. He half expected a driver or butler to approach him, but neither did.

"We're talking serious berries here. Joint must be worth a small fortune."

He lit a cigarillo and strolled towards the main entrance. The gravel crunched beneath his feet as he went. To his surprise, the door was standing wide open. There was no sign of forced entry.

"Mrs. Barnes?" he called out from the threshold, giving the door a few hard knocks. "It's Samson Valentine; we spoke on the phone. I'm the private investigator. I'm coming in."

Samson pushed the door open further. The hallway where he stood was set in semi-darkness. Shadows danced on the walls. Somewhere close by, a fire crackled.

"Mrs. Barnes?" He now stood at the foot of the staircase.

"Mr. Valentine? Do come up," Violet answered.

"I've been going out of my mind with worry!"

"Whatever for?"

"You've not been answering your phone. I thought I was too late." Samson climbed the stairs with caution—he'd been in this business long enough to know that subterfuge was easy to walk into. "Where have you been?"

"I was probably in the shower when you called. Please, come up. It's much warmer here to discuss business."

Samson kept his back to the wall. For all he knew, she had bruisers up there waiting to box his ears.

Maybe she's a femme-fatale, or on XRay's payroll? A gangster's moll?

"When's your husband due home?"

"Not for another few days."

When he got to the top step, he asked her where she was.

"Third door on your right, Mr. Valentine."

He meandered along the landing, wary of hatchet-men lurking within her home. "Are you decent?" He stood at the room's threshold.

"Why yes," she laughed. "Don't be coy."

Samson removed his hat and entered. His breath hitched. She lay across a chaise lounge wearing a white, silky negligee with gown to match. The attire showed off her curvy frame and exposed her legs from her knees down.

He averted his gaze.

Miss Chicago 1940, he thought. She smoked Pall Malls without the cigarette holder. *Shame,* he added.

Her pretty face was flanked by luscious, raven-coloured hair. All that was missing from the scene was a grand piano—she'd gone all Rita Hayworth on him.

If I look at that face for too long, I'll go all rubber-legged!

"Scotch, Mr. Valentine?"

"I only drink Old Bushmills or Glenfiddich. And please, call me Sam, Mrs. Barnes."

"Violet, please.

"I always find it disrespectful to refer to a married lady by her first name if I don't know her. Call me old-fashioned."

"Sam, you are old-fashioned!"

He smiled.

"Help yourself to a drink—I don't cater your brand, but I do have a wide range of expensive scotches. Please, have one. I hate drinking alone."

He then noticed a glass of bubbly on the side table next to her.

We have a classy little muffin on our hands here, Sam, but her charm could be a death dealer. Watch her.

"Thanks, I'll take one drink whilst we talk business and berries. Tell me, what's the skinny with your husband?"

She exhaled smoke and let out a sophisticated laugh. He didn't know such a thing was possible.

"Something amusing, miss?" He narrowed his peepers.

"No, not at all. Just you," she smiled, blowing more smoke.

"Why?" He poured himself a scotch.

"You talk funny. The things you say. I was told you were... *nutty*."

"Nutty? Is that right?"

"It would seem that some of the coppers around here are *not* your biggest fans, Sam. They see you as a bit of a laughingstock."

He washed his temper down with a slug of scotch and laughed. "I thought I was here to save you, and not myself from a character assassination."

"Sorry, am I making you uncomfortable?"

"Let's get on with the job at hand, yes? I can't say I care what they make of me down at the station. I'm still the best damn private eye Chicago has ever seen."

"*Chicago?*"

"Cardiff, sorry. Hell, I'm the best all over."

"Yes, I was told you had an impressive score

sheet, which is why I came to you."

Samson poured himself another drink. "Well, it would be too late to ask for a refund, lady. If you want me gone, I'll be taking my petrol money and callout fee—"

"Wow, steady on, Sam. I'm not saying that. I like what I see. I think you're an honest guy; a little rough around the edges, but honest. Hard working, too."

"Let's get down to business, then."

"Of course, Sam. Has anyone ever told you that you ooze charisma? You should slacken up on the booze—"

"Look, lady, I've just about had enough of your smart mouth. I'm beginning to see *why* your husband wants you rubbed out!"

She gasped, and her eyes flinched as though someone had slapped her.

"Sorry," Sam said in lowered tones, "that was a mean thing to say."

"Apology accepted. After all, I was riding you a little hard. I asked for it. Besides, I wasn't lying when I said you have charisma—you exude character. Anyone would swear you'd walked out of a hard-boiled detective novel, Sam. You're one of a kind."

Even the way she smokes is graceful. "Thanks." He helped himself to another drink.

"Please, sit down." She indicated to the soft chair in the room's corner.

"Mind if I smoke?"

"Go right ahead, Sam."

He removed a cigarillo and lit it. "Okay, so when you're ready, maybe you'd like to tell me exactly what's going on? I know about your suspicions."

"That's right, Sam."

"Care to refresh my memory?" He wanted to make sure he had *all* the details correct.

"*Huh*. Well, it's my husband. He's trying to kill me."

"Okay. Why?"

"For this!" She waved her hands around her.

"The house?"

"Yes. My money, too. You see, he's a lot younger than me. I'm what they call a 'sugar mama', Sam."

"I see. Do you have life insurance?"

"Of course, yes."

"How much are we talking?" He sensed the question may be too personal. "I just want to get the full picture, Mrs. Barnes."

"Between the house and what I've nestled away, probably close to ten million."

He whistled, got up, and helped himself to another drink. He then sat back down. "I could see that being reason enough to put a person six feet under."

"Quite, Sam." She studied the drink in his hand with an eyebrow raised. "Enjoying *my* scotch?"

"Yes, thanks. Proceed."

"My, you are a delight." She smiled and shook her head. "For a man who was 'only having the one'…"

"It helps me think and keeps the shakes away."

"Oh?"

"I'll warn you now, Mrs. Barnes—I'm not the man I used to be. I've lost my spark, and it's been a long time since I worked a case of this magnitude."

"I was told you're the best…"

"By whom?"

"Bill Arbogast."

"Billy's been out of the game a few years—he's lost touch with what's going on within the world. But he's right, I *am* good, I just need a clear head."

"Remind me to hide the scotch next time you call, Sam."

"Ha, yeah. Listen, I'd like half the cash upfront to cover my expenses and the work I'll be doing in catching your husband red-handed."

"Don't beat around the bush, do you?"

"No, ma'am, I like to get on with things."

She smiled. "When and where do we start?"

"Not sure there's much I can do, at the moment, if your husband's out of town—"

"So, he says. I believe he's holed up close by, plotting my death with his latest squeeze."

"Care to share *how* you came to believe all this, Mrs. Barnes?"

"Well, you see, he works a lot from home—he's a financial advisor to local businesspeople. He deals mostly with small firms. So, instead of working out of an office, he uses a section of my house to run things. Occasionally, he'll leave for work trips out of town and out of the country."

"Seems he's making a pretty decent living—why would he want *your* money?"

"Because his business is failing, Sam. I've caught snippets via eavesdropping on phone calls and snooping around his mail. Naturally, I wouldn't invade his privacy in such ways, but I became concerned when his business partner came to me to inform me that they were in trouble. That he thought my Peter was on the verge of a breakdown."

"I see. And did you confront your husband about this?"

"Why yes, of course. But he pooh-poohed me away. Shot me down in flames, as it were. He made out as if nothing was wrong. A few days later, after checking up on him at various locations, I came to learn he had another woman. I even caught him in her arms one evening."

"Oh?"

"Yes, they were cavorting… in his office. On his desk, of all places, if you can believe that. He had her bent over it like a filthy beast."

He couldn't help but laugh inwardly at that one, but didn't show it. *You're much too classy for that sort of behaviour, Mrs. Barnes,* he thought, watching her take a delicate sip of champagne and play with her beads with her free hand. *You're a prim and proper lady, just like my Claire and Angie were. You don't get such refinement with gals these days.*

"Are you okay, Sam?"

"*Hmm?*" He snapped out of his trance. "Oh, yes. I was just mulling things over, tossing things around inside the old noggin. So, right," he cleared his throat. "Did you interrupt when you caught them cavorting?"

"I'm a lady, Sam—I wouldn't have walked in on them and caused a scene, even as mad as I was. I'd planned to confront him later that day."

"Did you catch them talking about you?"

"No, that happened a few days later."

"You never told him about what you saw?"

She shook her head. "I planned to, but I was too upset. He broke my heart, Sam. I made him."

"You *made* him?"

"Yes. Before he met me, he didn't have two pennies to rub together. I sank my money into starting his business, and that's how he repays me, by *fucking* his personal assistant."

"Right, okay, you held off on telling him."

"Yes. Then two days later I was about to challenge him about it in his office. But before I could, I heard him on the phone. He was plotting, with *her*, about how they would murder me and make it look like an accident. I heard him laugh as he told her how they would run off with my money."

"*Hmm.* And they were going to pull it off that easy? I don't think so." Samson chuckled.

"Yes, *that* easy. My Peter knows a lot of suspect people, Sam; people who don't do business in ethical ways."

"Thugs?"

"Criminals. Organised ones at that."

Samson's interest peaked. "I've had my dealings with such bozos throughout my career, Mrs. Barnes.

Such ruffians have kept whisky in my belly." He arched an eyebrow and lit a second cigarillo. He felt smooth. No, he *was* smooth.

"I'm sure. But he's in deep, Sam. I think he owes these people money." A tear rolled down her cheek. "He's made a deal with the devil and I'm the offer, Sam. I feel like such a fool."

"Hey, sweetheart, there's no need for tears. You've got Samson Valentine in your corner—ain't nothing going to happen to you. You're safe." Samson wanted to hold her, to chase her concerns away. Instead, he swallowed the remainder of his scotch and decided to leave it at that.

"Well, that's kind of you, but I'm not really looking for a gallant knight, Sam. I need my husband taken away. Prosecuted."

"Before we get ahead of ourselves, I'm going to need to either catch him in the act or get a confession on tape. Let me do some snooping." He stood and put his hat on.

"Wait, where are you going?"

"To get some sleep, Mrs. Barnes. I'll be back early tomorrow morning to start work."

"But—but what if he comes for me tonight?"

"I didn't say I was leaving you completely. Whenever I take on a case such as this one, I normally do stakeouts. I'll be outside your home in my car. Is it just the one way in and out of the estate?"

"Oh, right, I see. Yes, just the one entrance. Where will you park?"

"Across the street from your gates. When is he

due home?"

"Friday. But, as I said, he's close by. I know it. He's—"

"Yeah, setting up your murder. Tomorrow morning when I come for my coffee, I'll get further details."

"Okay, Sam. Thanks."

"I'll need that first instalment of cash as soon as possible."

She nodded. "Of course."

"I hope you're an early riser, because I like to get started at the crack of dawn."

"Don't worry—I'll be waiting for you."

"Good. Now get some sleep," he said, leaving.

"Thanks once again, Sam. I already feel much safer."

"Thank me when it's over, Mrs. Barnes. G'night," he called from the landing.

Five minutes later he was parked opposite her gates. Samson had his window down and a cigarillo in his mouth. From where he sat, he could see her bedroom light burning and wondered what she was doing, as he smoked and listened to Jazz FM.

When three a.m. rolled around, he set the alarm on his watch and called it a night. There was no sign of the husband making a return. Even if he did, Samson would hear the approach of a vehicle or the gates moving.

He settled in his seat to the soothing sounds of a saxophone and drifted off to sleep. It had been some time since he'd done a stakeout.

Chapter 9

When his alarm beeped at six in the morning, Samson was already awake and standing outside his car; the case had his mind working over-time. He was smoking, excited and eager to get the day underway. He felt alive.

The street was deserted. The only sounds were the birds singing and his car radio.

Once he finished his cigarillo, Samson locked his Ford and moved across the road to the Barnes' residence. He shook the gates. Locked. Out of curiosity, he walked alongside the wall and rounded the corner to where the path came to an end—there was no way past the thicket of trees and bushes: a person would have to cut his way through with a bulldozer.

To double-check, he went the other way and was met with the same resistance. He was satisfied nobody could sneak around the back or get over the twenty-foot wall.

Even though Violet had told him nobody could access the house other than by coming through the gate, he wanted to make sure. *If someone wants access to somewhere by surprise, they can, because they wouldn't let anything get in their way if they were determined enough,* he thought.

He rang the buzzer on the gate and hoped Violet was awake.

The gates clicked and groaned as they swept

backwards. He walked up the drive and was inside within a couple of minutes, finding Mrs. Barnes in the kitchen. A thick smell of coffee and bacon hung in the air.

"Would you like some eggs with your bacon and toast, Sam?" she asked, watching him enter the kitchen.

He noted she was still wearing her silky gown, which hung to the floor. "It's been a while since a lady cooked me a meal," he admitted. "Eggs would be good, thanks."

"I thought we could eat as we discussed your day's plans?"

"Sounds good, but I don't want to waste a load of time gabbing. We need action."

"Huh, I like a man of action. Your money's on the table, by the way. It's all there. Every promised penny."

"But—"

"I know you said half, but I trust you, Sam."

He didn't argue; instead, he picked up the cabbage and stuffed it inside his breast pocket. He'd never been in possession of such a large sum of cash.

"Are you sure you can afford this gesture?"

"I wouldn't have offered otherwise. Besides, it could get hairy out there, knowing the people he's involved with."

"True. If anything does happen, make sure I get a nice Chicago overcoat and some expensive flowers."

"Chicago overcoat?"

"A coffin, muffin."

She shook her head, laughing. "My, you really do have a charm about you. Married?"

"I was, twice."

"Couldn't live with your huge personality, huh?"

"They were taken by cancer." A silence grew between them. "Huh," he cleared his throat. "It's okay, you weren't to know."

"I'm sorry…"

"Don't be, it was a long time ago. May I?" He indicated to a seat at the kitchen table.

"Gosh, yes. Please, sit."

He removed his hat and placed it on the seat next to him just as she set their breakfast and coffee on the table. "Looks delicious, Mrs. Barnes." He picked up his cutlery and tucked in.

Between mouthfuls they conversed about Mr. Barnes: she went over details of places he liked to hang out and where he did business, and so on. She also supplied him with a file filled with lists of properties and clients her husband looked after.

"You'll find everything you need in there. I've also supplied you with his little black book that contains numbers for his contacts."

"The woman, his PA—"

"Her details are also in the file. Patricia Selks. I mean, how much of a cliché is it, Sam, putting it to your secretary? I'm a blind *fool*."

"Love does that to you, Mrs. Barnes. When I lost my first wife, Claire, I said I'd never remarry."

"What changed your mind?"

"Love, of course. Angie, my second wife, took

my breath, sight and mind away—she rocked my world..." He looked down at his plate. "However, cancer came back into my life and took her from me and shattered my world all over again." He felt a knot develop in his throat. His cutlery rattled against the table as his hands shook. Samson always tried to steer clear of the subject of past wives. "I guess what I'm trying to say is, don't be too hard on yourself. It happens to the best of us; we put our trust in others and they break our hearts."

"But your wives didn't let you down, Samson—they didn't break your heart through mistrust, lies or threats of death." She wiped a tear from off her cheek.

"No, but at the time I did feel let down by them. It was selfish of me, I know that now." Samson's voice cracked, but he managed to hold firm. "How about another mug of joe and some for the road, possibly?"

After clearing his plate, he suddenly felt claustrophobic, as if the walls were closing in on him. Samson loosened his tie and pushed his chair away from the table. He was done. He needed fresh air.

"*Phew*, is it hot in here or is it just me?" *It's roasting! Between the heat and her perfume, it's making me nauseous; who wears a bottle load to breakfast? Who wears* any *to breakfast?*

"Sorry, the heating is on. Are you heading off?"

"Yes, muffin—I need to get cracking, especially if your husband is planning on coming to kill you soon. Who says he's going to wait? He could sneak back at any time. Besides, I have a lot to do by the looks of this file," he said, getting up and moving towards the door.

"Okay. I'll fix you a flask of fresh coffee to take with you."

"Can you lace it with scotch?"

She laughed. "Of course."

"Thanks," he said on his way out.

When he got outside Samson filled his lungs with the crisp morning air. He felt weak, his hands continued to tremble, and his chest ached as he breathed.

"Need a drink."

"Take it easy, Sam. I'm here."

"Angie, where did you go, gal?"

"Nowhere, I've been here all along, I just don't like disturbing you whilst you work."

"You weren't in the car last night, either—you abandoned me."

He was sweating profusely; his head spun. Samson made a grab for the short handrail connected to the steps that led off the home's front porch, and in a daze, made his way down them. From behind he heard Mrs. Barnes.

"Don't forget your coffee, Sam."

He turned and took the flask from her. "Thanks." Samson zigzagged towards the gates. "I'll be back later this afternoon. Try not to worry too much. I have your number, and I'll keep you updated and check in on you from time to time. Thanks once again for the breakfast and coffee."

Seconds later, Samson was in his car with the

windows down. He removed his coat and fedora. As he flicked through the file, he tried to cool down and focus his vision. Samson needed to figure out where to start looking for Mr. Barnes.

He lit a cigarillo.

"He's probably holed up in one of the local businesses he does the books for. It's what I'd do."

Samson took a few puffs on his cigarillo. *Perhaps he's shacked up with his PA muffin? Yeah, hers might be a good place to start looking.* Samson searched for her information and found the details Mrs. Barnes had written down for him: home address, mobile/landline number and a small photo of the woman in question.

"Okay, let's have a look-see here," he muttered, his smoke clenched between his teeth. "A pretty little thing." After removing all the information on her, he tossed the file onto the passenger's seat. From what he could tell, she had a fancy house just outside of Newport city.

"Hmm..."

Samson placed her details on his seat and opened the glove box. Inside were items every good PI needed: camera, Dictaphone, binoculars, notepad and pen. Samson removed his camera and checked it was loaded before looking to see if there were spare tapes for the recorder buried in the small compartment.

"Been a while since I used some of this stuff."

Before closing the hatch, he removed the pad and pen then replaced everything else. Samson then started his car and pulled off. As he drove down the street, he couldn't help but admire the array of stylish cars parked in the driveways: Cadillac sedans, Chrysler Highlanders and New Yorkers, Chevrolet Fleetmasters and station wagons—they were some of the finest models the late thirties/early forties had to offer.

We live in one hell of a time.

As he drove through the apple of Newport, he noted the place was as rundown as Cardiff, if not worse.

"At least with Cardiff being the capital, the government spends a bit of money tidying up and seeing to it that businesses move in and do well. But Newport? *Pfft!*" He looked at the people and the streets as he drove: most of the shops were boarded up with druggies, homeless and flunkies hanging about in their doorways, and some of the suspect characters were pestering passers-by for spare change and cigarettes. Others asked them to buy booze and drugs for them.

Newport is a place down on its luck, he thought. *My Chicago will see its glory days again, once I've cleared out XRay and his goons.*

Crossing a bridge out of the city and into the neighbouring town of Cwmbran, Samson didn't think things could get much worse, but he was wrong. *The joint looks as though the Luftwaffe have returned to finish what they started!* He shook his head.

But as quickly as he'd entered the spit of a town, he was leaving and was now looking for Patricia's street.

It took him less than fifteen minutes to locate her house and pull up outside.

Samson checked his watch.

Eight o'clock, on the button.

"A little later than I would have liked, but still."

From this distance he couldn't see too much, but could make out the closed upper and lower curtains. Her car wasn't parked on the drive, neither was his. Samson rechecked the notes to remind himself of what make and model vehicles they drove.

Also, there didn't appear to be any sign of life in or around the property, not that he could be entirely sure, of course.

Looks so damned quiet, he thought. *Hell, they could be in there all right, with their cars hidden or in storage.*

Samson sat there for a few minutes and eyeballed the house.

Finally, he got out of his car, locked it, and then as bold as brass made his way across the street and tried to peek through the tiny part in the curtains. He couldn't see movement so he decided to try the other front window, but found the curtains on that side were closed tight. Before heading off around the back of the property, he lifted the letterbox slot's door and peered inside. Nothing—it was too dark inside to see anything. He put his ear to the hole. No sound. Samson double-checked the street to make sure he wasn't being watched, then made his way to the rear of the home.

He tried the back door and found it locked. Then, in the window, he thought he saw a flash of movement.

"Hello?" he called, giving the door a rap. "Are you looking to change your windows?" Samson had used the salesman routine a few times over the years.

No response.

He moved to the window and gave it a couple of hard knocks.

Cheekily, he pressed his face against the glass and looked in, as there were no blinds blocking his view here. The building appeared abandoned.

Pretty sure I saw something...

Samson stepped back and looked up at the top windows—the curtains were drawn there, too.

Hmm. I wonder if it's worth staking the joint? He shook his head. *Nah, I can come back later this evening and see if anything has been disturbed, once I've checked out the local businesses.*

He returned to his car, picked up his camera, and then reeled off a few shots of the place before getting behind the wheel. As he swung his Ford around to face the opposite direction, he gave the upper and lower windows one last look.

I'll be back, palookas, he thought, pulling away.

***

By eighty-thirty Samson was walking the mean streets of Newport. He had a few businesses in mind he wanted to check first, before heading out to the biggest one, which was situated on the edge of town: a hotel by the name of Zzleep Easy.

First on his list was a Laundromat by the name of World of Whiz.

Cute, he thought, standing outside the shop with a smile on his face. But his mirth soon turned to confusion on seeing the sign on the door. It read 'closed'.

"*Huh?*" he scoffed. "How can it be closed...?" His words trailed off as he looked at his watch. "Shouldn't they be open at this hour?"

To be on the safe side, I best hang round for a short while—maybe they're a nine, nine-thirty kind of establishment. Samson looked at the sign once more before putting his face to the glass to peep inside.

Deserted.

He looked about him. The town centre was slowly waking up. *Maybe I'm slightly early*, he thought, spotting a coffee shop across the street. *Aye, why not?* He crossed the road and entered the joint. It was a homely, family-run place, that immediately reminded him of Alice and her coffee shop.

Damn! he chastised himself. *The frying-pan. I need to return it.*

"Large black coffee, please, miss," he told the woman behind the counter, stopping himself from asking if she could put a few shots of something stronger in it.

As he waited for his drink, he shuffled through his notes to see if any of the other businesses were close by. He looked up and out of the window every so often to see if anyone had turned up at the

Laundromat.

Looks like World of Whiz is the only business on this street he takes care of, unless I'm missing something.

His coffee was plonked down in front of him, a bit splashing over the rim and spattering onto his papers and hand. It was hot.

"Thanks," he tutted.

"Anything else, love?" the waitress groused. She had a fag dangling from the corner of her mouth. Ash hit his table. The stench of grease and sweat that rolled off her caused him to wrinkle his nose.

"No, thanks," he replied. "But I do have a question for you. What times does the Laundromat open?"

"You some kind of woodenhead?" She hung over his shoulder like a parrot.

"Woodenhead?"

"Yeah, a copper, love."

Listening to her talk was like hearing someone run their nails down a chalkboard. He winced, his top lip twitched. "Something like that, yes."

"Around nine o'clock, I think. Today could be their close day. Anything else?"

He shook his head. "No, thank you. Now, if you don't mind, I have important work to be getting on with, miss." Samson gave her his best smile, but she was already gone, heading back towards the counter, as another customer entered.

***

Samson sipped his coffee and continued to stare at the Laundromat as the clock ticked down the minutes—nine-thirty, nine-forty-five, ten o'clock… By ten-thirty there was still no sign of someone opening up shop, even though the street was now jumping with shoppers and workers alike.

After draining his third coffee he got up to leave and called his thanks to the wannabe barista.

"Bye, love!" she called back, though with hardly any enthusiasm.

Samson pulled up his lapels, tucked his file under his arm and walked across the street to the World of Whiz.

"Okay, so maybe today *is* the day they're closed. I could ask someone else? Forget it, let's see who's next on the list—I can always come back here later—*ah*, the Pig and Whistle. Hmm, sounds like a pub."

The stroll along the high-street to the Pig and Whistle was longer than he would have liked—his cheeks were a bit flushed by the time he reached the ale house's front stoop. But whatever thoughts he had of popping in and having a drink on the job were dashed when he grasped the door handle and realised that it, like the Laundromat, was closed.

The same was true of all the other businesses on his list: the butcher's, bicycle shop, key cutters, snooker hall, a second pub (this one called The Slaughtered Sheep), a gift shop, a small parcel company… Every single one of them was shut, and by their decrepit appearances, had been abandoned for a long time. Samson stopped in the middle of the street and lit a cigarillo. "It's a shakedown."

With no sign of Mr. Barnes, Miss Selks, or anyone connected to the pair to talk to, finding out what's going on is going to be tricky, he thought. *I have three options: go back to the Selks' house and wait to see if someone shows, wander over to the Zzleep Easy, or go back to Mrs. Barnes and stay put. After all, if Mr. Barnes does truly intend on killing her, then there is where he'll eventually turn up.*

Samson decided on the former, seeing no point in checking the hotel just yet: the Selks' home was on the way to the hotel, so checking her place first made more sense. Besides, he knew now there were no leads to follow in town.

"A shakedown, all right, especially if he's involved with the mafia," he thought aloud. "Mrs. Barnes did warn me that he was in deep. Maybe he borrowed the cabbage and hired a gun from them to rub her out? Is XRay mafia or mafia-connected?"

He was determined to figure it all out.

Nobody, but nobody, pulls the wool over Samson Valentine's eyes, he thought, getting into his car and driving off.

Chapter 10

When he arrived at the Selks' place it was after six. The sun had started to set, a spattering of premature stars twinkled in the sky and the moon had begun its climb from behind a group of rogue clouds.

The street had a totally different vibe: children were now playing with a football in the dying light by kicking it up against garages and parked cars; dogs barked, barbeques smoked, neighbours conversed.

Samson double-checked he had the right road, which he did. *It was much quainter earlier. What happened?* All he remembered seeing were high-end cars and nice homes but all that was here were patched-together bone shakers and rundown council homes. He scratched his head. *Maybe things just looked better in the daylight?* But he knew that didn't make sense. Before Samson crossed the road to Selks' house, he studied it. Something seemed different, but he couldn't tell what. He looked up at the top windows then back to the bottom ones. The curtains were disturbed.

No lights could be seen from within.

Samson looked over his shoulders and saw nobody paying him any attention. Mothers were calling their children; others, their pets; and Selks' neighbours on either side of her home were nowhere to be seen, giving him the confidence to move closer to the property.

Standing by one of the front windows, he checked again to make sure there was nobody eyeing him. The street was getting quieter: most of the children had gone in, along with the chatting neighbours. There was a lone dog walker in the distance, but they were headed in the opposite direction.

Streetlights burst to life.

The sun had fully set and the moon was now hidden behind the clouds.

Samson pressed his face to the glass and, even though the curtains were parted, he couldn't see into the living room from how dark it was inside. However, on closer inspection of the window, he saw bloody fingerprints on the inside of it.

His heart spurred to a gallop.

She must have been attacked upon returning home, as I would have seen the blood earlier. Was the person awaiting Patricia's return? Possibly, as I'm positive I saw movement whilst looking through the kitchen window earlier—Maybe Mr. Barnes has been injured? Perhaps he's hurt her? Did she know too much?

Slowly, he snuck around the corner of the house and moved to the rear. Samson was thankful there was nobody about to disturb him. He heard noises coming from one of the neighbouring houses; it sounded like someone was having a party in their garden.

He didn't let this halt his progress. After all, he was a PI, and had every right to snoop. When Samson rounded the next corner, he knew immediately that all was not well. The back door was fully open, its window smashed. Most of its glass lay on the concrete.

Facing the opening, he looked through it and into the house—there was nothing to see except gloom and moving shadows. He stepped over the threshold and announced his presence.

"My name's Samson Valentine, I'm a local PI and I'm coming in." His feet crunched broken glass as he crossed into the kitchen. "If there's somebody in here, hiding or otherwise, let yourselves be known, as I'm armed and have a nervous trigger-finger."

He stood still and listened for a moment.

A water pipe groaned.

A board creaked.

"Well, *anyone*? Miss Selks? Mr. Barnes? Speak up, goddamn you, or are there only palookas and hatchet-men waiting in the shadows?"

When he came across a light switch, he flicked it. The room was thrown into a pool of light that illuminated blood trails and destruction in the kitchen: the table and chairs had been overturned—some smashed to smithereens—splinters of wood were scattered across the floor and counters. Bloody handprints smeared the fridge door that had a massive dent in its middle.

Samson followed the blood trails.

As he entered the sitting room he flipped the lights on. The room had succumbed to the same fate as the kitchen: it was positively wrecked. He continued to follow the blood, which had marred the cream carpet, out of the door and into the hallway.

He checked the front door. It was locked.

As I'd thought, considering the mess on the back door.

Not wanting to touch the rail on the wall at the side of the stairs, Samson made his way up slowly, being careful to avoid the pools of blood on the steps.

Jesus! It's been a while since I've seen anything like this.

"Be careful Sam—the perpetrator could still be lurking."

I know, Angie.

When he reached the top step and saw someone standing in front of him in the room opposite, he thought his heart was going to explode in his chest—his breath hitched, and the hairs at the back of his neck and on his arms pricked.

Before he could yell, Samson noticed he was looking at himself, that it was a mirror image. He took a few deep breaths and moved closer to the room. A weak light escaped from somewhere within.

"Hello? My name's Samson Valentine and I am a private detective." No answer. "I'm coming in." He moved through the entrance fast and noticed immediately that a single lamp was burning on a bedside table. The room was empty, the bedding ruffled.

No blood trails.

He returned to the landing and pricked his ears.

Silence.

Samson looked down and noticed the blood led to a room at the far end of the landing. As he headed in that direction, he passed two more bedrooms and a bathroom, all of which were empty.

When he got to the end room, he found the door to be closed. There were smears of blood all over the white exterior and doorknob.

He pulled on his collars and swallowed hard.

Sweat broke across his brow and his hands trembled. He was in need of a drink and a smoke. Samson hated to admit it, but he was rattled.

"Is anyone in there, damn it?! If I have to come in and get ya, you aren't going to like it!" Samson put a hand to the doorknob, careful to avoid the blood, and turned it, slowly. "I'll give you to the count of three. One..." He held his breath. "...Two..." He turned the knob until it wouldn't go any further. "...*Three*!"

Samson threw the door wide.

He was hit by the foul stench of death, piss and excrement—it smelt like gone off milk, mixed with dead animal. "Oh, *Jesus*!" he blurted, covering his nose. The room lay in darkness, so he reached for the light switch. When the space was cast in a milky glow, he gagged at the sight before him: Miss Selks lay dead and naked on her bed. Her body had been split from abdomen to sternum, and her intestines lay in a coiled pile by her side. An impossible amount of blood was spattered all over the walls, carpet, photos and other trinkets and décor.

Samson stepped closer to the body. It was definitely Miss Selks. She no longer looked as pretty as she did in the photo he had of her in his folder: her blonde hair was soaked red, her face ashen. Purple marked her neck. Her right arm and fingers on that hand were broken—bone split skin. There was also bruising around her cheeks and eyes. Her lips were split.

"Someone gave the poor dame a good battering before ending her." Samson dug out his camera from his coat and reeled off a few snaps. He then noticed something odd, something he'd never seen or heard of before—she had something protruding from her vagina.

He put his camera down and plucked the offending article from her body. There were minuscule spatters of blood on the paper, which was rolled up as tight as a rollie.

"Dear Mr. Barnes," Samson read aloud. *"If you are reading this then I am safe in assuming that you have come out of hiding and are wishing to pay me my money. I do hope this is the case. If so, good. We can proceed with our business arrangement as planned. Bring the cash to Cardiff pier tonight, midnight, sharp. Once I have your payment, Mrs. Barnes will be no longer. Signed, The Sandman."*

It's always midnight with these idiots! he thought.

Samson looked down at Miss Selks and shook his head. "Poor thing. You were nothing more than a pawn in a twisted game of chess." Samson screwed up the note in his hand and pocketed it. "What did he send you back here for, I wonder? To see if the coast was clear? Did he honestly think he could pull the wool over the eyes of a ruthless killer? What did he promise you, sweetheart?"

He stared into her unblinking eyes. He knew it was no good—the broad was never going to tell him anything. She had taken her secrets to the grave.

Samson left the bedroom and checked his watch. He had plenty of time to get to the Zzleep Easy before going to the pier.

"Hell, I might even call in on Mrs. Barnes before I go and talk with The Sandman. *Pfft*, The Sandman—how inventive!" Samson headed downstairs and out the back door. "Best I call this in at some point." He got behind the wheel of his car and drove to the soothing sounds of jazz to help clear his mind.

***

The Zzleep Easy was a rundown hotel situated on the outskirts of Newport apple. It didn't belong to a chain, but a family—a mother and son. By all accounts, the father had passed away a number of years before the mother had purchased the place out on the old road connecting Cardiff and Newport.

It was a relic, a place time had forgotten; and from what Samson could see from standing outside, it was in desperate need of refurbishing and trade.

"At least it's open." He stepped up to the entrance. "I still can't think why the others were closed. I mean, if it's a shakedown, what's the point? It's not like he has money in them."

Questions, questions, he thought.

Samson walked to the reception desk and gave the bell atop the counter a couple of dings. The hotel was deathly quiet.

When there was no sign of anyone answering his call, Samson was about to hit the bell again, but stopped when he heard high-heels click-clack along the floor towards him. From behind a curtain at the rear of the reception area stepped a woman in her early fifties. She wore a figure-hugging red dress that showed off her curves.

Samson was glad his mouth was closed, because he was sure his tongue would have rolled out otherwise.

"A room?" she asked. Her voice was as fine and firm as her body. Samson couldn't get over how piercing her jade-coloured eyes were, which burned a hole through his forehead. "Sir?" she pushed, filling the silence.

"Sorry, er—no, I've come in search of a person and to ask a few questions, if that's okay?"

"What sort of questions? Are you a police officer?"

"I'm a private eye, ma'am." Samson showed her his credentials. "Are you the owner?"

"Why yes, my name is *Ms*. Peters."

If she is hiding Barnes here, then she's acting as cool as ice about the whole thing, he thought, looking her in the eye. "I see. And is it 'Miss', as in the unmarried kind?"

"No, as in the widowed kind, Mr. Valentine."

"I'm sorry to hear that."

"What is it I can do for you, exactly?"

"I'm here about your bookkeeper, Mr. Barnes. You see, his wife is very concerned about his well-being, considering one of his employees has turned up dead at her home," he informed her. He was hoping the information would rattle her, and that she would expose her hand. "The quicker I find Mr. Barnes, the safer others will be."

She held firm. "Oh, dear God—that's awful! Who was it?"

"His PA, a Miss Selks."

"Dreadful. Who would do such a thing?"

"Rumour is Mr. Barnes was having an affair with Miss Selks. Do you know if that's true?"

"Why, I couldn't possibly tell you."

"Are you hiding him here, *Ms*. Peters?"

"Most certainly not! I haven't seen Mr. Barnes in days, as a matter of fact. The last time I *did* see him was on Wednesday of last week. He came here on business." "I see. And if I wanted to check the premises, I'd need a warrant? Or would you allow me to have a look around? I mean, if you're not hiding anything…"

She scowled at him and crossed her arms in front of her chest. "Are you calling me a liar?"

"No, not at all, I was—"

"Good. But you can still go and get yourself a warrant."

"You'd be saving me an awful lot of trouble if—"

She shook her head.

"Hardball, eh? Well, that's fine by me. I just hope I can get back here in time." He turned to leave.

"And just what is *that* supposed to mean?"

"It means I've been talking to a dead palooka." Samson exited the hotel, frustrated by the fact that he was nowhere closer to finding out what was going on.

***

With a little over three hours until he had to be at Cardiff pier, Samson decided to check back with Mrs. Barnes.

He rang the buzzer on her gate and she let him in almost immediately.

"At least she's still among the living! It would be a shame for such a pretty, elegant woman to wake up on the wrong side of the dirt."

Her front door was standing open, which slightly angered him. *Silly woman, she should have waited until I'd knocked—anyone could have been lurking.* With that thought, he checked around him.

There was nobody there.

He pushed the door wide open, it creaked.

"Mrs. Barnes?" A chill inched its way up his back and settled in his gut. But the feeling dispersed as fast as it had set in.

"I'm in the kitchen, Sam. Please, come on through."

He didn't need telling twice. When he reached her, he found she had a cup of coffee and a hot meal on the table for him.

"Why, Mrs. Barnes—"

She pooh-poohed him with her hand as she took a sip of her coffee. "I'll hear none of it. Please, sit down and eat. I'd like to hear about your day and what you've managed to find out. Besides, it's nice having a real man to fuss over."

"You had Mr. Barnes."

"*Huh*!" she scoffed. "You must be kidding. He didn't want me, as much as I tried to be the good 'little wifey'. He was disinterested. He only wanted my money."

Samson took a seat. On the plate was a piece of chicken, new potatoes and vegetables. *I remember you cooking for me like this, Angie.*

A forgotten time emerged in his whisky-addled mind, but Samson didn't allow it to fully materialise.

His guts rumbled.

"This looks good."

"I know how it is with you police officers," she smiled.

"You do?"

She nodded. "My uncle used to be on the force. I always remember my aunt complaining about how she rarely saw him and how little he ate. 'He's always thinking about the job,' she'd say."

"Sounds like he was one of the good guys, Mrs. Barnes—there's so many bad apples in the force nowadays, which makes it hard for us straight-laced Joe's."

"Are you the one good cop in a bad town, Mr. *Ness*?"

He huffed a laugh. "An *Untouchables* fan? I

didn't think such a classy lady would be into such violence."

"Maybe I'm *not* that classy under the surface, Sam. Now, eat up and tell me what you've found out."

"You could have fooled me." Samson removed his coat and hat before starting his meal. It felt strange—never had a client treated him this way, or with such respect. Maybe a long time ago, but he couldn't recall. His early days as a PI were buried beneath a thick, golden haze of whisky. Maybe this case and Mrs. Barnes were the best things to happen to him.

It's been a long time since I've been thinking this straight, this sharp. Even though I cracked a big job not too long back, it was a mere fluke. Not only that, it was a straightforward stalk and snatch.

"Did your husband ever mention The Sandman when you were eavesdropping?"

She shrugged. "Never. Who is he?"

"He's either some sort of Bruno—a tough guy, enforcer for a mean bunch of bastards, pardon my French—or The Sandman is a button man—a professional killer; a hitman. If that's the case he's either a lone businessman your husband sought out, or The Sandman is working for a big player."

"What makes you say all this, Sam? What have you discovered?"

"Well," he said, between mouthfuls. "There's definitely something fishy going on with Mr. Barnes, and I think he's in way over his head."

She put a hand to her mouth. Her eyes glassed

over.

Samson couldn't help but feel for her. She was clearly scared. A single tear rolled down her cheek. *If she's this shaken by that, then God knows how she's going to react to the rest of it.*

He didn't hold back. He told her about Miss Selks, the information he'd recovered from her body and about the businesses all being closed, apart from the hotel.

"I think he's hiding there, to be frank."

She started shaking and crying, her hands curled into fists.

A lump developed in his chest, which wasn't indigestion, no matter how much he tried to convince himself it was. Samson wasn't a soft, whimsical man, but there was something about this broad. *If I'm not careful, I'm likely to get dizzy over this dame, which isn't a good thing.*

He put an arm around her. "You're safe. You did the right thing contacting me."

"Oh, Sam—what am I going to do?!"

"You don't have to do anything. I'm going to go to the pier and have a chat with Sandman, to see if I can get the dirt about your husband. Do you have any idea *why* all the businesses would be closed?"

He felt the shake of her head against his chest.

"What about this Peters woman at the hotel?"

"I have no idea, Sam. I'm scared. What if you come back here and find me cut open?"

"That's not going to happen."

"How can you be so sure?"

"Because I plan to relocate you, that's how."

"Where?"

"My place, but not tonight. Tonight, you'll have to sit tight. I'll get you out of here tomorrow morning."

"Where will you be?"

"I'll be outside, on watch. You're safe, trust me."

"Thanks, Sam," she sniffled.

"No problem, kid." He let go of her and returned to his food.

"Now's the time to lay off the booze, Sam! This is your chance to get straight."

I know, Angie.

"A return to the glory days..."

With his food finished, Samson chewed the fat with Mrs. Barnes over a second coffee, before heading out the door to his car. The pier was calling, and he had forty minutes to get there.

Chapter 11

The pier was a relatively modern structure situated in Cardiff Bay: a snooty area that reeked of money, Porsches, Ferraris, yachts and speedboats. Only the likes of doctors and lawyers inhabited the flats that came with a seven-digit price tag; Samson and his ilk were relegated to the slums and middle-class parts of town, which suited him fine. He'd never seen himself owning a fancy boat, car or a house that dripped materialistic possessions.

Also, he'd been lucky in marrying two great ladies who'd felt the same way—they'd been happy with their simple set ups, knowing Samson's end goal wasn't a fancy lifestyle.

The way he saw it, there was more to life than glossy objects.

Samson parked his car a few streets away, thinking a walk to the pier would do him good. He lit a cigarillo and started ambling towards his destination. He was in no rush. *The hatchet-men in the shadows can wait—it's not like they're prone to decency or sticking to house rules, such as being somewhere on time. They run with the fox and hounds*, he thought, looking out across a sea that reminded him of an oil slick.

The posh streets of Cardiff were quiet. There were no raucous strip joints, overzealous nightclubs or boozers filled with brawling knuckleheads. The avenues were clean and tidy—druggies and flunkies didn't hang around in doorways and for the first time in nights Samson saw good ole' boys walking the beat.

"Well, will wonders never cease?" He watched as the boys in blue moved a couple of youths along who seemed to be doing nothing wrong.

Another thing he noticed was that all the streetlights worked. Hell, even the air smelt cleaner, fresher. It wasn't choked with fumes, but that could have been his imagination.

"Angie, I bet you would have loved a place down here."

"Maybe, but you know I liked our little home, Sam."

"It's so empty without you."

He stubbed his cigarillo and threw the butt in a waste bin that was nailed to a lamppost before pressing on.

When he arrived at the pier's entrance he noticed the barriers were down, the doors locked. *Access denied*, he thought then spotted a large concrete bin that was cemented to the ground. *If I hop onto that, I should be able to get onto the roof of the pay booth.* Without further thought, Samson put his plan into action and was soon on top of the ticket stall.

He looked down over the other side and saw another bin, which he hopped onto. When he was on the planks, he strolled quickly up the pier, assuming the meeting would take place at the far end where they'd be out of sight and away from prying eyes.

Samson slowed his pace as he drew nearer to his destination. The pier was in complete darkness—the moon and stars concealed by clouds. Beneath him he heard the waves crashing, masking his footfalls. At the far end of the structure he knew there was an arcade, a coffee shop and some stalls.

As he neared the end he could see the outlines of the buildings—they looked like badly drawn lines against the night sky. His breath caught in his throat when he saw plumes of smoke rising from a hidey-hole in the dark.

"Stop right there, Mr. Barnes," a voice called in the near silence. "I take it you got my message?"

Samson could almost hear the smile in the meathead's tone.

"I wasn't sure if you'd show up or not," the palooka went on.

"Yeah, I got it. How did you know I'd go to the house ahead of this meeting?"

"A hunch, I guess. Besides, you didn't really have anywhere else to run to, did you?"

"What do you mean?"

"Come, come, Mr. Barnes. Let's not play dumb."

"Why don't you enlighten me, boob?"

"Tough talk for a man in your situation, don't you think?"

"Sorry, I just—I'm rattled."

"Understandably so, I guess, but this is what happens when you play with the big boys. You wanted your bitch dead, but had no means of paying me for such a job. You tried to trick me, Mr. Barnes, but I found out about your money woes."

"I see. And you came looking for me at all the places I look after in Newport, isn't that right?"

"You're a quick learner."

"I guess you didn't know about the Zzleep Easy, as I was holed up there."

The Sandman didn't answer.

"I guess you ain't *that* smart, bruno!" Samson jeered.

Footsteps shuffled towards him.

"Yes, I knew about the hotel, and I was on my way there to flush you out, but I ran into that pretty little secretary of yours. She parted with information."

Again, Samson heard that smile.

"What did she tell you?" he asked.

"Where's my money, Mr. Barnes? I suggest you hand it over, or it'll be *you* who ends up dead, not your lovely wife."

"If I hand over the cabbage, do you promise to do the job and leave me alone?" Samson asked.

"Of course. I'll eliminate her tonight."

"But the deal was for the weekend?"

"Do you have a short memory, Mr. Barnes? We agreed—who the *fuck* are you?!"

Samson had become engrossed in the conversation, failing to notice the big shape looming out of the blackness before him. A glint of steel to his left caught his attention.

"You're fucking dead!" the man roared.

The hunting knife cut through the air, barely missing Samson as he clumsily side-stepped, almost tripping over his own feet. "I'm with Johnny law!" he said, hoping it would make a difference, but it didn't—his attacker kept coming.

After regaining his balance Samson saw the serrated, red-coated steel come at him from a different angle. In one fluid movement, Samson blocked the attack and knocked the knife out of The Sandman's hand—it skittered across the pier's planks.

The Sandman grabbed him and twirled him around, ramming his back against the rail. Below them, the waves crashed. Samson tried to struggle free, but the man's large paws wrapped around his throat.

"Who the *fuck* are you? It doesn't matter, soon you'll be dead anyway, just like the Selks—*oomph*!" Sandman cut off as Samson raised his knee hard and fast, ploughing it into his attacker's balls.

The grip loosened from around his throat, but didn't completely fall away until after he'd delivered a second and third knee to the guy's bollocks. The Sandman doubled over in pain and wretched up his lunch onto the boardwalk.

Samson was about to give the man a sharp chop to the neck, but a second and third assailant stepped out of the darkness—he thought he saw Tommy guns.

"Hold it right there, lawman," one of them said.

The second mobster cocked his machine gun. "I say we pump his guts full of lead, Johnny!"

Samson put his hands in the air. "I only want this palooka. You're free to walk."

"Who—who are you talking to?" Sandman wheezed, collapsing to his knees.

Samson looked down at the man and then back at the chopper squad: they were heavily scarred and smoking thick cigars.

"Check him for a smoker, Knocks," the first gunman said.

"I'm unarmed, fellas."

"We're still going to check you, friend—you might have what we're looking for," Knocks said, lowering his gun and patting Samson down.

"The stone?" Samson asked.

"Maybe, now shut your yap!" Johnny said.

"He's clean—" said Knocks.

Samson grabbed Knocks and threw him over the pier's railing—his screams were cut dead when he hit the water below. Bullets cut the night apart as Johnny's Tommy gun opened up, spraying lead and illuminating the area with Chicago lightning.

"*Christ!*" Samson jumped, rolled and picked up The Sandman's knife as he went. When he came to a stop, he turned and threw the blade, which slammed into Johnny's chest. The mobster lowered his still-firing gun, which peppered his feet and the planks, before he crashed to the ground, dead.

"So, you thought you could rub me out with your hit squad, hey, Sandman?" Samson went to the man and dragged him off the floor. "Who do you work for?"

"There's only you and me here!" he spluttered.

Samson screamed in the man's face and grabbed him by his coat's collars, "I'm placing you under arrest, palooka. They'll throw the book at ya: assault with a deadly weapon, the murder of the

Selks woman, and the attempted hit on me, one Samson Valentine. It's just a shame your brunos aren't alive to do time with you."

As he reached for his handcuffs at his side, he noticed the man he'd killed with the knife was missing. Also, there were no bullet holes or blood to be seen. "*How—?*"

He was shoved off balance. This time, he did trip, but Samson managed to take The Sandman to the ground with him. They rolled about the floor, throwing fists. Samson caught one to the nose, which started gushing.

"Get…off…!" Samson gasped as he struggled with the bigger, heavier man.

Another fist caught him on his right cheek, and then the left. A head-butt came from nowhere and ignited a galaxy of stars before his eyes, but he didn't release his hold on The Sandman.

A few digs to his ribs: left, left and a right. With a push, Samson drove himself up and off the floor, using all his weight and might to drive his opponent against one of the stalls. He let rip with three lunging head-butts of his own, which left his assailant dazed.

The Sandman slumped in his grasp. Samson let go. The man hit the deck with a solid, satisfying thump. He cuffed him to a section of railing. Knowing his man wasn't going anywhere, Samson staggered backwards and slumped onto a bench.

He dug a cigarillo out of his pocket and lit it, noting it was his last. "Well, at least luck's on my side." He leaned back against the bench and smoked as he waited for his head to clear, and The Sandman to wake.

"I want answers out of that palooka before I take him downtown."

His nose and ribs hurt, but the tobacco helped soothe him. He turned and looked over at the spot where the gunman had lain dead. He couldn't understand where the body had gone.

"He couldn't have been dead. He's probably scuttled back to his boys to regroup."

Samson looked up at the sky—some of the clouds had parted, exposing a cluster of stars. "It's too beautiful a night to worry about escaped hitmen. I'll fall on him at some point. They can't outrun me."

Fifteen minutes later, with his smoke finished and The Sandman still down, Samson was out of ideas as to what to do next. *The gates are locked and I can't lug him over the roof. I could wait until the pier opens? Damn, that'll be a waste of time.*

Samson got up and walked over to the downed goon. The Sandman was unconscious. To be sure, he checked the cuffs. They were secure. He was going nowhere, so Samson returned to his seat and sat with a huff. Before he knew it, he'd drifted off into sleep.

***

Someone was yelling.

They sounded distressed. He opened his eyes—the sky was still dark.

"*Hey*! Wake the fuck up. You're fucking dead meat, pal. Do you hear me? Fucking *dead*!"

When Samson moved his head, his neck screamed in agony. "God*damn* it!" He put a hand down the back of his collar and massaged the hurt from his muscles. His eyes flicked to The Sandman. He was a tall burly chap with a thick, blood-coated beard. His nose was flat against his face, broken. He spat and snapped at Samson like a rabid dog, and had the circumstance been different, he would have howled with laughter. Even the man's teeth were stained red.

"You better let me go, *punk*!"

"*Punk*?" Samson smiled.

"Who the fuck are you? Answer me."

"A friend of *Mrs*. Barnes."

"You piece of shit. You've no idea what you've done. Nobody gets in my way. *Nobody*. You're a copper, right?"

"I'm a PI, and I have you under citizen's arrest, jug head. As soon as the pier opens, I'm taking you downtown, see?"

"A PI? A private investigator?!" The Sandman shrieked with laughter. "You're nothing more than a glorified, fucking curtain twitcher. Fucking snoopy cunt."

"You have a potty mouth, son, and your kind is what's wrong with the world nowadays. Now, start answering some questions. Where did your goon run off to, the one I poked with the knife?"

"I ain't telling you shit, pal."

"What if I say please?"

"You have no power. You have nothing. You can't make me do or say anything."

Samson rose, lifted his collar, and walked to the man. He got down on his haunches and looked him in the eye. "I might not have power, but I know plenty of ways to make you scream while I extract information, hop-head. Now, in general, I'm a friendly guy, but when I have my buttons pushed, I tend to hit back."

The Sandman seemed disinterested, unafraid. "You can't scare me, dickhead."

"Is that so? You know, Magic Mike pushed my buttons…"

The look on The Sandman's face changed.

"I see you know the pimp," Samson went on. "Yeah, I crippled him by all accounts. Now, I'm going to tell you once more—I want information, and if I don't get it, well, let's just hope you can swim. I'm done screwing around with you, bruno."

"You can't threaten me—you're a *copper*."

"No, I'm a 'glorified curtain twitcher', remember?" Samson pressed his nose to The Sandman's. Both men gritted their teeth.

"I'm calling your bluff."

Samson shook his head. "Many times, I've run into hard cases such as yourself," he said, spotting the Bowie knife on the pier and fetching it. *Hmm, the palooka must have pulled it out of his chest before running off,* Samson thought, pulling on a pair of gloves before he picked up the blade. "An impressive knife. Do you hunt?

"With a flick-knife?"

Samson turned to face The Sandman, who shuffled closer to the railings. "In order for me to not hurt you, I urge you to start talking. Who do you work for?" Samson thrust the tip of the steel closer to the man's eyeball. "I could pop it like a water balloon. Don't forget, nobody knows I'm here but you."

"Jesus, get it out of my face!"

"Is this the blade you used to kill Miss Selks?"

"Piss off!" The Sandman spat in Samson's face.

A hot rage slipped down Sam's insides and nestled in his guts. He slowly dragged the tip of the knife down The Sandman's face.

"Argh—*fuck*! Get off—"

"Is this the knife you used? I'm not messing with you, Mr. Hard Case. Is it?"

"Go to hell, pig!"

Samson pulled the knife down the other side of The Sandman's face. The early morning was split asunder by yelling and sobbing.

"I'm going to cut your nose off next, palooka! I really detest a man who hurts and threatens ladies."

"I can't... They'll *kill* me."

"*Who'll* kill you?"

The Sandman shook his head and pursed his lips.

Samson ran the blade down the man's nose, over his lips and then his chin. The sound made him think of a razor cutting through stubble.

"*Arrrrgh*! Please!" The Sandman was wailing like a baby throwing a tantrum.

"The nose comes off next. Now, *talk*."

"You're just a PI, for fuck's sake."

"True. However, before I became a private investigator, I was a regular cop, but the force kicked me."

"What? *Why?*" The Sandman asked, spitting blood.

"You've never told anyone about your dark days on the force, Sam," Angie warned. *"You only told me because you were drunk that night..."*

"*Nothing!* Forget I said anything. Just answer my goddamn questions."

"Look man, I can't. They'll do much—*arrrgh!*" he screamed again as Samson ran the knife across his forehead and then placed it against the bridge of his nose.

"Talk or it comes off."

"This is brutality! You can't go—yes," he quickly said, as the blade dug into his flesh.

"Yes, what?"

"Yes, it's the knife I used."

"Who are you working for?"

"I... I—*arrrgh!*" The Sandman cried as the knife bit into his nose further. "Alligator. Alligator, damn it."

Samson eased up with the blade, a smile stretched across his face. "Got any smokes?"

The Sandman sobbed. "Left pocket."

Samson found what he was looking for and dug a Pall Mall out of its box. He stood up and lit it. "That's good. That's very good. What's your name?"

"Sandman—"

"I know your moniker. I mean your real name.

First and last?"

"Robert Dalesford."

"And you're a hired hitter for Alligator, is that right?"

Robert nodded.

"Where can I find Alligator? Who is he?" Samson asked, advancing with the knife.

"He's a crime boss on the West Coast. You can cut me up all you want, but I don't know where he lives. Nobody does—not even his closest soldiers."

"Soldiers? *Pfft*, that's a laugh. Is this Alligator connected to XRay?"

"Hey, fuck you!"

"Watch it, or I may cut your tongue out. Answer the question."

"*Easy, Sam, baby—try not to revert back to that Sam. Get the balance right. Return to glory.*"

"You're right, Angie."

"What? Who in the fuck are you talking to? And what goons did I have with me?"

"Never mind, palooka. Answer me!"

"You're insane, and I'll get you on brutality."

"Who do you think the cops are going to believe—a woman-murdering scumbag like you, or an upstanding private eye such as me, Sam Fucking *Spade*?"

"You said your name's Valentine?"

"Ah, pipe down. You might not be able to tell me who Alligator is, but I'm sure *one* of his goons will be able to."

"Best of luck, dickhead."

"Is he connected to XRay?"

"I told you, I don't know anything—I just get handed my orders, I swear."

"Do I have to use the knife some more?" Samson threatened, raising the blade.

"*No*! Jesus. Look, okay, there's bad blood between Alligator and XRay, but I don't know what it's about. Honestly. You have to believe me!" The man was close to tears.

Samson shook his head and looked at him. He wanted to smash Sandman's nose with the haft of the Bowie, but managed to swallow his rage. *I need a drink*, he thought. His hands shook.

"Just keep quiet. The boys at the big house will get all the information we need from you. Now, we've got a few hours together yet and the last thing I want is you yip-yapping, so keep your flapper shut."

Samson took a seat on the bench. After two hours of silence, Samson got up to stretch his legs and to check on Robert's cuffs before walking down the pier towards the gates.

Best I check the opening time.

"Six a.m.," he read. He looked at his watch—it was four minutes to five. "Not long now," he muttered, walking back up the boards to his charge.

"Hey, do me a favour and loosen one hand so I can have a smoke? I'm starting to lose circulation here."

Where's the blood gone from his face? The slice marks, too? Samson thought.

"Did you hear me?" Sandman asked.

"Er—they aren't *that* tight."

What's going on? Am I losing my mind? I cut him up, didn't I? How did I get the information out of him…?

"Come on, man—I ain't going anywhere. Besides, *you* have my knife."

"Yeah, er…I do, don't I? Any funny business and I'll stick you. Got it?"

Robert nodded.

Samson bent down, undid one of the cuffs and quickly snapped it to the railing.

"Thanks." Robert rotated his hand. "Smoke?" he offered, digging his fags out of his coat.

"Please," said Samson, taking one and lighting Robert's.

"What time can we leave?" Robert asked.

"Place opens at six which gives us less than an hour."

"Great."

Samson went back to the bench and sat down. When he turned to look at Robert, he noticed the man had his hand digging inside his coat pocket.

"What are you doing?" Samson leapt to his feet and shoved Robert, who collapsed to the floor. He put his hand in the man's pocket and dug out a mobile phone. "What did you do? What's the code for this…this *thing*?"

"*Ha!*" Robert bellowed, lashing out with his foot and kicking the phone from Samson's hand. It sailed through the air and over the pier's railings.

"Damn. That's it, we're getting out of here right now, palooka." Samson removed the cuff off the railing and secured Robert's hands behind his back.

Robert struggled and cursed as Samson strong-armed him up the pier.

"Hey, you—you're not supposed to be on here," someone called, rushing towards Samson. "Who are you?"

"Samson Valentine, private eye." Samson showed the breathless man his credentials. "This jug head is under citizen's arrest. Are you able to let me out of here?"

"Oh... I see... Yes, right this way. I don't normally come down this early, but someone reported seeing people on the pier."

"That would be us," Samson said.

"Hey, mate—you've got to help me," Robert said. "This man is taking me hostage."

"*Quiet!*" Samson stepped outside the pier and dragged Robert to his car.

Once he'd bundled his man inside, Samson wasted no time in getting behind the wheel and driving off. His tyres screeched. When he looked up to check on Robert in the rear-view mirror, he noticed there was a car tailing them.

Chapter 12

"Friends of yours?" Samson asked, keeping an eye on the car behind.

"Don't know what you're talking about, friend."

"I'll just bet you don't!" Samson looked at Robert in the rear-view, who was trying to look over his shoulder and out the back window, before taking a sharp right, a left and then another right, which took him onto the motorway back to Cardiff. He hoped the series of quick manoeuvres would shake the car behind, but they were sticking to him like flies on a corpse.

They were driving along a quiet stretch, with nary another car on the road. Suddenly, Samson's car swerved amid the crash of metal and an explosion of breaking glass. As Samson fought the wheel for control, the other driver pulled up alongside Samson's car and side-swiped him. His door buckled, his side window shattering in a blizzard of flying glass. The driver wrenched his car free of Samson's for another pass, prying off Samson's wing mirror.

"*Bastards!*" He glanced over at the two men—their faces were hidden behind animal masks. The driver was a bear, the passenger a fox. "Who are they, Robert?"

"*Who?*"

The car slammed into his side again and again, before dropping back and shunting his rear bumper.

Samson hit the accelerator and swerved into the fast lane. His car shot by others as he increased his speed to ninety, but still they kept coming, and rammed into his side again and again, sending him into the steel barrier that separated the traffic moving in the opposite direction.

"*Jesus*!" Samson screamed.

"What the hell is wrong with you?" Robert asked.

When Samson looked in the rear-view, he spotted a four-by-four hurtling towards his back bumper. Seconds later, it smashed into him, jerking his car. His head snapped back from the impact.

The masked men then came in from the side once again, aiding the four-by-four. They closed him in and forced Samson's car against the divide again, gradually slowing him down to seventy, sixty, fifty…

"Shit, shit, shit!" Samson slammed his fist against the console and pressed his foot down hard on the accelerator. All the while he yanked the steering wheel to his left with all his might, trying to force the car off him, to no avail. They had him pinned in.

Forty, thirty…

His car was now crawling and chugging. Samson had to do something, because if they stopped him, they would free their man and execute Samson. His eyes darted left and right, sweat stung them, and he spotted his wheel lock in the passenger well. Samson bent over and retrieved it. Knowing his car was stuck fast to the barrier, he undid his belt and clambered into the passenger seat.

With the window gone, he was able to reach out with the locking device and smash it through the other driver's window and club the Bear with it.

Their car skidded and smashed into a brewery tanker marked Brains Bitter.

By the time Samson was back in his seat and in full control of his car, he saw the tanker's driver get out of his cab moments before it caught fire. The whole sorry mess exploded a heartbeat later, and the car was thrown into the air before smashing back down on top of the lorry.

The air filled with the stench of charred metal, ale and flesh.

Samson mashed the accelerator and pulled away from the four-by-four, taking the vehicle's bumper with him.

"What the hell kind of driving is this?" Robert asked. "I'm being thrown around like a fucking ball, dickhead! There's no need to go like hell, man."

"Shut up!" Samson couldn't see the four-by-four now, allowing him to gather more speed and a bigger gap. "Who are they, Robert?"

"Who are you talking about?"

Samson jumped on the brakes, throwing Robert forward and smashing his nose against the passenger headrest.

"Talk, damn you!"

"They're my boys, but you lost them before we got on the motorway—they won't catch us now."

"Don't act so stupid—they just tried ramming us off the bloody road!"

"What the fuck are you talking about?"

Samson slammed the brakes again. "Don't mess with me or I'll throw you out onto the motorway."

"I don't know what you're talking about. You *lost* them. There's nobody on the road with us!"

"They've gone Sam, calm yourself and get this bozo behind bars," Angie said.

Samson dropped into his seat as the rear window shattered in a rain of bullets. He snatched a glance in the rear-view and saw a gunman hanging out of the passenger window of the four-by-four. In his hands was a Tommy gun.

"It's a chopper squad, all right. Looks like your friends caught up, Robert."

Bullets pummelled the passenger seat and sheared off his remaining wing mirror.

"I don't see anyone!" Robert said.

Samson ignored his prisoner and took an exit ramp off the motorway. He sped through the city as fast as he could, but then a dreadful banging erupted from the engine, like a desperate man hammering for release from a coffin. Smoke oozed from the edges of the bonnet.

"Come on, come on—I've got to make it to the station!" He gritted his teeth.

The car swerved and careened around the city. As soon as he got into a more populated area, the four-by-four fell away—it screeched around a corner and disappeared.

Samson released his held breath.

"Your palooka friends have gone. Nobody is going to save you, Robert. You're off to the big house, friend."

Robert said nothing.

Samson brought the car to a screeching halt outside the police station and dragged The Sandman from his seat. Police officers swarmed them.

"It's okay, I'm a private investigator, and I have this man under citizen's arrest."

They were both hauled into the police station and separated, with Samson being escorted to D.I. Davis' office.

"*Come!*" the D.I. called from his office after the young constable with Samson had knocked.

"Sir, we have someone here for you."

"Valentine? Bring him in."

Samson walked in, his face locked in a mute expression.

"What the hell happened?" Davis asked shaking his head. "You look like shit."

"It's a long story."

"You can leave us, constable."

The young policeman acknowledged with a nod and left as asked.

"Well, Sam?" said Davis. "And the *truth*, mind you."

Samson sighed. "I'm onto something big."

"Word is you've been causing trouble for certain people…"

"Who's been yakking?"

"Relax. You can trust me, Sam—not all of us coppers around here are bent." Samson eyed the older man for a second. Since they'd thrown Samson out of the force, he'd found it hard to trust any of them. "Whisky?"

"You still keep that bottle of Glen in your top drawer?" Samson smiled.

"I'll take that as a yes?" Davis poured them each a drink.

Samson relayed what he knew about The Sandman and what he'd done to the Selks woman—he also handed over the knife that had been used to butcher her. However, he left out the parts about the goons he'd dealt with on the pier and motorway.

Can't spill my guts completely.

"You'll find his prints on that and her body, which is at her house," Samson said, giving the detective Patricia's address. "I have to keep quiet to protect my client, Davis. I owe her that."

"And this husband of hers, you think he'll show up? Maybe do the job himself?"

"Possibly."

"I can have a guard on her property, if you'd like?" Davis offered.

"No need, I'm heading there now." Samson drained his glass and got up to leave.

"One thing, before you go?"

"Yeah?" Samson turned to face the D.I.

"Did you visit Magic Mike?"

Samson smiled. "That no good palooka of a pimp down on the docks?"

"That's the one."

"Never heard of him," Samson said, winking.

***

A few hours later, in a car that could barely move, Samson was back at Mrs. Barnes' place with a ton of information. Before they'd sat down to talk, she'd insisted on him taking a shower to freshen up—he'd also changed into some of the clean clothes he had in his car.

Once he'd finished, and she'd tended his cuts and scrapes, they'd gone into the kitchen for coffee.

"So, Robert, this Sandman—my husband hired him?"

"It seems that way, yes, but your husband had no money for him."

"But he has plenty," Mrs. Barnes said.

"Then why double-cross a man like that, a man who could easily snuff him out?" She didn't reply, and so he went on. "I have a feeling your husband stole the money from the businesses he was looking after, which would explain why they're all closed down. You've been lied to. I don't think he had *any* money of his own, Mrs. Barnes, and I think he planned to have you killed by The Sandman and then swindle him. Or, worse, kill him. My guess is, Sandman didn't know who he was getting into business with."

"But—but—where did the money from his business go? I'd also given him some."

"I'm not sure, but I'll figure it out. Is Mr. Barnes who he claims to be? Was Miss Selks a gold-digger?"

"I'm not sure, I just thought he was a down-on-his-luck businessman, and I have no idea about the woman. She's a complete mystery to me."

"I'm starting to think he's nothing more than a goon—a foot soldier for XRay, and that Miss Selks was a drain on him."

"Who's XRay?"

"Not a very nice man, and from what I can gather, he and The Sandman's boss, Alligator, don't like each other very much."

"If I wasn't scared before, I am now!"

"Don't worry. Like I said, I'll be moving you today. I think this thing is bigger than either of us thought. Whilst I finish up here, go and pack a few things, enough for a week or so."

She put her cup down and left the room.

"One more thing," he called after her. "Is there any chance we can use one of your cars? Mine's out of action for the time being."

"Of course."

***

Within minutes he heard her banging around upstairs: drawers slammed, cupboard doors opened and coat hangers rattled.

"Dames," he muttered, shaking his head. "Got to pack everything but the kitchen sink."

As he drank his coffee he paced the kitchen and eyed her various trinkets and décor. He went to fish a cigarillo out of his pocket, but remembered he had none, that the last smoke he'd had was off The Sandman.

Samson moved to the foot of the stairs. "Remind me to pick up some cigarillos and whisky on the way to my place, Mrs. Barnes."

"Yes, okay."

He then continued his mooch around the kitchen and came across a stack of letters. Samson turned to make sure Mrs. Barnes wasn't coming, before going through them. He hoped something would jump out at him, not that he didn't trust her.

I have a job to do, he thought, *and that job can lead to not trusting anyone, including my own mother. Not that she's alive' n' jivin'.* When he reached the bottom of the pile he found a piece of scrap paper with a bunch of numbers written on it. There was no name. *A telephone number?*

Thinking it might be important, Samson jotted down the digits in his notepad before putting the papers back as they were. Then he noticed the addressee on the paperwork he'd been rooting through—these were Mr. Barnes' personal effects.

Hmm. You'd think his stuff would be in his office, not lying around here in the kitchen for the whole world and his wife to see. I'll give this number a ring when I'm out and about—find out who's on the other end.

"*Maybe Mrs. Barnes has been doing her own investigating?*"

"Could be, Angie. Could be." He tapped his pen against his pad.

"What was that, Sam?" Mrs. Barnes called. "Can't quite hear you."

"Oh, nothing, I was just thinking aloud—I do that a lot, sorry. Something you'll have to put up with."

She laughed. "I won't be much longer, Sam."

"No worries, muffin." Samson continued to roam around the kitchen, but nothing else seemed to spark his interest. *Might be an idea to have a poke around Mr. Barnes' office?*

"*I think that's a fine idea, Sam,*" said Angie. "*But first, you should take Mrs. Barnes back to your place. If XRay puts two and two together, linking you to the diamond, The Sandman, Alligator and now Mrs. Barnes, then they'll head this way, or possibly to yours.*"

Panic consumed him. Samson's guts tightened and his mind became a derailing train of thoughts.

How much time have I wasted since leaving the police station? Is it possible the four-by-four followed me here? Would Alligator send his men to see The Sandman and pump him for information? Goons can't just walk into police stations—depends on if the good ole' boys are on the books or not.

Sweat broke across his brow.

His eyes fell on the phone; he went to it and snatched the receiver out of its cradle.

"Number... What's his number?" He patted his coat down and discovered his wallet in his breast pocket. Samson opened it and removed the slip with the D.I.'s direct number. He couldn't recall the last time he'd used the dog-eared, yellowing card.

Samson punched the numbers into the phone's keypad.

It rang a dozen times before the D.I. picked up.

"*Davis*? Samson, here—"

"I was about to ring you," the D.I. cut him short.

Samson ignored him. "Have your boys questioned The Sandman?"

"That's what I was going to call you about—he's dead."

"*What*? Dead? How? When, goddamn it?" Samson felt heat rise up his neck and into his face; his forehead felt hot enough to fry bacon on.

"About forty minutes after you brought him in—there's somebody involved on the inside, Sam."

Samson's grip on the phone tightened. "Who had access to him? Have you checked your tapes? Did he part with *any* information before he was killed?"

"We're in the middle of going through our surveillance now, Sam. And no, we didn't get a chance to sit and talk things through with him."

"Jesus *Christ*!"

"Is everything okay, Sam?" Mrs. Barnes called.

Before he could answer, Samson heard tyres screech to a halt outside. Car doors opened and slammed shut, followed by the sound of crunching steps on the gravel.

Samson dropped the phone.

"Sam? *Sam*?!" he heard the D.I. call down the line.

"Get on the floor, Mrs. Barnes!"

Machinegun fire opened up. All around, glass popped, china disintegrated and chunks of plaster were thrown airborne as bullets pelted the walls. The decorative ceramic tiles around the sink were smashed to pieces, hurling waves of shards at Samson; some of the debris landed in his hair, with bits of glass biting into his skin.

"*Hellfire!*" Samson put his hands over his head. He commando-crawled through the hallway and into the living room. There, he got behind the window and stayed low.

After a few tense seconds, the guns fell silent; Samson heard their exhausted hissing sounds. Then a voice.

"Go check round back, Paul. I'll go through the front door."

I have to get to Mrs. Barnes!

Samson got to his knees and chanced a peek over the windowsill. He saw a lone gunman standing in a pile of brass casings, reloading his Tommy gun. He was a nondescript white man dressed in a suit and trilby hat. Samson didn't recognise him from a rogue's gallery. Once the gunman had reloaded, he moved towards the house with a slow, careful gait.

"*Shit!*" Samson took his chance and ran for the stairs leading to the second floor. He fully expected a hail of bullets to rain down on him, but they didn't.

Halfway upstairs, Samson heard the back door being kicked in. It thumped against the wall.

Someone must have heard all that noise, he thought, continuing his way up the stairs and reaching the landing. Not wasting time, he rushed across to her bedroom and burst through the door. He didn't have to look hard to find Mrs. Barnes—she was hunkered down behind her bed, her hands covering her head. She was trembling.

"Are you okay?" Samson moved towards her and she looked up at him, her eyes filled with tears, her cheeks wet and red. "Come on, we have to get out of here."

She nodded, but seemed unable to speak or even move, so overcome with fright was she.

He pulled her to her feet and ushered her into her en suite bathroom. "Stay here and keep your head down. Don't come out for anything. I'll be back before you know it."

She didn't utter a word, nod or even shake her head—she merely stared through him.

As he turned to leave, she reached out and gripped the cuff of his coat.

"D-don... don't go out there."

He removed her hand. "I'll be fine, trust me."

Samson picked up on a set of feet climbing the stairs—the gunman was taking the slow approach.

He looked about the room in search of something to defend himself with, and spotted a letter-opener on the bedside table. He picked it up. Samson knew it would be next to useless against an automatic weapon, but he didn't have much choice.

As he stepped away from the nightstand he noticed something else—a wine glass stood next to the bed on the floor. It was half-full.

Perfect, he thought. *If it worked once...*

A floorboard creaked.

The gunman had reached the landing.

Samson went to the walk-in wardrobe and stepped inside.

He held his breath.

A second set of feet was now starting their climb.

Through the sliver he'd left in the door, he saw

the muzzle of a Tommy gun pass by. When the man's back was to Samson, he pushed the door wide and jumped out of the wardrobe. The gunman turned, about to fire, but Samson threw the wine in the man's face, blinding him, allowing Samson to punch the knife into the hitman's throat.

The gunman fell backwards, taking his weapon with him. His finger squeezed the trigger, spraying the ceiling with bullets. Brass casings showered down around Samson, but he didn't move. Instead, he watched the man hit the bed, his Tommy gun dropped to the floor.

Both the gunman's hands went to his mortal wound, which pumped blood. He tried to stop his life from slipping away but, within seconds, he was dead.

Samson scooped the Tommy gun off the floor and fired it into the wall nearest to the door, figuring the second hitman was now on the landing. Over his gunfire, Samson heard the man cry out, followed by the sound of wood cracking.

He released the trigger.

Mrs. Barnes was screaming.

"*Quiet!*" Samson crept out onto the landing and noticed the banister had been smashed. He peeked over the side and saw the second hatchet-man lying in a crumpled heap at the foot of the stairs—he was covered in splintered wood and snapped spindles. He wheezed and coughed up blood as he tried crawling to the door.

The palooka's right leg is broken, Samson thought, spotting bone jutting from the man's torn trousers.

"My God, what a bloody mess." Samson threw the gun to one side and went to check on Mrs. Barnes.

Chapter 13

By the time Samson reached the palooka at the foot of the stairs, he was dead. He turned the gunman over and saw that bullets had torn into the man's chest and left shoulder. A stray slug had lodged in the guy's neck.

In the distance, sirens wailed.

"Well, I'm glad this wasn't urgent—it's taken them long enough! Mrs. Barnes, you can come down now." He heard her feet shuffling around above. "And bring your bag—we're getting the hell out of here, *pronto*."

"Okay," she sniffled. "I'm coming."

As he waited for her, Samson bent over and patted down the palooka, finding his wallet with ID inside. "Paul Haythorne." On the licence was an image which matched that of the dead guy before him.

Where did his suit and trilby go? This guy's wearing jeans and a jumper. Why can't I think straight?

He pocketed the ID and wallet, thinking they might come in handy.

When he straightened back up, he saw Mrs. Barnes at the top of the stairs.

"Shouldn't we wait until the police get here?" she asked.

"I will, once I have you in a car first," he said. "Can you open the gate to the driveway?"

"I've already done it, Sam." Tears slid down her cheeks, but she offered a weak smile.

"Good. Come on, let's get you to safety."

When they got outside they saw police officers making their way up the drive. Blue and red lights flickered off the house and grounds.

"I'll talk to them. You get your car out here and ready to go," he told her. "But I don't think a sports car will be inconspicuous enough!"

"Sure, Sam." As she made her way over to her garage, Samson couldn't help but watch her go.

Fine legs, he thought, and then made his way down to the good ole' boys.

"Is D.I. Davis—" he was about to ask an officer, then spotted the D.I. coming up the drive.

"What happened here, Samson, World War III? And the *truth*, Valentine! No more fairytales. Since you started snooping around I've had carnage and bodies stacking up all over the place—you're not Clint Eastwood!" He jabbed a finger at the PI "Where the hell do you—?"

"Let me stop you right there, *chief*! I'm not asking or looking for trouble, it just so happens to come my way."

"I suggest you get out of whatever it is you're mixed up in, or you're either going to find yourself dead or in prison. Come on, spit it out. What happened? What's going on?"

"I'm not parting with any information yet. I know how crooked the department is—one of your goddamn rats almost had me and Mrs. Barnes ventilated by a couple of goons. We're lucky you aren't heaving us into Chicago overcoats, palooka. Now, stay out of my way, I have a client to protect. I'll come to *you* when I have a punk who needs putting in irons." Samson turned to leave. "And be warned, the stiffs inside look like Swiss cheese."

"Where are you taking the woman, Samson?"

"Somewhere safe," he said, knowing that the walls had ears.

"We're going to need to talk to her, Sam. You're not above the law!"

"It can wait. I'll give you a call when we're underground—fill you in on exactly what happened here."

"Do it now, damn it!"

"No, I don't fancy our chances out in the open. I'll ring you later."

"*Samson!*"

The D.I.'s words fell on deaf ears as Samson made for the driveway.

Mrs. Barnes pulled onto the drive in a silver Nissan four-by-four. The bodywork gleamed.

"Hop in!" she told him through her open window. "Where are we going, Sam?"

"First we'll head to my place. I want to check up on a few things. Then I'm going to stash you somewhere safe, like a hotel."

"*Alone?*"

"Yes, but I'll be close by at all times, Mrs. Barnes. Don't worry—nobody'll know where you are."

"Okay, fine. I can live with that. Are you going to give me directions to yours?"

"Of course." He looked at his car as they approached it—there were no bullet holes or missing glass, just dents and chipped paintwork.

"Jesus, Sam—they really did a number on it."

"Umm—yeah, I'm just glad I managed to walk away from it with my heart still ticking! They had guns and hand grenades, too."

"You *were* lucky. Do you need anything from inside?"

"No, it's fine. Keep going."

When they got to the end of the street, he guided her out onto the main road and then gave directions to his flat in Cardiff.

"Those men at the house wanted to kill me, right?" she asked.

"Something tells me they wanted me more."

"For foiling The Sandman?"

"Maybe." He avoided telling her about the diamond and his own involvement with XRay. "I spoke with the D.I. on the phone before those goons turned up and he told me that The Sandman had been murdered. Cut up into tiny pieces, or so he told me."

"In *prison*?!"

"Yeah. There's got to be men on the inside. *Must* be. They probably pumped The Sandman for all the information he had before snuffing him out."

"But why would they want to hurt *you*? You were only doing your job."

Do I tell her yet?

"Sam?" she asked, looking over at him. Their eyes fused.

"I'm already involved with XRay and his gang. I got dragged into something a few nights ago. I'm in deep." He told her about the stone, Vampire, Magic Mike and everything else he thought she needed to know. He felt that Mr. Barnes was connected to it all, but couldn't figure out the puzzle just yet. His gut was telling him that Mr. Barnes was either XRay or a high-level foot soldier within that criminal organisation.

"If that's the case, then why would he need to pay a hitter that worked with another gang?" he went on. "It doesn't make sense—he could have had his own boys do it."

"Who are you talking about?"

"Hmm?" He looked at her. "Oh, I was just thinking aloud and harking back to a theory I had about your husband. What if he's XRay?"

"What, a criminal mastermind?" she laughed. "He couldn't keep a simple book-keeping business afloat."

"True, but there's something fishy going on."

"I think you might be on to something, Sam, when you said he took all the money from his businesses to finance my murder."

"After I drop you off, I'm going back to the Zzleep Easy with a warrant, but first I need to see *if* Davis will sort me out with one. I want a good snoop around."

"You think he's hiding there, don't you?"

"Yes, and I think if I don't get back there soon, he'll have moved on. I also need to get more dirt on XRay. I need inside info. Anyway, the *first* thing I need to do is get you stashed."

"We're still heading to your flat first, right?"

"You bet, kid," and then he went silent as he chewed things over. *I need to give the D.I. a ring when I get home. After that, I'll hit the meaner streets of Chicago to see if I can get someone to talk about XRay. Then, maybe I'll pop back to see that pro skirt. What was her name? Ronnie? No, Roxie. Yeah, good idea. Perhaps I can drop that frying pan off to Alice, too!*

"Sam, am I heading the right way?" Mrs. Barnes asked, coming to a set of traffic lights.

"Take your next left. The complex has parking bays at the rear."

"Great. Are you sure you won't stay at a hotel with me, Sam? I'd feel much safer."

"No. Besides, you'll be fine. Like I said, nobody is going to know where you are. I've been keeping an eye out for a tail."

"And is there one?"

"No, nothing, we're safe." He peeled his eyes off his wing mirror. "There's nobody suspicious back there for sure. I've been watching ever since we left your place."

"I thought a police car might have followed us."

"Oh, why?"

"Because that D.I. didn't seem too pleased with you, Sam."

"*Huh*, Davis is a pussycat. If you take your next right, it'll lead you into a car park behind my building. Whilst I go up, I want you to stay put. I won't be long—I've got to make a quick phone call."

"Wouldn't I be safer with you, Sam?"

He didn't want her to go up there with him in case there were bozos waiting to bushwhack them.

"Sam, are you okay?"

"Hm?"

"You seem lost. A bit—spaced out. Are you feeling fine?"

"Oh, I'm okay, just a little rattled after all that gunplay."

"Ooh, I didn't know they had guns, Sam!"

But you must *have heard the roar of the Tommy gun and exploding glass?* "Ugh, yeah…Would you like to come up for a coffee?"

"Yes, please."

If there are thugs up there, they'll be no match for Samson Valentine.

They got out of the car and led her around to the front of his building where the homeless were sitting on the front steps, drinking and smoking. One was even taking a piss against the apartment door.

"Watch out, Trev—Dick Tracy's back," one of them said to the man urinating.

"Oh, fuck him! Got no balls."

"Yeah, no hairy nuts between 'em legs," another homeless piped in.

"I'm sorry, Mrs. Barnes—the neighbourhood isn't what it used to be," Samson said, holding the door for her. When she was inside, he turned on them, a fire burning in his gut. "I want you lot gone from here by the time I get back, do you hear me?"

The group of five laughed at him. "Wha' ya goin' to do, put us in the *clink*?!" the pisser said.

"That's exactly what I'm going to do, for drinking, smoking drugs and going to the toilet in a public area. Now, I'm off up to my flat to ring the police on a different matter. If I were you lot, I'd be gone by the time my back is turned."

Through the door, he heard the men mutter amongst themselves.

"Trouble?" she asked, standing at the foot of the staircase.

"Nothing I can't handle."

"Who were you talking to?"

"The bums outside."

"Oh, I see. What were they doing?"

"Loitering, Mrs. Barnes."

A smile pulled across her face. "Which floor are you on, Sam?"

"Third. Door six."

"Okay." She took the stairs briskly, Sam followed suit.

When they reached his door, he caught her by the arm and eased her out of his way.

"Let me go in first. I want to make sure nobody's lurking." Samson unlocked the door and depressed the handle. He felt confused for a second, not knowing where he was or what he was meant to be doing. He put it down to coming out of a whisky stupor.

After a quick peek around the door, feeling it was safe, he let her cross the threshold. "Ladies first," he said, ushering her inside. "Excuse the mess—someone broke in the other night and ransacked the place."

"Why, it's lovely," she said, stepping inside. "It's quaint, and for a fella who lives on his own, it's pleasantly clean and tidy. I'm impressed. Then again, you do strike me as a man who likes prim and proper."

"*Huh?*" Samson moved into his flat. It was spotless. Nothing was overturned and all the drawers and their contents had been replaced. *I don't understand; I cleaned most of the mess up, but—* A sound from the kitchen derailed him.

"A flatmate?" Mrs. Barnes asked.

"No, I don't have one!" He lightly grabbed her arm again and pulled her behind him. It sounded as though someone was sifting through his china. "Who's in there? Come out, *now!*"

The sound stopped.

Samson braced himself, his body tensed and then relaxed as a female walked into the living room to greet them. "I did your dishes and squared up a bit, I hope you don't mind?"

"*Roxie?* How—why?" His words lodged in his throat. Samson suddenly felt embarrassed.

"You know this scrag-end?" Mrs. Barnes asked. He looked at her and she looked at Roxie—her face was a mask of distaste. "Is she a *hooker?*"

"Hey, fuck you, bitch!" Roxie jabbed a finger at Mrs. Barnes. "You look like a lowlife chav, with your fake gold rings and tracksuit bottoms."

"You cheeky little—"

"Ladies, ladies, *please!*" Samson said, getting

between them. He turned to Roxie. "What are you *doing* here?"

"I came to see you."

Samson's eyebrows knitted. "Why? And how did you get in?"

"I have something for you, and since you helped sort out Magic Mike, I thought I'd come and tell you."

"How did you get in?"

"Your door was off the latch. You really should be careful—this isn't a pretty part of Cardiff."

"Have you been snooping around in here? Did XRay send you?"

"Jesus, I just told you—I have some information. Are you nuts or just paranoid?"

"It's my job to be on edge, young lady."

"Well, *fuck*. There's no need to get all fucking pissy about it, pal. You came to me, remember? And cost me a fuck job, too."

"Good, God! What a potty mouth," Mrs. Barnes said.

"Ah, up your knickers, bitch! Don't act like your shit don't stink. You probably live on some fucking council estate."

"*Hey*!" Samson snapped. "There's no need to talk to her like that, okay? Tell me what you need to and get the hell out."

"I was hoping for some privacy. I don't know *that* woman from Eve, so I'm sure as shit not speaking in front of her."

"You don't have to worry about—"

"I'm not talking in front of her, okay?"

Samson turned to Mrs. Barnes. "Look, I think it's best I take you to where you need to be," he told her. "You," he addressed Roxie, "wait here—I'll be back in an hour or so. Just sit down and sit tight! Got it?"

Roxie nodded. "Okay."

"Come on, Mrs. Barnes; let's get you taken care of."

Samson couldn't believe it. Within minutes of arriving, he was leaving. Not only that, the thought of Roxie alone in his flat unnerved him. Also, he never got to make his phone call to the D.I. *What was she really doing there?* He felt as though she was a smokescreen to something else, but what?

Once they were outside, Samson told Mrs. Barnes to grab her things from the car, and that the vehicle was better off left where it was.

"I know of a hotel just across the street," he said as they got out of the car.

"Fine, yes." She sounded angry.

He didn't know if it was about the car or Roxie. *Why would she be jealous of another woman?* "I had no idea she was going to be there, believe you me, I'm just as infuriated."

"No, it's fine, I'm being silly. It's your place. Who am I to get upset if you have hookers calling in?"

"It's not like *that*." He crossed to the other side of the road. Mrs. Barnes followed.

"As I said, it's nothing to do with me, as long as you concentrate on your task at hand and stop me from catching a bullet."

He huffed. *Dames*!

Samson took up the front and led her around the back of the street. "You should be safe here. I know the guy who runs the joint; fella by the name of Lewis."

When they stepped into the hotel's foyer, he saw Mrs. Barnes give the place the once-over. She didn't appear impressed.

What do you expect, a lady of her calibre? he thought. *She's probably used to fine dining and fancy hotels—she has wonga up the yazoo!* Samson smiled at that one, and then rang the bell on the reception desk.

Lewis, a squat, fat and balding man in his mid-forties presented himself from behind a curtain at the back of the reception counter. "Hey Sam, what can I do you for?"

"Need a room for the lady. A couple of nights should do it for now."

"Okay," Lewis said, "sure thing."

Mrs. Barnes was then asked to sign in and was given a key to her room.

Samson escorted her to her door and saw her inside.

"I'll drop by later to check in on you, okay?"

"You promise?"

"Of course. Besides, if your husband is hiding at the Zzleep Easy and I find him, this will be over and done with."

"Yes, I guess."

"What do you mean?"

"You'll need a confession from him, some form

of proof."

"Don't worry, I'll figure something out."

"Thanks, Sam."

"That's okay. Now, lock the door," he instructed, stepping out into the corridor. He heard the locks clack behind him. "Don't forget, I'll tap five times so you know it's me."

"Of course," she said, her voice muffled.

He left the hotel and headed back to his flat.

Chapter 14

His stomach knotted and his mind raced as he strode across the street back to his apartment block. Samson was eager to get to Roxie and find out what she had for him.

He raced up the steps, two at a time, breaking a sweat and wheezing by the time he reached his door. When he stepped inside his apartment, he found her sitting in his easy chair, a whisky in one hand, a cigarette in the other.

"There's a drink and a cigarillo on the sideboard for you," she said, puffing rings of smoke out of her mouth and looking at him with half-open eyes. "I noticed you were out of both, so I bought some."

He studied his drink, and then faced her. "Kind of you. How much do I owe you?"

She shook her head. "Call it a gift."

She was sat, not very lady-like, with one leg crossed over the other—her micro skirt had ridden up her thighs, almost exposing everything she owned beneath her fishnet tights.

"Am I making you nervous, Sam?"

Did I even tell her my name at the docks? Must have. "Frankly, ma'am, yes, you are."

She smiled, took a drag on her fag and blew a cloud of smoke in his direction. "No need to be, Sam. I'm only here for the stone."

His guts flipped like pancakes; his mouth opened but his words were slow in coming. "What *stone*?"

"Come on, don't be coy. You *know* what I'm talking about—the one you nicked from the train station when posing as Vampire."

"Who are you, *really*?" Samson asked, raising his voice. He stepped up to Roxie until he was towering over her. She didn't flinch. "Best start yakking, muffin."

"Sam, we both know you're not—"

"I'll haul your damn arse in for selling your body on the streets. Now, start flapping, or so help me God I'll take you in."

The look on her face changed.

"You wouldn't."

Samson squatted until he was eye-level with her. "Why don't you go ahead and try me?" He winked. She looked everywhere in the room to avoid meeting his stare. "*Well?*" He leaned closer to her face.

He saw the cracks appear in her tough muffin routine: her chin wobbled and sweat broke across her brow.

"Hey, back off!" She tried to get up, but Samson pushed her back into the chair.

"*Talk.*" His teeth clenched, his fingers dug into her forearms.

"You're hurting me!"

"You came to me, remember?"

"Yes," she winced.

"How did you know about the stone? Are you here off your own back, or did XRay send you?"

"No, I—"

"Tell me!"

"I—I—"

"Spit it out!"

"Okay, I came on my own accord—nobody knows I'm here. However, I do have information for you, which I'll trade for the stone."

He dragged her from his chair and turned her around, bending her arm behind her back. "I'm through playing games—there's two women dead, with another in jeopardy, and they're all linked to XRay and his goons. Now, I'm not messin' around. Tell me what you're up to."

"*Argh*! You're hurting me."

"I'll break it. *Talk*, damn you."

"Argh—*Please*! My arm… I thought you liked me—that we were friends?"

"What gave you that idea, palooka?"

"Magic Mike—you saved me from—*argh*!"

"Don't make me snap it." Her sobbing brought a lump to his throat, but Samson knew he'd have to overstep some boundaries to get to the truth.

"Okay, okay, I'll talk. Just, please—let go of my arm."

"Not until you give me something. I don't trust street-walking dames, see."

"I promise you, I came here on my own. You can trust me. I even made sure I wasn't followed, I swear."

"Okay, I'll believe you, for now." He slackened his grip on her arm.

"XRay and his boys know exactly where you live, hang out and who you're friendly with. They know *everything*."

"Tell me something I *don't* know."

"I heard a couple of Magic Mike's guys talking about the stone yesterday—there's something particular about it, but I'm not sure what. They saw me snooping before I could get much info. Whatever it is, it's connected to something huge—there's a lot of bad people out there looking for what you've got, Sam."

"Any idea what it could be?"

"I think it's connected to some arms or bomb deal that's going on—there was something on the news about it last night."

"I don't own a television. What's happened?"

"Give me the stone and I'll tell you."

Samson applied pressure to her arm. "Spill."

"*Bastard*! There's codes or some shit gone missing, but that's all I know. I swear. Please, let go of me."

"I can't give you the stone, Roxie, but I can give you cash."

"How much?"

"Five thousand. More, if I'm satisfied with everything you have to tell me."

"*Ha*! You ain't got that kind of dosh, Sam—don't take me for a mug."

"I wouldn't lie. Don't you have children?"

"A little girl. Charlie."

"Then the money'll come in handy to get you off the streets and give Charlie a better way of life."

"If they find out I've been talking, they'll slit my throat."

He shuffled her over to the window.

"*Hey!*" she protested.

"Quiet." Samson looked out—there didn't appear to be anyone lingering by the phone, across the street or outside his apartment block. "I think you're safe—nobody's watching the place. Besides, you can stay here. You'll be safe. Promise. However, you get nothing if you lie or skip off or leave anything out. And, if I think there's even a hint of sabotage, I'll throw you out and let the big fish devour you. It'll be the big sleep for you," he whispered in her ear, "and I'm sure it won't be pretty. Hell, I'll even take you to the flat above and show you what's been left behind of my friend, your colleague. I'm sure her blood will never fully wash out of the walls and carpet."

He felt her shaking, tears ran down her face, but Samson didn't think it was his words alone.

"I won't lie or do anything! Let me sit, Sam."

He let go of her arm and watched as she lowered herself into his chair. She was a broken doll; her face ran with mascara. Her bottom lip trembled. Samson offered to top up her drink. She took it.

I guess she hasn't poisoned it, then.

"*Still, it was a good thing to be wary of it, and her, Sam.*" Angie sounded proud.

He smiled.

Samson watched as Roxie devoured the firewater and asked for another. She'd finally stopped shaking and crying, but her cheeks were still wet and flushed.

"When I overheard them talking about the stone, they said you had it."

"Who was it you eavesdropped?"

"Big O. He runs—"

"I know who he is. I've already had a run-in with him and that palooka who runs the slot place. They're a right couple of bozos."

"Oh, okay, I didn't know. I heard O talking to Jim Graves, Magic Mike's right-hand. Now that Mike is out of action, Jim's running the show at the docks."

"I see. But why would O report to Jim? Why not XRay?"

"Because only a handful of people know who XRay is, Jim being one of them."

"Okay. It seems odd that a right-hand man should know and not the fella running the snooker hall—surely it's a main enterprise, just like the whorehouse?"

"Jim knew through Mike, who wasn't just a guy who looked after the whores and dockyard. Oh, no, he's much higher up the chain than that, or so I've come to learn after listening to O and Jim. Most of XRay's boys answered to Mike. So you pretty much crippled someone who could have told you everything."

"*Damn!*" Samson slapped his hands together. "I guess I need to speak with Jim, or head to the hospital and yak with Mike."

"Best of luck—nobody knows how, but someone punched his ticket. But yeah, Big O went to him and told him you'd paid a visit about the stone. I'm guessing they've come looking?"

"They offed Mike? Cold-blooded bastards!

Yeah, they've come, also threatened people close to me, but they've given me until Saturday, midnight, to return the stone."

"What are you going to do? They'll kill you once they have it."

"They've been trying anyway."

"Only because you're in the way."

"What do you mean, 'in the way'? Of what? What are you holding back?"

"Sam—"

"Tell me, and I'll give you *ten* thousand."

She licked her lips. "The stone alone is worth millions, that's what I want, not your money."

"You *can't* have it."

"I could disappear with Charlie. Tonight. Please, give me it."

"How do I know you're not trying to trick me, and that you'll run it back to your organ grinder?"

"XRay? No, you've got it wrong—I'm out for myself. I told you."

"You can't have it, and that's final. Now, I'm going to ask you once more, and if you don't tell me, you get *nothing*, and I'll turf you out."

"But—but—okay, okay! They've been trying to kill you because of your meddling with the Barnes woman."

"*What*?!"

"You heard. I'm not saying it again. Barnes is in with them."

"I bloody knew it. Is *he* XRay?"

"No—he's the outfit's bookkeeper."

"What was his involvement with The Sandman?"

"He hired him to kill his wife. The Sandman's not part of XRay's organisation, but of a west Wales one."

Alligator, he thought. Samson decided against telling her he knew this. "And you got all this from one overheard conversation?"

"Yes, but that's pretty much all I got. If you need more, I suggest you talk with Big O or Jim—I'm sure they'll enlighten you," she smiled.

Yeah, right. Fat chance. "I can't see them opening up." Samson chuckled, stood and dished out five grand. "I'm off to see if I can find someone to chat with. Once I'm done, I'll be coming back here for the night. When I do, you and I are going to speak further, okay? I'll give you the rest of the money then, *if* I'm satisfied."

She nodded. "You'll come back, right?"

"Of course. Make sure you bolt the door when I leave. I'll ring when I'm on my way back."

"Great."

"Make yourself at home, which you've pretty much done already, and use whatever you want. There's not much food in, but you're welcome to it."

"I'll rustle us up something for when you get back."

"Okay, excellent. One thing before I do go, who has Charlie?"

"She's fine. A friend of mine is watching her. I got spooked after I was seen snooping and thought it best to stay low for a few days."

He nodded. "Yeah, good thinking. Right, I'll see

you in a couple of hours." Samson walked through the door and closed it behind him.

When Samson got outside he decided to head to the Jazz Hole first to check in on Steve and to make his call to the D.I.

"I could be waiting a couple of hours for my warrant, that's *if* I can sweet-talk him into giving me one, so I may as well kill the time at the Hole."

As he walked, Samson mulled things over. *I've got until Saturday as far as the stone is concerned, and I can't see them coming to my flat to turn me over or try anything else for that matter, as they would have acted by now. I guess I was just in the wrong place, at the wrong time when I was at Mrs. Barnes' home.*

"*XRay might not try anything, but if Mr. Barnes is in with the gang, then* he *may send goons after you,*" Angie chirped.

Not if Barnes has annoyed his underworld boss, muffin. Besides, they're going to want me alive, just in case I don't show on Saturday.

"Good point! Now, what's this arms deal business Roxie was going on about?"

I have no idea what the arms deal is all about, but I plan on learning more about it, fast.

"*Just make sure you take that stone to the docks Saturday, Sam.*"

"I plan to, muffin, definitely."

"What the fuck did you just call me, *love*?" a drunken female yelled, but he ignored her. "Fucking perv bastard!"

Samson continued strolling until he came to a

corner shop. He stopped, remembering he'd left the cigarillos Roxie had bought him at the flat. He went in, purchased two tins and a newspaper, then left.

After scanning the paper and finding nothing about missing codes, Samson unwrapped a cigarillo and lit up. He took a few puffs before crossing the street and taking a back alley that would lead him to the Hole quicker.

By day, the side streets weren't that bad—the level of risk to one's life wasn't as great as it was after dark. But still, a lot of deadbeats, homeless and flunkies hung about.

No place for a woman with her child, that's for damn sure! he thought, looking straight through the winos and crack heads who asked him for spare change. His snub brought insults, which didn't bother or surprise him. *When a man has no home, money, wife, or anything else in the world but his words, what can you expect?*

He crunched needles and kicked empty, discarded cans of booze out of his path as he went. When he sidestepped a large pile of dog shit, Samson stood on a condom. Its contents jettisoned out, causing him to gag. Samson put a hand to his nose and mouth, and then quickened his pace to be free of the alley and the stench that clung to the air.

When he took a right, he found himself in a lane that ran alongside the river Taff. On the opposite side was the looming rugby stadium. Just beyond this stretch of walkway was civilisation. Samson glanced over his shoulder to make sure there was nobody coming, and spotted the steel plant in the background. It was polluting the air, causing a thick, black curtain of smog to form.

Jesus, between that place, the buses and the work traffic, I'm surprised Cardiff hasn't corroded into a massive pile of steaming rubble.

At the end of the path, Samson turned left, finding himself on a main street that led directly to the Jazz Hole. He stood for a moment to take in his surroundings—police cars shot past him, sirens blaring.

Across the street he witnessed a gang of thugs rush by a group of middle-aged women and snatch their bags; nobody responded to the women's pleas for help. Elsewhere, drunken fights were underway—a knife was pulled, a bottle broken. Instead of stepping in to break it up, people stood by with their phones and recorded the action.

Samson shook his head and moved on.

He was sick of the apple—it was rotten to the core.

The goddamn palookas of the night own the place. I'm only one man. I'm not a super cop. I can't help everybody, *and I can't prevent* every *crime.*

He flicked his coat's collar up and walked on. He needed a drink; it felt like an eternity since he'd last had one.

His mouth sagged when he opened the door to the Jazz Hole, which almost cost him his smoke. The place had been turned over—tables, chairs and glasses lay smashed, along with mirrors and light fixtures. The bar looked as though someone had taken a hatchet to it. Chunks of wood had been hacked out of fittings. Even the stage had come under attack.

"*Jesus!*"

The joint was empty, which was unusual for this time of day.

"Steve?"

Samson stepped through broken bottles and glass as he progressed deeper into the club; he almost slipped on the saturated carpet.

"Bloody hell. Steve? *Steve?!*"

When he got to the bar, Samson stepped on the brass foot rail and boosted himself up so he could look over onto the other side. He half expected to see his friend sprawled out on the floor, but there was nobody there, just a sea of broken glass and splashed blood.

His stomach flipped. He felt sick. This was *his* fault.

"Steve? Steve, for Christ's sake, answer me."

Samson heard someone approach from behind. He turned to see a young couple standing in the doorway. "We're closed," Samson growled, moving in their direction. When they cleared out, he closed and locked the door, engaging the deadbolt.

Maybe he's in the cellar, or upstairs? Samson moved to the bar hatch and found no trails of blood. *If they did kill him, then they didn't do it here.* He then went to the door behind the bar, knowing it would lead to the cellar. On opening it, he was met with nothing but solid darkness.

"Steve?" Samson strained his ears, fancying he

heard something. "Are you down there?" He searched for the light switch and flipped it. The space below exploded with harsh fluorescent light.

His eyes dropped to the staircase, finding specks of blood. "Oh, Christ…"

Samson took the first step, which creaked under his weight, and ducked his head to try and see between the spindles in the banister.

"Thing's as solid as a rock, Sam!" he remembered Steve saying once. Many a night the pair had locked themselves inside the Jazz Hole and drank into the wee hours of the night.

The smile that pulled weakly across his face died as fast as it had formed.

When he got close to the bottom, Samson looked into the room and saw a pair of upended feet sticking out from behind a few barrels. "Oh, *no*!" He rushed down the remaining steps.

There, behind a stack of steel kegs, Samson discovered Steve. He was tied to one of his chairs, his clothes plastered in blood.

"*Shit*! Steve?" Samson screamed, bending over and grabbing his friend. He righted the chair and saw that Steve was still breathing, even thought he'd been beaten to a pulp; his face was nearly unrecognisable.

Samson removed the man's gag.

"*Water*!" he gasped. His head flopped and his chin came to rest on his chest.

"Okay, okay, one second," Samson said, rushing up to the bar to grab a bottle of water from one of the fridges.

He uncapped the chilled drink and tipped the bottle to Steve's mouth. When he was finished, Samson replaced the cap and undid the ropes holding his friend in place.

"What happened? Who did this?"

"Where—where have you been, Sam? I thought…" Steve tried to talk, but coughed, bringing up blood and phlegm. "You would have been in to see me after that threat."

"Did *they* do this?!"

Steve coughed violently. He nodded.

"But why? I have until Saturday to return their property, for Christ's sake." Samson balled his fists.

"This—this was a reminder…" he wheezed, "'just in case you forgot.'"

"*Bastards!*"

"Take it back to them, Sam. *Please*. They made off with my takings and scared my customers away. I'm ruined. They may…" Another cough. "… They may as well have burned the place down. My customers won't come back now, not after this."

"I'm here, aren't I?"

"Sam, they're coming back tonight for *another* payment, and they said if I don't have it, they'll give me another beating. After that, Saturday night, if you haven't been to them, then they are going to burn the Hole to the ground with me inside."

"Take it easy, Steve." Samson put a hand on his friend's shoulder. "I can help with the money, trust me. What time are they coming, and how long have you been down here?"

"Since yesterday, I think. I can't remember

exactly. They expected me to release myself, knowing full well I wouldn't be able to. I guess they're eager to give me another hammering. They didn't say when they'd be back." Steve slurred and stumbled over his words.

"They'll pay, alright."

"*You* don't have that kind of cash, Sam."

"I do, and I'll make sure I'm here to give it to them in person."

"*Ugh!*" Steve heaved, throwing his guts up. Bits of teeth were mixed with blood and vomit.

"You need to go to the hospital, friend."

"No. I need to be here for the sake of my bar."

"I told you, I'll be here to greet them." Samson turned and made his way upstairs to call for an ambulance. As he went, he noticed a pair of brass knuckles and a blood-stained baseball bat lying on a crate of bottles.

I can use those to dish out my own punishment! thought Samson, pocketing them both before heading up the creaky steps.

Chapter 15

After ringing for an ambulance, Samson phoned D.I. Davis and asked him for a warrant to search the Zzleep Easy hotel. "I'm sure you can do that for an old pal, Davis," Samson had said. "We go back a bit and I've helped you plenty in the past."

"Of course! No problem, Sam"

Samson had expected to plead a lot with the man and was surprised by how easy he'd won over the copper.

Wouldn't have matter if he'd sorted me out or not. I would have snuck in and snooped, he'd thought.

"Got a good lead, have you?" the D.I. had pressed him.

After slipping the good ole' boy a lame excuse as to why he wanted to sniff around the hotel, the D.I. again agreed to his request and said that it would be ready by tomorrow afternoon. Samson then tried the number he'd written down on a piece of paper at Mrs. Barnes' house, but found it rang through to a disconnected number.

"Sandman's phone?" he asked himself.

Five minutes later, Samson heard the ambulance screech to a halt outside the Hole. Beaten to within inches of death as Steve was, he was in no shape to climb the stairs unaided. Samson carried him up the steps and set him down onto a chair in the barroom. He then unlocked the doors and opened them just as two paramedics alighted from their ambulance.

The older one of the two medics went straight to Steve and checked his vitals. "What happened to him?"

"He was mugged. I'm a friend of his—his name's Steve."

"Steve, can you hear me?" the second medic spoke.

Steve nodded, though it was clear that he was only somewhat conscious.

"Do you need a hand getting him into the meat wagon?" Samson asked.

The first medic looked at him sharply.

"No."

It then took them ten minutes to get Steve onto a stretcher and into the ambulance, with Samson standing behind them.

"I'll look after the Hole, pal, don't you worry," Samson told him.

Steve didn't reply.

When the paramedics had him safely inside, they jumped in and left, leaving Samson alone in the street.

"Not much I can do now," he said, turning to the pub, "apart from getting ready to greet my guests." Samson walked in and closed the doors. He was of two minds whether to straighten the place up but thought against it.

The hatchet-men could drop by any minute now, catching me unaware. No, the best thing I can do is wait for them to arrive. Poor Steve; they sure gave him a working over—damn near rang every bell in his head.

Samson pulled the bat out of the interior lining of his coat and choked up on it, following through with a slow-motion swing for the fences as though he were a professional baseball player. He hefted its weight in his hand, eyed it over. It was an aluminium bat, dented in places and caked in dried blood. Some of the red spots had clumps of human hair stuck to it where it had broken someone's scalp.

Those palookas are going to pay.

"What if there's more than two or three of them, Sam?" Angie said.

"I can't think about that right now, muffin."

Samson placed the bat on the bar before searching the shelves and finding a near-full bottle of whisky. "It'll have to do."

He grabbed Steve's barstool and sat.

It was almost nine o'clock.

Where did the day go?

Samson unscrewed the bottle's cap and tossed it to one side. He pressed the container to his lips and upended it. The firewater poured down his throat and flooded his guts in a warming glow.

He slammed the bottle down on the bar.

"Tastes good." He smacked his lips and turned in his seat. Steve kept a small radio under the counter, which Samson decided to grab and turn on. "May as well. I could be in for a long wait."

He picked the whisky up and guzzled more.

I could avoid a fight, a world of trouble and possible pain, he thought, listening to the soothing sounds of a saxophone—it brought to mind the young lad he'd seen here a few nights ago. *I have the money. I could just pay them and leave it at that.*

"You know that's not going to happen, Sam. They won't allow it."

He guzzled some more whisky. "I know, Angie, but there's a possibility."

"You need that money. Not only that, it would be morally wrong."

"I know, I was just thinking. If I did go that way, I could save myself a trip to the hospital... maybe the morgue."

"Sam..."

"I'm not going to; I'm just spit-balling." He took another slam of whisky, almost finishing the bottle. "No more," he burped. "I need to keep a clear head. Then again, the alcohol will deaden the pain I'm bound to be feeling later, *if* they manage to get their hands on me."

"Get off the whisky, Sam—you won't be as confused."

He got off the stool and walked the length of the bar and back. His legs and back had stiffened. Samson stretched his arms and rotated his shoulders until they popped. Then he went to the phone and dialled his home number. On the fifth ring, Roxie answered. He filled her in on what had happened, and that he might be back a lot later than expected. After their conversation, he rang the hotel where Mrs. Barnes was staying and told her everything.

Back on the stool, he was tempted to finish the whisky.

It was ten-thirty.

When are these palookas—?

His heart smashed against his chest when he heard the sudden squeal of tyres outside.

A car door opened and thumped shut.

To his disappointment, he heard a second slam closed.

There's definitely two coming my way, that's if these are my guests arriving.

Samson stood and slipped his hand into the knuckledusters. He made a fist—they felt good. He took one last swig of the whisky as the door to the Hole was kicked open by a fat palooka in a baseball cap. The lock popped, but remained intact. The thug didn't notice Samson until his partner walked in and closed the door behind them.

"Yo, who the fuck are you?" Baseball Cap asked.

Samson eyed him up and down. He was squat and dripped gold: chains, rings and bracelets.

He looks like a walking advertisement for a jeweller's, Samson thought.

His pal, who stood at his heels like an attack dog, was much taller, taller even than Samson. He had tattoos on his neck and one on his left cheek of a teardrop.

It's pretty obvious which one's the mouthpiece and which is the muscle.

"Hey, fuckhead—he asked you a question," Teardrop said.

"A friend. Got a problem with that?"

"That's my fucking bat!" Teardrop pointed at the bat atop the bar counter.

"I was keeping it safe for you."

Baseball Cap stepped forward, his attack dog followed. "Who the fuck are you, *friend*?"

Spittle found its way onto Samson's face. "I'm Steve's money man. How much does he owe you?"

The thugs laughed.

"I don't think you get it," Baseball Cap said. "We want the fucking lot—every penny that's on this property. And once we've taken it, we'll be back again and again and again, until we're happy. Got *it*?"

Samson stood defiant. "How does ten grand sound? Will that be enough to keep you palookas away for good?"

"You don't listen, do you? Whatever you give us, it isn't going to be enough." Samson watched Teardrop remove his jacket—he had muscles that would make Arnie blush. "And since *you're* here, protecting that piece of shit in the basement, the payment has gone up. Not only that, but you're both in for a beating," Baseball Cap said, slamming his hands down on the bat to stop Samson from lifting it.

"There's no need for violence. I have money. More than enough."

"Jason," Baseball Cap said. "Teach this arsewipe a lesson."

"But I *have* your money."

"This goes beyond money, *friend*."

"You're making a big mistake, palooka." Samson turned to face Jason, who was sauntering around to his side of the bar with a cocky smirk on his face.

"I'm going to enjoy this," the thug smiled, cracking his knuckles. When he got close to Samson, he grabbed him by his trench coat and pulled him up to his face. "I'll beat you like I beat your bar buddy—*oomph*!" Jason huffed, doubling over and crashing to his knees.

Samson brought his leg up, smashing Jason under his chin with his knee, knocking him backwards. He was out cold.

"What the—?" Baseball Cap started, but was cut dead.

"You forgot the brass knuckles." Samson reached over the bar and punched the smaller man on his nose, shattering it, and sending him to the floor.

Before Samson made his next move, he finished the whisky. "Was there any rope in the cellar?" he thought aloud, gasping and wiping his lips dry. "Not too sure, but I can look. Before I do…"

Samson grabbed hold of Jason's arms and dragged him around to the front of the bar where Baseball Cap lay. Once he had both goons side by side, he used his handcuffs to cuff them together.

"It won't stop them from running, but it'll hamper them, not that I think they're getting up any time soon," he muttered, checking to make sure they were secure.

Satisfied, he headed down to the cellar in search of rope or anything that could be used to lash them to chairs; he wasn't quite done with them yet.

A few minutes later, Samson had unearthed a

length of rope from Steve's 'Aladdin's Cave', as he called it, and currently had both hatchet-men tied to chairs, sitting back-to-back. He'd also gagged Jason, intending to interrogate Baseball Cap.

Samson now circled them with a cigarillo in his mouth, the steel bat in his hands. Baseball Cap was slowly coming around, but Jason was completely out of it. Had Samson not felt the guy's pulse when tying him up, he would have sworn the fella was sleeping the big sleep.

"Where...?" Baseball Cap muttered. Strings of blood dangled from his nose like horrific snot. "Where—where am I?"

Samson was tempted to tell him "Hell," but he bit his dark sense of humour back. "You're at the Jazz Hole, jug head." He grabbed a half-filled pint glass off the bar and threw the liquid in Baseball Cap's face.

"*Ugh!*" he gasped, spitting stale lager. "Bastard."

"If you're going to keep sweet-talking me, 'least offer to take me out for dinner and drinks."

"Fucking pig *cunt*, I'll kill you! You have no idea who you're fucking with."

"I think you'll find that I do, and my, how the tables have turned!" Samson swung the bat. It whooshed as it cut through the air. "Now, I'm going to start asking you questions, and if I don't get the answers I want, I'm going to hurt you. Do we understand each other, goon?" Samson popped his cigarillo back into his mouth.

"Are you some tough nut Steve employed to kick us around? Well, there's more like Jason and myself out there—we're an army, and we will come down on you, your little friend and everyone and everything else in your—*argh*!" he screamed as Samson clubbed him across his knees.

"That's just a friendly tap, hophead. Next time, it *won't* be so soft."

"What do you want?"

"Don't you even *recognise* me? God, XRay needs to get himself thugs with brains. I'm Samson. I'm the whole reason you're smashing this joint up and sending my friend to the hospital."

"*You're* Samson?" Baseball Cap gawked.

"Idiot." Samson rolled his eyes.

"We weren't shown a photo of you. Hell, we didn't even think we'd see you. Word is, you're nothing but a broken alcoholic who spends most of his time in La La Land. A private eye on the scrap heap."

Samson got close to the man's face. "That's what I *want* people to think, punk—it makes scum like you drop their guard." Samson pulled up a chair and sat. "You see, before this, the whole gumshoe for hire gig, I was a cop. Before that, a military man, and I took no shit from anybody, which earned me lots of shiny medals."

Baseball Cap stared, his mouth gaping.

"You see, in my youth, I was bad-tempered. I had no control over myself until I found something I truly liked. Noir. Crime fiction from a past *almost* forgotten. An era of sophistication. But this didn't fully put me on the straight and narrow. Oh, no. My father enrolled me in the army, and boy did that sort me out. A drilled life, combined with my passion for 40s crime drama, helped mould me into a better person, pal."

Samson got off his chair and went around the bar. He unscrewed the cap from another bottle of whisky he was fortunate to find and took a hearty mouthful before going back towards his seat, noticing Jason was coming around. He clubbed him in the face.

"Lights out, palooka!"

Jason hardly had time to scream as the bat came down, knocking him leagues back into unconsciousness.

"What the hell, fucker?!" Baseball Cap cried.

"I can't have both of you whining at me. One at a time, fella. One at a time. Besides, I need to finish telling you my story first, boob."

"You're going to fucking die for this, pig—*argh*!" Baseball Cap cried as the bat smashed across his knees again. "*Fuck*!"

"Next time you get the bat to your beezer, bruno. How does that sound?"

"*What*?" Tears ran down his face, snot clung to his chin.

"Shut it, and pick up your friggin' ears."

Baseball Cap eyed him. "You may have the upper hand now…"

"I met so many like you in the army, which is why I was forced out. Out of the police, too. With them, I was classed as being too heavy-handed with suspects. I kept interrogating them too forcefully, but it's the only way to deal with yobs like you."

Samson thrust the end of the bat into Baseball Cap's chest. "The army also didn't take to a man who hurt and bullied troublemakers. Sure, they tried to discipline me, but it was no use. I just liked hurting the bad apples *too* much." Samson continued to circle the tied men and lit another cigarillo. He returned to the whisky for another hit and smiled on the inside, for he knew his tall tales were rattling the hoodlum.

"I can't leave this stuff alone, which brings out the violent side of me; the Samson who takes no nonsense—who wants, no, *needs* to hurt the filth. I became a pushover sober. A loser. I guess losing two wives to cancer can do things to a man. To his mind. It pushed me to the edge. But now I've walked into this little mystery, where people have been pulling guns and knives on me, it's helped me get back where I need to be." Samson slammed some more whisky. "I've lain off the booze a fair bit the last couple of days, too, so you might not get that much of a thumping. However, it's helped sharpen my mind. You know, I was drinking four to five bottles a day at one point," he exaggerated.

The hard face Baseball Cap had been wearing was now starting to soften. He resembled a terrified rabbit caught in a car's headlights.

He's beginning to think that ole' Samson isn't completely all there—that he's dealing with a broken, fragile mind. Samson wanted to laugh. *Let's really scare the hell out of him.*

Samson put his face to Baseball Cap's. "If you palookas had left that girl alone, you'd be dealing with a pushover; I would have given that stone back in the blink of an eye, but you lot killed a friend of mine—the only person I had left in this whole miserable world, see. And now you're pushing my bar-keeping friend about and another lovely lady by the name of Mrs. Barnes. Well, I'm not going to sit back and watch you bozos ruin any more lives. I'm prepared to go to the big house for my actions on this one—I'm going to burn your organisation down from the inside." Samson smiled the craziest grin he could muster. He then gave Baseball Cap a few light slaps on his cheek. "Now, there's still a way for you and your bruno friend to get out of this alive and walking. Understand?"

Baseball Cap nodded. His bottom lip quivered, and Samson saw tears in the man's eyes.

"I'm just about holding it together, and one more shove from you or your friend will tip me over the edge. I'm pretty scared about what I'm capable of." Samson pressed his nose to Baseball Cap's, who gulped. Sweat trickled down his face and peppered his upper lip. "I cut Sandman up with a machete…"

"You can't do this," he whispered, his voice breaking.

"Oh, but I can. You jokers think it's fine to terrorise a whole city—to keep the innocent living in constant fear. Well, things are going to be different around here now, because Samson Valentine is starting to feel like his old self again, and he wants Chicago back!"

"*Huh*?!"

Samson got up and took a few drags on his

cigarillo. "I've given you enough background information on me, pal, so now I need *you* to start talking. I have a series of questions, and, if your replies don't please me, then you're getting the bat, and I'm sure I'll be able to crack your kneecaps." He grinned his insane grin once again, and the look on Baseball Cap's face told Samson that he knew the gumshoe was being serious.

I've got him fooled.

"I'll let that sink in for a moment, shall I?" Samson went back to the whisky for another mouthful. "Or are we ready for some Q&A time, buster?" He walked to Baseball Cap and swung the bat before him.

"Please, don't do this. We can work something out. *Please!*"

"There's nothing to work out. You have information which I need. Do you work for XRay?"

"I—I—"

Samson was about to slam the man's thighs when there was a knock at the door.

"Hold that thought," he said before heading to the door.

Chapter 16

Samson was apprehensive about answering the door. His gut told him to leave it, but his head said otherwise—*I'm a gumshoe, it's my job to be nosy!* He stuffed Baseball Cap's gag back into the man's mouth.

When he reached for the deadbolt there was another knock, followed by a pounding. It was urgent, alright.

"Who's there?" Samson called, unwilling to snap the bolt back. He was nosy, not stupid; even in a whisky stupor he was still street smart. "*Well?*"

"Er... Got a delivery for ya, wise guy."

"At this hour? You taking me for an idiot?"

"Hey, I just deliver the stuff, pal! I was told there was a barrel of beer needed? You rang for one a couple of days ago."

"Again, at *this* hour?"

"We do drops at all times. We're in the city, not a town in the arse-end of nowhere. Now, are you going to let me in or should I take it back?"

Shit, Samson thought. "Can't you come back tomorrow? We're closed—"

The door's lock, which was clinging on, exploded off the door and hit Samson in the chest. The sudden burst cast him tumbling backwards and onto Baseball Cap's lap.

Through the door walked a large, square-shaped fella with a nose as flat as a burst tyre. One of his eyes was pearl white and sightless—a scar ran the length of his right jawline. The thing Samson noticed the most was the size of the guy's hands—they were huge. *Shovel-like*, sprang to mind.

Even though the oak tree of a man was slow in moving, he was all over Samson. His thunder-like punches were heavy and effective. The first bloodied his nose; the second deadened his cheek, but the third missed him as he pushed off Baseball Cap and lunged to the floor.

A muffled '*Ugh*' rang in Samson's ears as he hit the deck. He took a fleeting glance over his shoulder as he tried to scramble towards the bat and saw that Baseball Cap had taken that last punch for him. He wanted to smile, but he was grabbed by the legs and dragged along the floor, back toward the beastly palooka with the crushed nose.

Before he knew it, Samson was flipped onto his back and was receiving a shower of lefts and rights to the face, before being pulled to his feet by his collar and head-butted. When his attacker let go of him, Samson was unable to stay standing and crashed to the ground. His head connected with the wooden flooring and black spots danced before his eyes.

Samson was powerless to stop the barrage of blows. In the background, he heard Baseball Cap scream beneath his gag. And, even though it was muffled, Samson could make it out.

"Untie me, Jean. Untie me!"

This bruno must be the driver. What took him so long? "*Ugh*!" Samson cried upon receiving a harsh round of kicks to the ribs, and then a stray one to his balls. His mouth filled with bile and whisky, but he choked the vomit back down. "Argh!" He rolled onto his side and curled into a ball. A flash of electric agony whizzed up from his scrotum and nestled in his guts. His head flooded with pain; the breath was crushed out of his lungs.

Samson screwed his eyes shut.

Then, the muscle was gone.

"I said, un-fucking-tie me!"

"Sorry, boss—I couldn't understand you."

"Just fucking do it, dickhead!" Baseball Cap was shouting freely, suggesting the gag had been removed.

Got to get to my feet! Samson thought, clutching his nuts and straining to his knees. *If he gets one of them free, I'll never make it out of here alive.*

He pushed the pain to the back of his mind and got to his shaking legs. The bat was lost, but Samson remembered the knuckle dusters in his pocket. Through his good eye, he saw the huge palooka lumber towards him.

"Hey, Jean, I'm not fully untied, damn it!" Baseball Cap yelled.

"Let me finish him off first, boss."

Samson's good eye flicked between both men. He saw Baseball Cap wriggle free from the rope as the behemoth closed the ground between them. Samson ducked under the palooka's swing and drove his brass covered knuckles into the guy's ribs with all his might. He pounded him like a machine, his arm pistoning back and forth, smashing the same spot on his assailant's body. The sound of ribs cracking brought a satisfying smile to Samson's grizzled chops. He kept punching, feeling the bones splinter and cease offering resistance. His fist met tender meat, smashed it with his brass knuckles until the bruised skin popped like an overfilled sausage and the blood ran.

Samson lunged into an uppercut and his fist met bone again, but this time, he had struck a loose rib fragment. Jean screamed breathlessly as the bone shard punctured his lungs. Blood welled up in Jean's mouth in a fountain of red; he choked and sputtered on it as it filled his throat.

Jean collapsed on top of Baseball Cap and then rolled onto the floor. He didn't move. Slowly, a pool of blood spread on the floor beneath the big man.

Samson went to him and put a finger to his neck. There was no pulse.

"Oh, shit! He's dead," Samson muttered to himself. "It was self-defence..."

In that moment, sobriety, reality and the realisation of the situation he was in hit him like a subway train, but he didn't have time to reflect upon it, as Baseball Cap threw himself onto Samson's back, forcing him to the ground. A few sharp blows ignited fresh hurt at his lower back and kidneys, but the guy didn't have the strength Jean had.

Thank God for small mercies! Samson thought, spitting a gob of blood that spattered the floor before him. He then turned onto his back, throwing Baseball Cap off.

Jason was still out of it.

Maybe he's died, too! God, what have I done?

Angie answered him. *"It was self-defence, baby."*

Samson managed to get to his feet and grabbed the chair Baseball Cap had been tied to. He raised it overhead and brought it down on his attacker. It burst into a shower of splintered wood.

"*Ugh!*" Baseball Cap cried, falling silent. He didn't move.

Taking advantage of the momentary lull in action, Samson dragged Baseball Cap to a new chair and tied him to it. Then he shut the doors to the Hole and propped a chair up against it before perching himself atop Steve's stool once more.

He nursed his battered eye and split lip with a cloth filled with ice, then took a slug of whisky for the pain. He stared at Baseball Cap. It was him and his goons who were the biggest threat to the city.

"Oh, you're going to talk," Samson said through a clenched jaw.

Jason was starting to come around.

"Wha' ya say, ya punk ass bitch?" Baseball Cap slurred, baring his teeth.

"You heard me, fool, you're both going to start shitting information. And before this is over, you're going to be begging me to take you in. But I'm not going to. The days of me playing nice are fucking over. I'm sick of trash like you—you're everything that's wrong and ugly about this world."

Revenge burned in his guts. Samson was vengeance on two legs.

He put the makeshift icepack down and picked up the bat as he stood. "I think you've had long enough to calm down and to think things through. So, here we go—a simple question to start you off. Do you work for XRay?"

"We ain't saying shit!" Baseball Cap said.

Jason said nothing but the whimper in his throat betrayed him.

The weaker target would be the best to pick on, he thought. "And what about you, tough guy?" he asked, circling around to Jason. He jabbed the end of the bat into the bigger man's chest. "Do you feel like talking, or are you going to let me beat the living piss out of *both* of you?"

"I—I—gots nothin' to tell you, dude!" He looked as though he was going to cry.

"*Really?*" Samson smiled. He went back to Baseball Cap and slammed him across the knees once, twice, three times with the bat.

"*Argh*, fuck!" he screamed.

Samson went back to Jason. "Anything now?" he smirked, watching the way in which Jason's mouth opened and closed repeatedly, with no words coming out. He shook his head and closed his eyes. His whole body wobbled.

"Okay!" Samson said cockily, going back to Baseball Cap with a whistle and a spring in his step. On the inside, he hurt like hell: his eye and lip were screaming in agony, but he had to see this through to the end. This could blow everything wide-open.

He raised the bat high above his head, ignoring Baseball Cap's pleas, and brought it down with all the force he could muster. The man's thigh bone shattered on the first smack. Without missing a beat, Samson wound up and swung crosswise. Some of Baseball Cap's teeth flew out of his mouth on a wave of blood as the bat slammed into his face.

All Samson could see was Stevie's dead body on Vampire's sofa, along with the battered face of the Hole's barkeep.

"Stop it!" Jason screamed. "*Please*, stop!"

"I bet Steve begged you to stop, didn't he?" Samson flashed his teeth. "I'll stop when I have the information I need, dickhead." Samson swung the bat over his shoulder in readiness.

"I'll tell, I'll *tell*!"

"Sh—p, *fo—ol*!" Baseball Cap tried to say, but his jaw appeared broken. More teeth slipped out of his mouth on blood that was as thick as liquorice.

"Be quiet, or would you like me to start smashing your toes up?"

"Christ, he'll never walk again!" Jason said.

"Maybe, maybe not, it depends on how quick you can get to a hospital."

"I said I'll talk."

"I'm all ears, muffin." Samson moved back to the muscle and got down on his haunches in front of him.

"Call Mitch an ambulance. He has kids. A wife—"

Samson laughed in the palooka's face. "Here I was, staring down a couple of hard cases who are now blubbering and begging for mercy like a pair of schoolgirls. I think your boss should have sent *men.*"

"Fuck *you!*"

"That's more like it." Samson lit a cigarillo and blew smoke into Jason's face. "Now, do you work for XRay?"

Jason looked everywhere but at Samson and his mouth continued to do a funny flapping motion, much like a fish out of water, with no words coming. "I…" Tears spilled down his cheeks. "If—I—can you protect us if we talk?"

"I'll see what I can do. I'm *not* a police officer, pal, but I might be able to help you. For now, concentrate on answering my questions."

"Yes, we work for XRay, but we don't know who he is or what he looks like. Our orders come from different people—people who are higher up the chain than us." Jason flicked his head backward to indicate Baseball Cap.

"Would one of these individuals be Big O or Magic Mike?"

"Big O sent us. He's one of XRay's biggest players, along with Mike, but you put him out of action. He's been replaced by—"

"Jim, yeah. I know."

"How?"

"Never mind. So, Jim and Big O are the big boys and you foot soldiers pretty much answer to them, right?"

Jason nodded. "Yes. One of them will know XRay. If not, they'll know someone connected to him. We're pretty much in the dark—the right hand doesn't know what the left one is doing. And, as for us guys, we don't want to know who pulls the strings. We just do as we're told and keep our mouths shut."

"What do you know about the stone I have? I take it you bozos know about it?"

"Yeah, we do—you did a stupid thing in taking that package. It's stolen property from a crime boss in Carmarthenshire. Our boys didn't think it would make it to Cardiff. We thought the mule would have been rubbed out."

"Someone pulled a heist?"

Jason nodded. "It was payback. XRay had been stung in a deal by another boss—a lot of money was lost. So, XRay had an inside man steal the stone which is connected to some arms deal or bombs that have gone missing. Vampire was meant to pick it up, who would have ended up dead had he taken the stone to Big O."

"*Bastards*! Vampire knew he had no way out of the hole he was in, so decided to off himself and take my friend with him." Samson stood up and shook his head. His grip tightened on the bat as he walked around the men and muttered to himself. *The world has become an uncaring, unsympathetic devil in disguise. There's no room for a man like me any longer.*

Right then, Samson lost himself.

Before he knew what he was doing, he was swinging the bat as hard as he could, caving in the back of Baseball Cap's head. The man didn't have time to utter a single syllable, not that he could have heard himself over Samson's animalistic bellowing.

Blood jettisoned out of the thug's mouth and splashed across the floor in wide arcs. Meanwhile, Jason screamed like a girl, flinching and squirming in his chair with each beat of Samson's bat, his face blanched and wide-eyed.

By the time Samson stopped, he was winded. The bat fell out of his hand as he doubled over and took in air in gulps.

"It was self—" He stopped himself. "Consider that one payback for Stevie, and tell the Big Man upstairs I sent you, pal." He looked down at his red-covered hands. They felt tacky. "Stevie... Claire... Angie... Mrs. Barnes..." His mind derailed, plummeting into a spiral. "They'll throw away the key. No—who's going to believe *them* over me? They had this coming."

"Jesus Christ, you've killed him? You crazy bastard!"

"Shut up!" Samson slapped Jason across his face. "Unless you want to end up like him, I suggest you keep yakking."

Jason closed his eyes and held his breath to keep from retching. The drips of blood spilling from Baseball Cap's head filled the silence.

"I told you I'd talk," Jason whispered. "There was no need to kill him."

"Oh, really?" Samson pressed his nose to Jason's. "Tell that to my friend who had her throat slit open by a no good, drug-taking bum. A *dead*, drug-taking bum, I may add. Now, keep that gob going."

"What else do you want from me? I'm just a

nobody—they don't tell me shit!"

"Well, you seem to know a lot about an important heist for someone who hasn't got a clue. Who does it belong to?"

"A guy by the name of Andrew Peterson. People call him Andy Alligator. Word is he feeds his enemies into a gator pit he keeps on his farmyard out in the sticks. Nobody knows if it's true or not. Like I told you, he stiffed XRay on a deal, costing him millions."

"And he's Carmarthenshire-based?"

Jason nodded.

"Good, then he should be easy to track down."

"Wh—what do you mean?" Jason stammered.

"I'm going to return his property, palooka."

"But—XRay will kill you, and everyone around you."

"I'll take my chances. Besides, it might help weed the bozo out. Maybe this Crocodile fella can help me, possibly set me up with a fine pair of crocodile boots."

"*Alligator*!"

"Yeah, him too," Samson said. "Take a joke, kid."

"If this whole private dick shit doesn't work out for you, maybe you could consider a career in stand-up."

"What part does Mr. Barnes play in XRay's syndicate? Why did he double-cross The Sandman?"

Jason started sweating. "Can't say I know *anything* about that!"

"And I guess you wouldn't know why Mr. Barnes would want to close down all those businesses he did the books for, even though he had financial help from Mrs. Barnes?"

"No, I swear…"

Samson went to the bar and stood the bat against it. "I can see we're in for a long evening, Jason, if you're not going to cooperate." He removed his hat and coat, and then grabbed one of the man's tied hands. "Still have nothing to say?"

Jason shook his head.

"Fine," Samson smiled, snapping Jason's pinky finger.

"I swear… I—a*rgh*! Oh, *fuck*!"

"Tell me about The Sandman, Jason. *Please.*"

"No, I don't… *Arrrgh!*" A second finger snapped at the joint, making a noise like dry kindling in a fire. "*Pleeease!*"

"Shall I keep breaking them?" Samson grabbed a third.

"*No!* Don't. The Sandman was double-crossed."

Samson's smile widened. "Good. Keep going. Tell me everything."

"Mr. Barnes is XRay's accountant. He keeps the books for all the businesses in the city—Mr. Barnes doesn't have his own firm, it was a front. All of it, man. Even his PA. It's a smoke screen to protect his real job, as XRay wants him nameless and faceless to his organisation, but Barnes' wife started sniffing around and got too close, so XRay brought The Sandman in but had no intention of paying him."

"Why?"

"It was another dig at *Alligator*, to show him who's the kingpin of the underground criminal organisation in Wales."

"So, it was XRay that hired him?"

"No—well, yes, but it was made to look as though Barnes had brought him in."

"Go on."

"It was to fool the opposition. If Alligator had known it was XRay hiring one of his guns, the deal wouldn't have gone down."

"Jesus, I'm involved in a bloody game of tit for tat!" Samson said to himself. "Is Barnes holed-up at his, I mean, XRay's hotel? The Zzleep Easy?"

Jason was reluctant to answer. "Yes, and he's being guarded."

"What for?"

"In case thugs connected to The Sandman come looking for vengeance."

"So why are all those businesses closed down?"

"Word is XRay forced them all out of business by draining them of cash—he needed to recoup some cash for what he'd lost thanks to Alligator."

"Was it your boys that rubbed The Sandman out whilst he was in custody?"

"Oh, man, come on!"

"I'll break *all* your fingers, palooka!"

"Yes. We have a couple of insiders."

"Please don't tell me D.I. Davis is rotten?" Samson held his breath. When Jason nodded, he thought his heart was going to stop.

He probably knew those palookas were headed my way at the Barnes' house. Bastard!

Chapter 17

Before marching into the police station to have D.I. Davis placed under arrest, Samson needed concrete proof; but no matter how many toes, fingers or anything else of Jason's he threatened to break, the man was not for writing anything down or going on tape.

It didn't matter, because Samson wanted to catch the man red-handed.

Just how deep does XRay's organisation go? I'm in it up to my neck, he thought, sitting on Steve's stool whilst watching Jason sleep. He'd pumped the man dry of info.

Samson was mapping out his next move.

Do I go to the cop house and pick up my warrant? Will D.I. Davis try and stop me when we're face-to-face? Scupper my plans? What about Mrs. Barnes? She's safe. Nobody knows her whereabouts. What about visiting Alligator? No, not yet. I think the best thing I can do is get down to the station and pick up my warrant first—there's no need to show Davis I know anything. Just play it like ice. Nice and cool.

With his mind made up, Samson stood and cleaned his face and hands by using a damp rag from behind the bar. He then took one last look at Jason and decided to leave him tied to the chair. *I'm sure one of his goons will happen along soon.*

He smiled as he straightened his hat and then

removed the table from in front of the door. When he stepped outside, the sunlight hit him, stinging his battered, sleep-deprived eyes.

I can't be tied to this place, he thought as he shut the front doors and walked along the pavement as nonchalantly as he could muster. *I need to be a ghost. Ninja Samson.*

Half an hour later, Samson was at the police station collecting his warrant. After answering a couple of awkward questions about his face, Samson had been told to head to Davis' office, where his paperwork would be waiting on the D.I.'s desk.

Sure enough, his papers were in order. He noted, however, that Davis was nowhere to be found. Part of him wanted to ask why this was, but he thought better of it and remained quiet. After collecting his authorisation, Samson set off to see Mrs. Barnes. He wanted to fill her in on what had transpired between him and the thugs at the Jazz Hole.

I'm sure she'll find it more than interesting that her husband is working close to XRay, and that he has no real business at all. Once I'm done there, I'll head out to the Zzleep Easy.

As he crossed the street to the hotel where he'd stashed Mrs. Barnes, Samson looked over both shoulders. He was worried about being tailed. So, to make sure the coast was clear, he walked past the hotel, ducked down a side street and hid behind some bins, which were standing in half-shadows.

He waited.

Samson looked at his watch.

I'll give it a few minutes, he thought, crouching.

After fifteen minutes Samson decided to creep out into the middle of the alley. There was nobody to be seen in either direction.

Always better to be too careful than not at all, he reminded himself. Samson continued down the lane until he came out the other side, behind the hotel. After looking both ways and behind him once more, he circled back to the front.

Before going in, however, he checked to make sure there was nobody parked nearby or watching from a distance. Satisfied, he moved inside to find the reception area and desk deserted. Not stopping to mooch, Samson went directly to Mrs. Barnes' room and rapped on the door.

The security chain rattled, the door swung inward, and there in the doorway stood his damsel in distress. She'd been crying, and was trying to hide it behind a false smile.

"Sam, what a nice surprise—I didn't expect to see you again so soon. What on earth happened to your *face?*"

"I cut myself shaving. Listen, I have things to tell you."

"Straight to the point as ever, I see. Please, come in. Are you sure you're okay? Your eye looks—"

"*Ah!*" He waved her hand away. "I'm a big boy, and I can take a lickin' every so often, lady. Anyway, who's rattled your cage? The tears, I mean?"

"Oh, nothing—I was just being a silly, scared, little girl. Please, sit. Tell me all. Would you like a cuppa?" She pointed to the teas maid.

"Thanks, but no, I'm not staying long. I just came to tell you about my encounter last night."

He sat on the edge of the double bed, lit a cigarillo, and poured his guts out. Samson even went as far as telling her about the two thugs he'd killed, one of which was in cold blood. "I don't know what came over me. I saw red. Besides, they lived by the sword."

"Jesus, Sam!"

"I've been thinking, maybe it'd be a good idea to get you out of Cardiff, put you on a train out to the west coast. You hanging around here is a bad idea, especially now—they'll be gunning for me."

"What makes you say that?" She was visibly shaking.

"I let one of the palookas live, and told him too much. It was stupid of me, but I wasn't thinking. My head is all over the place."

"Calm down, Sam."

"The situation does not call for calming down, Mrs. Barnes." He sprang to his feet. "If anything, I need to calm up!" A smile flashed across his face. "Poor Steve is in the hospital due to me, and your life, along with Roxie's, is in jeopardy. I need to end this. If I can find your husband, maybe I can put a stop to things. If not, I see no other option than taking the stone back to its rightful owner."

"But what will that solve? Maybe you should give it to me, especially if you're putting me on a train out of the city?"

"Yes, I thought of that too," he said. Right now,

he didn't want to tell her where Mr. Barnes was.

"What about taking the stone to the docks as you're meant to?"

"No, they'll just shoot me where I stand."

"Hmm, you may have a point there, so why not try tracking my husband down first, start there? If you come up empty handed, we could both get on a train to the west."

Samson nodded as he thought. "Might be a good idea..." He let his words trail off when he saw D.I. Davis stroll past the window. He was on the opposite side of the street.

"Sam, are you okay?" She put a hand on his shoulder.

"Hello," he said, going to the window. He pressed his nose to the glass and watched as the D.I. disappeared up a side street. "Where are you sloping off to, I wonder?" Samson pulled away. "I need to go," he told her, patting himself down. "My camera! Damn it, I left it in my car."

"What's going on?"

"Huh? Oh, nothing. Just something I want to check on. You don't have a camera handy, do you?"

"No, sorry."

"Can I take your car? I'll bring it back later."

"Yes, of course." She handed the keys to him from out of her handbag.

Sam placed them in his pocket. "I'll call you later. I'll ring three times, hang-up and call back. Okay? Don't answer to anyone else, you hear me?"

She nodded.

He went to the door, opened it, and turned back.

"Make sure you lock it behind me."

***

Samson reached the lobby and rang the bell on the reception desk.

"Come on, come on, where the hell are you, Lewis?" He tapped the bell a few more times.

"Hey Sam, what can I—"

"Lewis, I need a camera. Pronto."

"Well…"

"*Quickly*! This is a police emergency, man."

"Okay, okay, hang on—I'll get my digital."

Within minutes, Samson had Lewis' camera and had been given a crash course in its usage before leaving the hotel.

He decided not to take the car. Instead, he ran across to the other side of the street and up to the alley he had seen the D.I. scuttle down. *I bet I'm too bloody late. Damn.* But then he saw his man at the opposite end of the lane with three others, forcing Samson to duck behind a couple of dumpsters.

Easy, Sam, easy.

Taking his chances, Samson poked his head out from behind the large industrial bins and reeled off a few shots with the camera. He took his time, making sure he'd zoomed in on his targets; the three men talking to the D.I. looked like your bog-standard thugs.

Now why would the D.I. be having a cosy little confab in a darkened alley with a few bozos? Samson smiled and reeled off more photos. In the last set of shots, he'd managed to capture money and packages trading hands. *My, my, what are you involved in altogether, Davis? I'm sure your superiors would love to know.*

After snapping off a few more pictures, Samson ducked back behind the bins and waited a couple of minutes before popping his head back out again. The D.I. was now heading in his direction.

As the copper approached, Samson edged his way around the bins so he was out of sight by the time the D.I. was on top of him. Samson watched his target leave the alleyway before deciding to follow him further.

He walked down the city's main shopping high street, taking a series of turns that led him to Big O's snooker hall. Samson hung back and took a few photos of him entering the place before going around the back of the pub and standing on the bins he found there. The height was perfect, allowing him to see into the back rooms.

Samson witnessed the D.I. handing the packages over to Big O and a couple of his goons, before taking a large sum of money from them and popping it into a suitcase he'd also been given by the thug in the alley. All the while, Samson snapped off pictures before heading back to the front of the building in time to get a few more of the D.I. leaving.

Very interesting, Samson thought, continuing to tail the copper. *I'm going to make sure I flush you down the toilet, palooka.*

Several minutes later, Samson watched as the

policeman entered Slot's place. The joint seemed busy, but Samson followed him inside anyway, and sneaked about the one-armed bandits and pinball machines. His cunning paid off, as Samson was able to pursue his man up to Slot's office where the door was closed in his face.

Undeterred, Samson found a vent close by and bent down to listen after making sure there was nobody close by to see what he was up to. By placing his ear to the air duct, he could hear what was being said within the office. Samson removed his pad and pen, just in case he needed to make a note of names, times, dates or anything important that was said.

"What are we going to do about him, Davis?" said an unfamiliar voice. "He's killing XRay's men left, right and centre."

"Got any suggestions?" Davis fired back.

"*You're* the police—*do* something about him, like arrest him!"

"Arrest him for what exactly?"

"How about the killing of Mike, Mitch, Jason and Jean?"

"We don't know for sure he was behind the murder of the guys at the Jazz Hole. It looked like a gang hit to me. Besides, how do we pin Mike's death on him?"

"*Jason died?*" Samson mouthed.

"We both know that's a load of horse shit, Davis. We could easily place Mike's death on him. After all, he did push the man through a fucking window."

"Samson probably has a ton of witnesses who will say it was self-defence—you can't trust whores not to turn on you, Slots; we have to be smart. He'll fuck up soon enough, and when he does, he's mine. Besides, why don't you guys just rub him out?"

"After what the cunt did to my hand, I want to, but orders have come from above—we've got to wait. If the bastard didn't have property belonging to X, then he would be six feet under by now. Anyway, he's meant to be bringing the stone to the docks tomorrow night. And, when he does, he'll get his."

"Don't be telling me shit like that, Slots. I'm still a copper!"

"*Pfft*, don't make me fucking laugh, Davis. You've been on the take since day fucking one. You're one greedy pig."

"I don't have to sit here and listen to this shit. If it wasn't for me turning a blind eye to your boss's crooked business, there wouldn't be an industry for you fuckheads. I run the show, not X. Got it?"

"*Ha*! That's pretty tough talk. Maybe we should get the boss on the phone and ask him who's in charge?"

"Fuck you, Slots, just give me the stuff so I can get the fuck out of here."

There was a loud thump, followed by the sound of clacking. It made Samson think that the D.I. was placing more goodies in his briefcase.

"What time is the meeting at the docks tomorrow night?" Davis asked.

"Midnight, why?"

"Because I want to make sure I see that bastard go down. The little pisser has been a thorn in my side for long enough. He's fucking annoying, too."

"You can say that again. And what's with all the 1940s shit?"

"Long story," Davis said. "Anyway, keep me posted on everything—I've had to be extra careful these last few days, since Samson started poking his nose in everything. Do you know how hard it is to kill a fucking suspect inside a police station?"

"Hey! You work for X, and if X says you rub some fucker out, you do it. Besides, The Sandman had to go. You know that. He was a player for the opposite side."

"Did they really chop his body up and send him back to Andrew piece by piece?"

"From what I heard, they cut him into such small sections that they'll be posting him for the next six months."

"Jesus, that's fucking sick."

"Was it you who sent men to the Barnes' house?"

"Yeah, I thought I could have taken out two birds with one stone, but Samson somehow managed to dispatch them. I should have sent them with guns, not knives."

"How does a drunken bum manage that?"

"Don't be fooled—the man's army trained. Anyway, I need to get out of here. Take care of yourself, Slots. I'll see myself out."

Samson got up and quickly dashed behind a couple of one-armed bandits. When the D.I. rushed by, Samson couldn't help but grit his teeth as he watched the man go.

"Oh, you're going down, Davis!" Samson scrunched his notepad. The notes he'd taken would be useless as evidence, but might stand for something when used with the photos. "I'll make sure I get more." He then followed the copper out of the door and into the bustling streets of Cardiff once again.

Even though it was busy, Samson was mindful to hang back and hide amongst the shoppers.

Where's the boob headed now? he thought, almost losing sight of him.

"There he is, just ahead of that fat, bald man!"

I see him, Angie. Thanks.

Samson forced his way through the crowd. He was big and heavy, which helped. A few toes were stepped on, a rib elbowed. Some of the people he nudged out of the way like bowling pins ignored him, others muttered, some cursed, but he didn't stop in fear of losing the D.I.

Damn it, I held back too far!

Before the copper could disappear down an alley without a trace, Samson spotted him as he slipped out of the crowd. He kept his distance, ducking behind bins and into doorways when necessary, as the D.I. was now watching over his shoulder more frequently.

Cagey bastard all of a sudden, isn't he? Well, he has every right to be, as he has the best goddamn gumshoe in Cardiff tailing him. Samson eased into a doorway as Davis turned to look back. *That was close.*

On hearing a few stiff knocks at a door, Samson stepped out from his hidey-hole and continued to creep down the lane. When he got close to where the copper was standing, Samson hid behind a bin and looked up at the sign above the door Davis was knocking on.

"Dancing Queens," he muttered, making a note in his rumpled book.

The sound of locks clanging and metal scraping filled the alley as the door was pushed open. "You're late!" Samson heard someone say. "Got the stuff?"

"Yeah," Davis responded.

"Best you get in here, then."

The door was closed, the locks re-engaged.

Samson peeked from behind the bins and saw the coast was clear. He stood and walked over to the door, but he couldn't get past it.

"Damn it!" He thumped his fist against the wall and looked up to see if there were any open windows or vents, but there were none. "Nothing I can do but sit and wait."

Samson returned to where he'd been hiding and sat down. As the minutes ticked by, he removed the camera from his pocket and scrolled through the pictures he had taken.

"I've got you, pal," he said, grinning.

He then noticed some of the camera's other functions "And what do we have here?" he said, highlighting the icon of a camcorder. By pressing the play button, Samson realised he was able to record live action, meaning he could capture conversations as they happened. "*Excellent*!"

Thirty minutes later, Samson heard the door to Dancing Queens open, giving him a start as he ducked further into the shadows. He heard voices.

"Oh, I forgot—tell Gavin I'm off to see Jim later today, and that I'll talk to him about Sunday night's meeting. Okay?" Davis said.

There wasn't a response, just a grunt, as the door was closed. A few seconds later, Samson heard the D.I. approaching his hiding place. He gave the man enough time to walk a good distance then stepped out, intent on heading back to the hotel where Mrs. Barnes was staying to pick her car up.

"I may as well get down to the docks to Mike's whorehouse. If Davis is going there to see Jim later, then I might be able to record some evidence if I can get there ahead of him. That would seal his fate!"

When he finally got to his car park, Samson unlocked the Jeep and jumped behind the wheel. He kicked the engine to life and sped off, taking the backstreets and shortcuts.

Time was running out, and there was too much on the line for him to lose now.

Chapter 18

Samson parked opposite the whorehouse and reeled off photos of the seedy joint and scantily clad girls hanging around outside trying to pick up men.

"Nice to see they've fixed it," he muttered, looking at the boarded-over window.

Samson removed the camera from his eye when he saw a man step into the doorway. He was dressed in a suit, with a fat cigar jammed in his gob. He couldn't tell if he was a client, or Jim, or a goon. Regardless, Samson took photos of him too.

When the man in the suit stepped out onto the street, three others flanked him. They had the hallmarks of hatchet-men, and so Samson made sure to capture their images as well.

"He must be Jim. *Must* be." Samson zoomed in on the three flunkies and saw bulges beneath their coats. "I see they've stepped up security since I was here last. I must remember to congratulate Jim when I take him down."

As Samson sat there, watching, snapping pictures, cars came and went. Girls were picked up and dropped off, but there was no sign of the D.I. It was frustrating, but he tried not to let it bother him. After all, he had a job to do, and stakeouts—tedious as they were—were sometimes the best way to catch the bad guys.

The three men flanking Jim parted ways and started their own paths around the property. Samson suspected there would be more brunos patrolling inside, and he knew getting in or even close to the building would be near impossible with all this security.

I need to try and capture some conversation if I'm to flush Davis, XRay and the rest of 'em down the toilet, he thought, watching the three men disappear behind the building. *Maybe I could pass myself off as a client? Those clowns at the Jazz Hole didn't know me from Adam! What about the D.I.? I could be in there before he arrives.* Samson put a hand to his face and rubbed the bristles on his chops. Going in as a punter seemed crazy. *One of the girls might recognise me and raise the alarm.*

"Remove your coat and hat before entering, Sam. They may *remember your quirky dress sense, but not your face."*

"Good point, Angie."

The D.I.'s car rolled up just then, coming to a stop outside the establishment. Jim recognised Davis, stepped over to his car, and ducked down by the driver's window. He then raised his hand and made a gesture suggesting that Davis take his car around back.

"Damn!" Samson groused. "Ah, to hell with it. I'll still go in," he added, slinging off his hat.

Once he'd stepped out of the car, he took off his coat and put the camera in his pocket. He thought it best to get rid of his tie and to unbutton the top two buttons on his shirt too.

Slow down and wait until Davis goes in. It'll minimise the risk.

Samson stood watch on his side of the street—he was still far enough away as to not bring attention to himself. When he eyed Davis rounding the corner, Samson turned his back and gave it a few minutes before facing the building again.

With the coast clear, Samson crossed the road and noticed the goons were nowhere to be seen.

Did they all go inside? No, they're probably—

"Hi, handsome," one of the girls said, sidling up to him. "Fancy a *fuck*?"

He looked at the woman. She reeked of booze and seemed high—her eyes were glassy, unfocused, and her pupils were mere pinpricks. On closer inspection, Samson could see track marks up her arm. He felt nothing but pity for her.

"How much for the lot? Any rooms inside?" he asked.

"Of course, baby. And if you want the *lot*," she said, opening her ankle-length fur coat to reveal an emaciated, naked and tattooed body, "it will cost you two big ones."

"Sounds like a deal for such a sexy muffin." Samson winked, his stomach flipping—he'd been taught to treat a woman with respect. "Shall we?" he asked, holding out a hand.

"Of course, baby." She took hold of Samson and led him inside.

So far so good, he thought.

After they strolled up a few short steps to the entrance, Samson was led down a long corridor. Just ahead of him, he saw Davis, Jim and two bozos, which meant the third was floating around elsewhere.

Hopefully he stayed outside.

All around him, barely dressed women strutted their God-given stuff. Others watched him with suspicion—a couple of the ladies whispered in each other's ears. It made him nervous, but Samson held his bottle. *I need to do this and get as close to the D.I. as possible. God only knows what I could get out of him and the rest of 'em too.*

The pro skirt reached a door and opened it, inviting Samson inside. Before stepping over the threshold, Samson caught a final glimpse of his target disappearing into a room a few doors down— he was flanked by not only the men but a woman who Samson assumed to be a prostitute.

Samson stepped into the room and turned on the woman as she closed the door. He snatched a hand around her neck and gripped her as hard as he could. Within seconds she folded into his arms, unconscious, and he placed her onto the bed and tied her arms and legs to the posts. To be on the safe side, he gagged her, too.

"Sorry, sweetheart." He left her some money on the sideboard as he opened the door to leave. "Once this is over, I hope you manage to get clean."

The hallway was clear apart from a lone hatchet-man standing guard at the far end with his back to Samson. Samson hurried away from his door and proceeded down the hall to the room he'd seen Davis enter. He placed his ear to it, but couldn't hear what was being said inside.

Damn! There has to be another way. He looked

down at the handle. *What if I open the door a sliver and place the recorder just inside?* He knew it was a colossal risk, but what else could he do? If he didn't take action, then he could possibly miss out on something massive.

He held his breath, clasped the door handle and depressed it slowly. When it wouldn't go any further, he edged the door open a slender crack. He removed his hand and exhaled—nobody from within appeared to have noticed.

Samson removed the camera from his pocket and set it to record. He then placed it at the foot of the door. Now, with the door open, he could pick up on the conversation. What he heard made his jaw drop.

"*Oi*! You! What do you think you're doing?"

Samson stiffened with sudden alarm. The voice belonged to the guy standing guard. Instead of turning to look, he fled up the hallway.

"*Hey*!" the man yelled after him as he broke into a run.

Samson rounded a corner to find a men's toilet. He rushed in and hid in one of the cubicles. He heard a muffled conversation and tried to remain calm, even though his heart galloped and sweat poured down his face.

Has he alerted the others? Davis? Jim? I'm trapped!

The toilet door slammed open.

"I know you're in here, man! Come out, now."

Samson looked about him and wondered what to do. Taking his chances, he flushed the toilet and started whistling. When he opened the stall door, he stood face to face with the goon.

"Were you calling me?" Samson asked, raising an eyebrow.

The man grabbed him by his collar and forced him back into the stall until his back met the wall. "What were you doing, punk?"

"*Woah*! Hold on, palooka—I was just looking for the toilet. The muffin I was with told me there was one down the end of the corridor."

"Muffin?"

"Yeah, one of your fine skirts. I just finished up with her and needed the toilet. No harm in that, is there?"

The guy's hold on him relaxed. "Seeing as you're finished here, I'll escort you out. You're not welcome here any longer, *mate*."

"Jesus, okay."

The man then shoved him out of the stall. "Walk!"

"I'm going! There's no need to push me."

"I'll do as I—"

Before the goon could get his next words out, Samson had spun around and smashed his fist into the man's nose. It cracked and flattened in a spray of blood. The blow knocked the bozo backwards, his head slammed against the wall hard enough to crack the tiles. He slid down it, landing on his arse.

Samson ran out of the toilet and back to the office door, which hadn't been disturbed in his absence. He grabbed the camera and ran down the steps, not caring if he'd gathered enough, or any, information. He needed to get away from this place before the thug he'd knocked out woke up and raised the alarm.

He made his way back to the Jeep and unlocked it, then tossed the camera onto the passenger seat. He was tempted to play the recording immediately, but knew he had no time to do so. He rammed the key into the ignition, started up, and pulled off.

His tyres screeched, and his heart leapt into his mouth when he saw Davis, Jim and his goons appear at the whorehouse doorway. The man with the busted nose was also there, pointing in Samson's direction.

He ducked low and took the next corner by peeking over the steering wheel. Once he'd straightened out, Samson stamped his foot on the accelerator, feeling the back end of the four-by-four careen and then hit something. A person yelled but he didn't stop, just sped up.

"Got to get away!"

As he took a left, Samson looked in the rear-view mirror and saw nobody by the whorehouse entrance. No Davis, Jim, Broken Nose, or goons.

"They went back in without giving chase?" he wondered out loud.

Without thinking, he took another left turn and then a right, followed by another series of turns in the hope that he could lose anyone that might be following.

But there wasn't anyone. The streets were empty.

Samson risked another look in the mirror and breathed a sigh of relief. However, this didn't stop him from taking a few more turns until he eventually felt safe enough to head back to his flat.

After parking in his space behind the apartment building, Samson grabbed the camera off the seat beside him and got out.

Once outside the door to his home, he gave it a few gentle knocks before announcing it was him. When there was no answer, he knocked harder and raised his voice.

"Roxie, it's me. Samson." He heard the security chain rattle and the deadbolt clack. Roxie stood in the doorway with tears running down her face.

"Hey, what's wrong?" asked Samson.

She stepped into the corridor and threw her arms around him. "Nothing. I was scared, that's all. I haven't heard from you. You said you were going to ring before coming back and I was going to prepare supper for us. I thought you'd been killed."

He tugged her arms from around his neck and held her away from him. "Sorry, doll, but I had no time—it's been a crazy, hectic evening, but I think I *may,* hopefully, have what we both need to get out of this situation." He wiggled the camera before her.

"What do you mean?"

"I have photographic, and with any luck, audio proof that D.I. Davis is involved with the XRay gang. This could help shut down their criminal activity, especially if I take it to the top."

"That's pretty good news. But why 'hopefully'?"

Samson filled her in on what had happened down at the docks and suggested they listen to the recording together.

"Would you like a drink?" she asked, closing the

door to the flat after he'd walked in and slumped down in his easy chair.

"Please. Make it a large—actually, scrap that. I'm cutting back. You could hand me the telephone though, please." Samson flicked through the photos he'd captured, then started the recorder.

As Roxie placed the phone on the arm of his chair, the voices on the recording filled the room.

"That's Jim speaking," Roxie said. "I'd know that voice anywhere."

"You're sure?"

"Yes, definitely. I've met him a few times while working the docks. Mike would make me sleep with him for free because I was one of Jim's favourites. The man repulses me."

Samson nodded. "The other voice belongs to the D.I.," he told her.

They listened to Jim and Davis speak about a large shipment due at the docks in the wee hours of Sunday morning, and how Samson had to be dealt with if he didn't show up with the stone on Saturday night.

Other evidence against Davis on the recording pointed to him being involved in the underground criminal organisation. The men also spoke about Davis' plans on moving the 'shipment', 'money' and 'guns'; and how he was going to use other bent coppers to help him do it. Davis reeled off a list of names. Also, Jim mentioned the D.I. by name, along with a few of his associates.

However, there was no mention of the stone's importance.

"This bangs the palookas dead to rights!" Samson said, switching the recorder off. Excited, he got up from his chair and walked over to his sideboard where he pulled out one of the drawers. He rifled through it until he found some envelopes and a small black book with 'addresses' written across its front.

"What are you doing?" she asked.

"Making sure this evidence gets placed in the right hands. I have an old friend who used to work at the station—he's the ex-chief of police. Him and I used to be good friends and would bounce things off each other all the time."

"What good is he going to be if he's retired?"

Samson picked up the phone and dialled his friend's number. "He'll make sure this evidence is given to the clean, and not crooked, cops."

She went to speak again but Samson started talking hurriedly into the phone.

"Hello, Adam? Listen, I think I've cracked open something huge here and I need your help. Are you still at the same address?"

"Samson?" a gruff voice came through the receiver. "Yes, I'm... Jesus, would you slow down!"

"No time," Samson nearly cut him off. "Look, I need help and I can't really explain right now. First thing tomorrow, I'm sending you something through the post that I want you to look at."

Adam paused to let what he'd heard sink in, then said, "All right. I'll get on it as soon as it arrives and get back to you. You know I'm here for you if you need anything."

"Thanks, Adam. I knew I could trust you," said Samson, grinning. "We'll speak again soon. Goodbye." He hung up the phone.

"Well, what did he say?"

"He's going to check it over first and then get back to me before he makes his move. If he thinks there's enough to bring charges, which there is, then he'll help me take Davis and the rest down."

"Oh, Sam!" She put her arms around him. "I just want to feel safe again, and for Charlie and me to have a proper life together, away from the game and drugs."

"And you will. I guarantee it. Take some of my money and get out of here."

"I will, but not until it's all over. I want to know I'll be safe."

"Okay."

She took a step back; her arms fell to her sides. "I'll get started on dinner."

"Sounds great. Whilst you're doing that, I'm going to give Mrs. Barnes a quick call to let her know how the land lies."

No sooner was Roxie out of the room than Samson was on the phone again, the mouthpiece pressed up against his face between his shoulder and cheek. There was still work to do and too little time left to do it in. He rang Mrs. Barnes, who was slow in picking up.

"Hello, Mrs. Barnes?"

"Oh, hello Samson…"

"Just listen, please," he cut her short. "I have a

lot to tell you but I don't want to say too much over the blower. I've decided to take the stone west tomorrow, to another known criminal. If you want to come, meet me at the Zzleep Easy by midday tomorrow. I think your husband is holed up there. Also, be wary of D.I. Davis—I can't say what I've got on him over the phone, only that he can't be trusted. We'll speak again soon."

He hung up on her before she could say anything in reply, then cast a glance into the kitchen.

"Dinner won't be long!" Roxie called.

"Okay." He snatched up an envelope. After writing the ex-chief of police's address on it, Samson popped the camera inside along with a short note, sealed it, and placed a stamp on it before setting it to one side to take with him in the morning.

He felt good. Relaxed.

Almost home and dry, Angie! He looked toward the kitchen and saw Roxie pottering around. A smile spread across his face. *Nice having a woman in here again.*

"Dishing up!"

"Would you like some music while we eat?"

"That would be lovely, Sam."

Samson put on some light jazz, filling the room with *Georgia on My Mind*. "Do you like jazz?"

"My mother used to listen to it all the time." Samson heard plates and cutlery rattle. "Food's up."

"Who did she like?"

"Nina Simone."

Samson smiled and looked down at the feast

she'd cooked. "Looks lovely."

"Please, sit and eat."

He didn't need telling twice.

Throughout dinner they spoke of life, lost loves, missed opportunities, children and her girl, Charlie, who was thirteen years old—a product of rape. The confession drew tears from her.

Afterward they retired to the living area and continued talking into the small hours of the morning. Once Roxie had passed out, Samson carried her into his bedroom and tucked her in. He then returned to his chair and slept his first sober sleep in a long time.

Chapter 19

Samson awoke to the clatter of plates and the kettle grumbling to a boil. At first, due to his grogginess, he thought there was an intruder in his home and he leapt from his easy chair and grabbed an empty whisky bottle.

"Who's there?!"

"There's a mug of coffee in here for you, Sam," Roxie called from the kitchen.

He felt foolish and lowered his weapon immediately. After placing it on the sideboard, Samson rubbed his face with his palms, then noticed there was a blanket on the floor at the foot of the chair.

She covered me up?

"Come on, or your coffee's going to get cold."

"I'm coming." He shuffled through the living room and greeted her with a lazy, sleep-laden smile. His guts rumbled, his nose sniffed the air and his eyes sought out the bacon and eggs she was cooking on the stove. "Smells damn good, Roxie!" He picked up his coffee and took a hearty swallow. "Have I got time to grab a quick shower?"

"Nope, I'm plating. Sit."

"There really isn't any need for all this fuss, gal."

"*Sit!*" She turned on him and pointed the spatula at the table. "This is my way of saying thanks. For *everything.*"

"*Bah!*" He waved her away and took a seat.

"Any man would have done the same, doll."

"No, there's not many like you left, Sam." She placed his food in front of him and helped herself to some breakfast. "What's the plan today?"

"In what way?" he asked between mouthfuls.

"Am I coming with you?"

"Absolutely not! I want you to stay here until I return. When I get back, everything will be fine, you'll see."

"So, I sit tight and keep the home fires burning, huh?" She smiled.

"Something like that, yes. I'll leave you some spending money, not that you'll need it."

"Well, I don't know about that. There's not that much food here, maybe enough for a day or two."

"That should be fine. I don't plan to be gone more than twenty-four hours. As soon as I'm done at the hotel, which shouldn't take me more than an hour, I'll be heading off, and I'll keep you posted. Okay? And try not to worry." He reached his hand across the table and squeezed hers.

She smiled. "Thanks, Sam. I'll never be able to repay you."

"You've done enough."

After finishing breakfast and guzzling a second cuppa, Samson got himself in and out of the shower before throwing on a clean suit and his shoes. Within the hour, he was bidding Roxie goodbye and heading out the door to Mrs. Barnes' Jeep with the package tucked under his arm and the stone in his coat pocket.

Samson checked the area to make sure there was

nobody casing the joint, then pressed on. The roads and streets were deserted, which was a good sign.

Good. I don't think the thugs will try anything.

He posted the package in a post box and then headed around back of his apartment complex.

When he got behind the wheel of the Jeep, it suddenly struck him that maybe it would be a good idea to get Roxie to check into a hotel at some point today.

The goons may come here looking for me when I don't show at the docks. Hmm. Might be a good idea. But first, let's get to the hotel and see what happens.

He pulled away, heading for the Zzleep Easy.

When he entered the hotel he clapped eyes on *Ms*. Peters, who looked up at him upon hearing her door slam closed. She glared at him, and seeing her displeasure only made Samson want to grin back, but he thought better of it and kept to his stolid expression instead.

"Morning, *Ms*. Peters." He strolled towards the reception desk and placed the warrant down on its surface. "It's all above board."

The look on her face suggested fear. "I—"

"Didn't think I'd be back?" He smiled. "I'll start down here and work my way up. Are there any goons here protecting him? That's what I've been told..."

"But... But—no, there's nobody here!"

He pocketed the warrant. "You'd save me a lot of time if you came clean about things. Is Mr. Barnes here? I don't intend to arrest him, I just have some questions for him," Samson lied.

Her mouth opened, but she snapped it closed.

"Very well," he went on. "Can you give me a master key to all the rooms, please?" He held his hand out.

Before turning to grab it off the key rack at her back, she gave him an acid look and then slammed the key into his palm.

"Thanks." He gave her his best smile and then shifted over to the lifts and called one. "If you'd be so kind as to stay right where you are, *Ms*. Peters, I'd be awfully grateful."

"Go to hell!" She stormed into her back room, slamming the door behind her.

"Dames," Samson muttered, shaking his head.

The Zzleep Easy wasn't as big as it appeared to be from the outside. It consisted of four floors, with each level containing six bedrooms, three communal bathrooms, one cleaning cupboard and a fire exit.

After sweeping the four floors, Samson came up empty-handed. He felt beaten, humiliated almost, when he saw the self-righteous look on Ms. Peters' face.

"*Satisfied*?!" she asked with a snarl.

"Not quite, no. I want to search in there first, and then I'll be happy." Samson stepped behind the counter and made for her back room, but she put an arm out to stop him.

"You can't go back there—it's *private*."

"I have a warrant, *miss*." He removed her arm and shoved it to one side. "Now, step away or I'll take you in."

"On what grounds?"

He didn't respond. Instead, he pushed by and headed inside. When he opened the door he half expected to see Mr. Barnes quivering in a corner, but it was empty and scant of items—only a TV and old, beat-up sofa adorned the space.

What self-respecting, intellectual fella would choose such a hiding place?

"*Damn*! I was sure he was here," he said aloud. He walked further into the room and stepped on something that made a hollow sound. Samson looked down and saw he was standing on a large rug. He moved his feet. Something rattled. Pulling the mat back revealed a hatch built into the floor.

"Interesting…"

He grabbed the handle and yanked the trapdoor open. Below was a wooden staircase. The room below was lit. "Mr. Barnes, are you down there? If so, come out, or I'm coming in to *getcha*."

When no answer came, he made a move toward the steps. The door to the back room flew open, startling him.

"*No*! Don't go down there," Ms. Peters pleaded. She had tears in her eyes.

"Stand back. You had your chance to come clean, muffin." When he turned from her, she grabbed his arm and tried to pull him away. "Get off!" He shook his arm, trying to dislodge her, but her grip was firm. "This is not helping your cause, lady."

With a few more violent shakes of his arm, she

flew loose and stumbled out the door she'd come through. He heard her crash to the floor. Samson wasted no time in rushing down the steps and into the small, tight space below. In the corner, behind a desk with a PC and a lamp on it, he saw a man hiding behind a chair.

"*Please*! Don't kill me!"

"If I was here to kill you, you'd be dead by now, scum." Samson walked over to the desk and dragged the scrawny man from behind it. "Are you Barnes? Answer me!"

"Ye—yes! Who are you?"

"Your worst nightmare if you don't start cooperating, got it?"

He shook his head. "You're not here to kill me?"

"No, *idiot*!" Samson slapped the man across the back of his head and then shoved him into his chair. "I want answers. Pronto." He snapped his fingers.

"What do you want from me? I'm just a number cruncher—"

"I want you to tell me what's been going on, and why you're trying to kill your wife. You know Selks is dead? The Sandman, too? I'm guessing you do, because you're an inside man. Talk, damn it!" Samson hammered the desk with his fist. "*Now*!"

"Dead...?" He put a shaking hand to his mouth. "Oh, what have I done? Patricia..." Tears welled in his eyes.

"You didn't know?"

"Does it look like I fucking knew, you flamin' fool!"

"But—"

A scream from above silenced them. Samson looked in the direction of the hatch. *Sounded like Ms. Peters...* A second scream pierced the silence, sending a shiver down Samson's back.

He went to the stairs and ducked into the passage, trying to peer up the shaky, wooden staircase, but could see nothing. What he heard, though, where sluggish footsteps and sharp gasps for breath.

"Ms. Peters?" he called up the steps. "Is everything okay?"

There was no response.

When he heard the roller chair behind him move, Samson turned and ordered Mr. Barnes to stay seated. "I'll handle this, pal. I don't want you out of my sight." He faced the steps again and saw a shadow on the staircase. "Ms. Peters—?"

He choked on his words when she appeared at the hatch. Her hands were clasped against her stomach, which was bleeding profusely—blood trailed at either side of her mouth and she was gasping for air.

When she reached a hand out to him, her legs buckled, and she crashed to the floor. Half of her body flopped through the hole, including one of her arms; her hair hung down, covering most of her face but one unblinking eye stared at him.

"Oh, God!" Barnes screamed, his voice cracking. "She's *dead*!"

Drops of blood splashed the dusty steps.

"Stay where you are, Mr. Barnes." Samson looked about and saw a length of wood propped against a wall close by him. He grabbed it, hefted it in his hand to get a feel for its weight. It would be suitable as a weapon.

After taking a deep breath, he made his way up the steps, knowing there was no other option. He was cornered. "I'm coming up. I don't have a gun or knife, but I do have a weapon, and I'll use it if necessary. I'm sure we can talk about this."

"Is Barnes down there with you?" a man asked from somewhere above.

"Yeah, he's here."

"You're Samson?"

"Yes."

"Do you have the stone?"

"I do.

"Come out of there real slow and you won't get hurt."

As Samson climbed the steps a pair of feet came into view, then their knees, until he was face to face with the palooka who, he assumed, had dispatched the Peters woman.

The man smiled. "Goodnight, Samson!"

Samson's face crinkled with confusion and he was about to speak, when someone cold cocked him from behind. The world slanted. His lights went out.

***

When he came to, he was unable to open his eyes. His body was being jolted from side to side, and his head hurt like hell—Samson felt a lump at the back of his skull.

"Oh-*ugh*!" he moaned, his head rolling on its fat plinth. He wanted to move his hands to rub the nape of his neck, but they were cuffed at his back, and that's when he felt something hard jab his ribs.

They've got a gun on me!

He prised open his eyes. His head lolled as he looked around and saw he was in a car that was travelling along a motorway, or so he thought.

"So glad you could join us, Mr. Valentine!" someone said. The gun's muzzle was pressed tighter to his ribs. "We've been hearing so very much about you and your heroics, sir. Excuse the gun— it's merely a precaution."

The voice was coming from the front passenger seat.

"Who... Who are you?" Samson slurred. His throat was so dry it hurt, causing his voice to crack. He licked his lips. "XRay...?" he gasped.

"Come, come, Samson, I thought you were savvier than that."

"Alligator..." he moaned, his eyes fluttering. "What did you hit me with?"

"Oh, you can thank Tracy for that, Mr. Valentine. She's by your side, the one who has the gun jammed in your belly."

"Try the ribs, boob."

"Ah, that's the spirit; a warrior to the end. I admire you so much—it's a shame I'm going to have to break you."

"Best of luck, bruno." Samson gritted his teeth and forced his eyes wide open. He felt dizzy. Sick. Bile rushed up his throat but he swallowed it back down.

God, I'd kill for a smoke and a drink right now.

"Aren't you going to say hello?" Tracy asked.

His eyelids drooped shut again. *How could I have been so foolish?!*

"Well, Sam?" she asked, digging the gun into his ribs.

Keeping his teeth gritted, Samson pulled his lips back, exposing his gums, as he opened his eyes and stared Mrs. Barnes in the face. "I should have known it was too good to be true. You used me to flush him out, didn't you?" He pushed his face close to hers but he was grabbed by the shoulder and pulled back by the thug sitting on the other side of him.

Samson turned to face him and slammed his forehead into the man's beezer, which burst in a fan of blood across the car's roof and the window. Samson went for him again but was reminded of the gun as its hammer clacked.

"Oh, *fuck*, he's shattered my nose!" the man wailed.

"Calm down, Sam," Alligator chimed in.

Samson turned to face her, ignoring Alligator. "Why don't you tell me what this is *really* all about?!"

She laughed in his face. "All in good time, Samson. All in good time. Oh, by the way, I took the liberty of relieving you of the cash and stone in your pockets."

"*Bitch*! A cold one at that. What have you done with Barnes?"

"You know, you probably could have worked things out a lot faster if you weren't such a lush!" she said. "But to answer your question, he's safe—for now."

"Yeah, I'll just bet he is," he seethed.

"She's quite right, Samson. He's in the car behind us," said Alligator.

Samson tried to look over his shoulder, but couldn't.

"Think you're pretty fucking clever, don't you? Breaking my fucking nose!" the goon at his side said, giving Samson a shove and putting *his* gun against Samson's head. "I could pop your fucking brains right now. Right. Fucking. *Now!*"

"Gary, put your gun away," Alligator said, turning in his seat to give his man a cold glare. "No harm is to come to him. *Yet.*"

"Yeah, *yet*," Gary whispered in Samson's ear. "Going to shoot you all up! Pow, pow, pow!" He smiled, exposing his red-stained teeth. Some of the blood had congealed on the man's upper lip, making it look as though he had ruby-coloured snot stuck to his face.

"God, wipe yourself off, man," Samson said. "You look a frightful mess, palooka."

Gary's face twisted with rage, and had he not been a bulldog on a chain, Samson feared Gary may have beaten him to a bloody pulp.

"You're going to get yours real soon!" Gary snarled.

"*Gary!* That's enough." Alligator slammed his fist against his seat.

"Care to tell me where I'm being taken to—possibly your underground hideout?"

Alligator laughed. "*Ha*! Your charm thrills me, Mr. Valentine. You're not 007, and you're not living in a Fleming novel, which I hate to break to you. Have I shattered your fantasy? Never mind. However, you're not completely off the mark. I'm taking you to my, er— *HQ*, shall we call it? Just for the merriment!" he tittered, and then turned in his seat to face forward.

"You're probably taking me to your goddamn gator pit!" Samson lurched in his seat, his jaws snapping.

"Oh, so you've heard about it? How quaint." He didn't turn to look at Samson.

"*Pfft*! Your cartoon fright tactics won't rattle me, pal." Samson then turned to Mrs. Barnes, or Tracy, as she'd been referred to by Alligator. "And you, well—what can I say apart from what I think about you? You're a diabolical, cold-hearted traitor, lady."

"Gary, you may make Mr. Valentine more comfortable. I can see he's not in the mood for playing nice."

"Huh?" was all Samson had time to say before being struck on the side of his neck by the butt of Gary's gun, turning Samson's world black once again.

Chapter 20

A splash of water in his face shocked him back to reality. A big, rough paw slapped him across his left and then his right cheek. Samson couldn't move—he'd been tied to a chair. The hand went away and was replaced by fists: a left, right, left, right combination pounded his guts.

"That's it, soften him up," someone said.

Close by a man cried. A woman screamed.

Samson's mind raced.

When the punching stopped, Samson unfolded his body and looked up—strings of bloody saliva clung to his drooping lip and chin. "*Roxie!*" he gasped, seeing the young woman tied to a chair. "You bastards. Let her go. She has no involvement in this, for Christ's sake. This is between us. Let's resolve it like men." Samson's gaze shifted. He appeared to be in a large metal barn with a mud pit attached to the rear. There was straw about his feet. The place reeked of wet animal. "Where are we?"

"I told you, Mr. Valentine," Alligator answered. "HQ."

"Out west, I'll assume. After all, you control those lines on the map, don't you?"

Alligator laughed. "Your resourcefulness and resilience are remarkable, sir." He walked over to Samson. "And for that, I shall fill you in on everything that's been going on. I'm afraid you've had the wool pulled over your drunken eyes—not that we had to try very hard. I know you used to be a big shot back in the day, but you're nothing but a washed-up whisky hound now, correct?"

"Tell you what, you let me free and I'll show you who's washed up."

Alligator bent down in front of Samson and lightly slapped his cheek. "That's gusto. Please, keep entertaining me, but there's a way you can walk away from this, Samson."

"What's the price tag, muffin?"

"Your silence. And of course, you'll belong to me, and I'll be after inside information from the police department on my rivals. Anything you can get, really."

"If I refuse?" Samson bared his teeth.

"Well, that's simple—it'll be into the gator pit with you."

"What happens to the girl?"

Alligator looked over his shoulder. "We'll have to wait and see, won't we?"

Samson eyed the small, stocky man, who walked with a cane and wore crocodile-skin boots. "You're a sack of shit in a cheap suit, jug head, and there's no way in hell I'll ever be a stoolie or mule for the likes of you." Samson wanted to spit on the man, but had more class than that.

"Then you know there's no other way out of this, Mr. Valentine?"

"A small price to pay in my opinion, pal—ridiculously small, in fact."

"My, my, what a brave man. You know, you would have been a right thorn in Capone's side back in the day." Alligator and his two goons laughed. "Gary, Dan—soften up my gator meat some more."

"With pleasure, Mr. Gator." Gary cracked his knuckles.

The other guy, Dan, removed his leather gloves and pocketed them.

He must have been the driver.

Gary stepped in. "Now you're mine."

"Do your worst, son," Samson smiled.

He pummelled Samson's guts with furious lefts and rights before delivering an uppercut, causing the gumshoe to bob in his chair.

"*No*! Leave him alone!" Roxie screamed. "You're going to kill him."

"It's okay, kid, I can take it—" Blood dribbled out of his mouth.

Gary stepped back and allowed Dan to take over. He started with Samson's face.

The two goons kept reshuffling every couple of minutes until a door somewhere opened and slammed shut.

"Okay, that's enough. Gary, Dan, give him some time to reflect."

"No, please... Please! I'm begging you!" Samson heard someone cry. Turning his head, he saw Mrs. Barnes enter the room with two more thugs—the muscle were dragging the bookkeeper along the floor whilst she kept a gun trained on him. "You said you *loved* me."

"*Ha!*" she laughed. "You never were the brightest, were you? Now, shut up, or I'll put a bullet in your head."

She'd undergone a complete transformation: gone was the suave lady who spoke with a plum in her throat. So, too, was her dress sense. Over the time he'd known her, she'd always dressed with elegance, even when he'd caught her unaware in the mornings and evenings.

But now?

Now her fashion choices portrayed her vile attitude. She wore black jeans and a jumper to match, with boots to finish the look. She looked tough, cold, and not like the glass figurine of a lady he had met a few nights ago.

Samson had been completely hoodwinked.

Never, ever, had he been tricked in such a way, but it was all starting to make sense—he could see what was going on—what the ruse was all about.

Samson continued to watch the men drag Mr. Barnes towards Alligator. Gary and Dan were flanking the crime boss whilst Mrs. Barnes strolled over to Samson. Even her walk had lost its finishing school strut.

"She's just a bloody common hood like the rest of 'em, Sam!"

That she is, Angie. I've been set-up good and proper.

"You thinking what I'm thinking?"

Yes.

"Mrs. Barnes. Why, it's so lovely to see you again." He tried his best to smile through the pain in his jaw and face. "I would love to entertain you, but I appear to be a little tied up. Do forgive me."

She scowled before cracking him across the

cheek with the flat of her hand. "We could have had something, you and I." She got close to his ear. "*Could* have." She licked his lobe and straightened.

Samson shuddered in revulsion.

"Sorry, I don't date women colder than the meat I keep stored in my freezer. Besides, doesn't your arm belong to Reptile Man over there, palooka?" Samson had never raised his hand to a woman, let alone struck one, but had his arms been free he would have slapped her across her smug chops.

He gritted his teeth, which hurt like hell.

She flashed him an icy glare. "No, I know the kind of women *you* like." She walked over to Roxie and pointed her gun in the woman's face. "Sad, lonely old men like you like young scrag-ends like this whore."

"*Bitch!*" Roxie yelled. "I knew there was something off about you when I first met you."

Mrs. Barnes pistol-whipped Roxie across the face. "Shut up, you little tart."

"*Hey*! You leave her out of this—she's nothing to do with what's going on around here. If you want someone to slug, give it to me, lady. Hear me?"

"*Arrgh*! No, no! Don't put me in *there*!" Mr. Barnes screamed, causing Samson to turn his head in the bookkeeper's direction.

Three of Alligator's men were standing on the gate to the swamp, dangling the unfortunate Mr. Barnes by his feet above the snapping jaws of an ancient reptile. The gator's teeth were inches from the man's face as he cried, screamed and begged for mercy.

"You don't have to do this, Andy! *Please*! I'll tell you anything you want. Please! Just call your men off."

"Jesus..." Samson uttered. "What are you *doing*?"

"*Hm*?" Alligator asked, turning to Samson. "Did you say something?"

"You barbaric son of a bitch."

"Why, thank you, Mr. Valentine! Coming from a man who likes to hit first and ask questions later, I'll take that as a compliment."

Samson wrestled with his ropes. "If I get loose..."

"Save your energy, Mr. Valentine. You may need it." Alligator turned back to his men.

I need to stop them from feeding that poor bastard to the gator!

"Hey, aren't you going to enlighten me on how you pulled the wool over my eyes?" Samson knew full well what was going on—he just wanted to hear it from the horse's mouth. Plus, it would buy him some time, time he needed to think of a way out of his current situation.

"Soon, Mr. Valentine, soon, I promise. Let's take care of one job at a time, shall we?" Alligator said without turning to face him. "Now, Mr. Barnes, can you hear me, dear fellow?"

"Yea—*yes!*" the number-cruncher gasped. "*Please*! Let me up. I'll talk. Anything you want—please..."

As the conversation unfolded, Samson worked at the knots keeping his hands tied behind his back.

What happened to the cuffs? Mental note: keep the rope.

Alligator and Mrs. Barnes had their eyes on the spectacle before them. With them distracted, Samson glanced over at Roxie and saw her doing something behind her back, but he couldn't tell what. She gave him a sign with her lips to be quiet.

There's hope if they stay distracted long enough.

"Are you quite sure you're happy to tell me all, sir?" Alligator asked, indicating for his goons to lower Mr. Barnes a little further, provoking a louder scream.

"*Argh*! Fucking hell, yes! Anything! *Anything*! Please, oh Jesus!"

"Okay, boys, let him up and place him in that chair," Alligator told them, pointing at the seat next to Roxie. "Let's see if he's willing to play ball."

Gary looked disappointed, making Samson think for a moment that the rogue would drop the hysterical Mr. Barnes on purpose, but he didn't.

"I do hope you're not wasting mine and my associates' time, Mr. Barnes." Alligator watched as his men placed the accountant in the seat and held him in place. "Tracy, his briefcase," he ordered, snapping his fingers.

The goon passed him the valise and Alligator snapped it open to withdraw a ledger.

"I'm going to make this simple, Mr. Barnes," he went on. "I know XRay has been dodging his taxes for some years, and that you, my friend, have been covering his tracks from day one. After all, you're the best in the business, right?"

"I... but I'm not XRay's only..."

"Do you want to be fucking dangled back over that swamp?" Alligator leaned on his cane and got in Mr. Barnes' face. "*Well*?!"

Mr. Barnes shook his head. "Yes—yes, I'm the *best*. I'm also the *only* accountant he has."

"Good, Mr. Barnes, good. We're finally making progress."

"Just tell me what you want, for Christ's sake!"

"My, my, such impatience. All I want is for you to show me *how* you've hidden his money. I want all the codes out of your book. You see, if I can't beat XRay with guns, muscles and territory, then I will have to get sneaky and flush him down the shitter in a different way."

"What good will that do you? You can't very well take him to court for tax evasion."

"Ha-ha! Oh, Mr. Barnes you make me laugh. You think I don't have judges in my pockets? Juries? People who will testify? Coppers? People to do just about anything I want them to do? When I have full control over XRay's organisation, I'll be one of the most powerful crime bosses in the UK. And, let's not forget, *the* most influential one on Welsh soil. Plus, I'll have my warhead codes back."

Warheads? Codes? Codes! Samson thought.

"You expect me to help you eliminate XRay? To double-cross a man I've worked with for almost four decades? You're mad. He'll do far worse to me than what you're fucking capable of, mate!"

"So, you won't help, not even after all your screams, begs, pleas and promises? This is most disappointing. For your cooperation, I would have placed you in my organisation." Alligator shook his head. "XRay must be a foolish man to allow such assets to be captured."

"Oh, and I suppose you stash your numbers-men on the other side of the world?" Samson chirped more to himself.

"As a matter of fact, I do. My most important people are hidden far and wide, Mr. Valentine." And with that, Alligator snapped his fingers. Mr. Barnes was hauled out of his chair and dragged back to the alligator swamp. They could hear the reptile writhing around in the muck, as though it could smell its dinner was coming.

"*No!*" Mr. Barnes protested again, digging his feet into the floor. His shoes squealed as he was dragged along by the three brutes. "Please, for fuck's sake! No!"

"I gave you a chance, sir."

"I'll talk, I'll talk!" he screamed as the thugs picked him up and turned him upside down. "I *promise!*"

"Put him in feet first," Alligator told them.

"You bastards! Give me the book! I'll tell you. I swear!" The man's scream reached its zenith, reminding Samson of a little girl having a tantrum in a supermarket.

The gator moved closer to the gate and snapped its massive, powerful jaws in readiness.

Samson felt his insides go cold. Mr. Barnes was inches from being fed to the thing. He couldn't watch, so he turned his head away, noticing Roxie had done the same, but not Mrs. Barnes. She watched on.

"*Argh!*" Mr. Barnes wailed. "No!"

The beast snapped its jaws.

"Give me the book!" Mr. Barnes yelled.

"Hold him there," Alligator demanded.

Samson looked over and saw what was going on. The crime boss had the accountant's book in his hands. "Show me. *Now*! Or they drop you."

"It'll take a couple of hours—there's lots to go through."

"If you're lying, then into the fucking pit you'll go, my friend. Do you understand me?"

"Yea—yeah!" Mr. Barnes was visibly trembling.

"Pull him outta there, lads, and throw him back in his chair." The thugs did as they were instructed. "You've got thirty minutes to tell me *everything*," Alligator threatened.

"But…"

"Clock's ticking, Mr Barnes, I suggest you get started."

Chapter 21

Mr. Alligator, or Andy for short, wasn't much of a timekeeper. Long after the thirty-minute mark lapsed, he and Mr. Barnes were still deep in conversation about XRay's money and empire.

Not that it bothered Samson, who had all but undone the ropes securing his wrists. The goons hadn't been paying him any attention. Gary and Dan were standing around smoking and chatting, whilst the other two flanked Mr. Alligator and kept Mr. Barnes still in his seat.

That left only Mrs. Barnes, who stood between Samson and Roxie. Now and then, she cast her gaze in his or Roxie's direction, but mostly focused on the conversation between her boss and husband.

With the ropes loosened from around his wrists, Samson pulled the slack into his fists so that the rope seemed taut. It would give the impression he was still tied up. Roxie continued to fidget, much to his curiosity.

Samson glanced about the room to take stock of the situation. There only appeared to be the one way in and out, which was through a large, steel door at the far end of the building. He had no idea whether more guards stood watch outside, but regardless, he knew he was up against far more than he could handle.

What am I going to do?! He moved his head from side to side as he tried to figure a plan. *Maybe*

I could get this rope around Alligator's neck and use him as a shield? That might work.

"...And that's all I know, Andrew, I swear. All the figures and codes I've given you are correct. I haven't held *anything* back."

"Good, very good, Mr. Barnes. You know, I like you. A lot—you have amazing skills at what you do."

Samson turned his head in the direction of the conversation.

"Now that we have this matter out of the way, will you let me come and work for you? You could hide me, like you've hidden your other key workers?"

"Yes, that was the plan, which still sounds awfully tempting. I could always do with people such as yourself, sir—one can never have enough numbers-men around, especially when dealing with such large amounts of cash as I do."

"If you let me go, or release me back to XRay, he'll hunt me down and rip my spine out."

"Barnes, Barnes, do you think I would let that happen to a man of your standing? You've pleased me by telling me what I wanted to know. However, there is one other thing I would like to know."

"*Anything*! Ask, and I shall tell. I've already shown how I can work for you."

Alligator put a fat Cuban cigar in his mouth and rotated it as he lit it. "Who *is* XRay, Barnes?" He pulled the cigar from his gob and blew a lungful of smoke in Barnes' face.

"I..." he stammered, "that, I *can't* tell you,

because I don't know who he is."

"Are you trying to tell me you've worked for a faceless man for almost forty years?! My, that *is* loyal! I admire that. And would you offer me the same amount of devotion?"

"Yes, of course. Anything. I beg you; don't toss me out there into the jungle or to your pet alligator."

"Of course not, Mr. Barnes. But you see, I have two problems: the first, I could probably overlook. However, the second is a little harder to swallow."

"I'm sure we can work out whatever it is. I'm a solver of problems."

"Hmm, yes… yes, you are, aren't you? Well, you see, the first conundrum I have is that The Sandman was led to his death because of you, sir, and he wasn't *just* a hitman on my books, he was my cousin. You killed my blood, Barnes."

"But… but… he was there to kill *her*!" he screamed. "That's what I was paying him for."

"Oh, Mr. Barnes, don't be foolish. He wasn't there to kill Tracy, he was there to kill, torture and extract information from you, obviously not in that order, of course. You see, when we got the call that you wanted to rub your 'wife' out, we couldn't believe our luck, knowing there was probably some form of a catch. Which there was. You stayed in hiding, making things difficult, and then this ape comes charging in like bloody Rambo!" Alligator turned toward Samson.

"Huh, my pleasure!" Samson coughed. His ribs and face ached.

"Yes, Mr. Valentine. We hadn't planned it that

way, but I'll come back to that." Alligator faced Barnes again. "You see, you've made things complicated. And of course, when my cousin was taken into custody, your lot had him killed." Alligator got in Mr. Barnes' face. "They're *still* mailing him back to me. This morning, I received his heart and lungs. Would you care to see?"

Samson fought back a surge of fresh vomit.

"If he was in custody, how could they be cutting him up and sending him to you?" Samson butted in.

"Don't be so naïve, Mr. Valentine—it's an inside job. And, if it's not, then someone got a handful of cash to see to it that body disappeared after it left the police station."

Samson fell quiet. *Something doesn't add up...*

"No..." Mr. Barnes whispered.

"And the second problem I have?" Alligator clicked his fingers; his men grabbed Mr. Barnes and pulled him from his chair. "I don't like people who rat out their employer."

"Oh, *Jesus*! No—help me!"

"Goodbye, Mr. Barnes. It was a pleasure doing business with you."

"*Argh*, no! Fucking hell. *Please!*"

Samson watched as the four brutes heaved Mr. Barnes over their heads and tossed him into the gator pit.

"Sweet Jesus..." Samson muttered, keeping his eyes fixed on the accountant.

Mr. Barnes rolled onto his back in the mucky water and tried to crawl back to the gate on his arse by using his hands and feet, but he kept slipping, unable to get traction in the mud.

Not that it would have done him any good, as the ancient beast pounced on Mr. Barnes in an instant. And when that happened, Samson had to look away, as the gator snapped its mighty jaws down on its prey's arm, breaking it like a dry twig.

Samson had never heard screaming like what came from Barnes, not even while on tour in the army—and he had seen some horrific sights during his stint in the Gulf.

Roxie couldn't bear to watch. She had her face turned as far away from the gator pit as her restraints would allow. Next to her, Mrs. Barnes watched on with something akin to glee in her eyes, never blinking, hardly moving except for the smile that spread across her face.

"Did you see that fucker swallow his head in one go!" Samson heard one of the heavies bellow with excitement. His mate replied with harsh laughter. Meanwhile, in the pit, the gator thrashed in the mud with Barnes's body in its jaws, ripping the mangled corpse to pieces.

Samson heaved, fearing more vomit was coming.

The sound of a chair being dragged in front of Samson stung his ears.

"You didn't have to do that, Alligator," Samson whispered. "My God, you're a savage."

"I'm glad you think so, Mr. Valentine. I also hope you realise how deadly serious I am, and that you've come up with an answer I'm going to find pleasing. Will you be my inside man?"

"I guess I'm gator dessert if not, huh?"

"Yes, but it doesn't have to be like that, as you know."

"If I agree to keep silent and be your puppet, I want you to spare the girl. Got it?"

"Do you think you're in any position to barter, Mr. Valentine?"

"I know I'm up to my neck in gator shit, but I must insist on you sparing her—she has a daughter who needs her. Me, you can do with as you please. I'm a lone wolf. The world won't miss a crazy old fool like me."

"Let me think about it—"

"You'll have me to bend any way you see fit. I'll get you all the information you want."

Both men stared at each other. Andrew laughed. "Okay, you have a deal. But the moment you double-cross me, I'll chop you into tiny fucking pieces and feed you to my pet alligator."

"You have my word," Samson promised.

Andrew nodded. "Release the girl." He snapped his fingers, his guards untied her.

Now's my chance!

"There's just one thing I want to clear up before we move on to being bosom buddies, Andrew."

"And what would that be?"

"I was hauled into a pathetic game of Tit for Tat, wasn't I? A pawn in *your* game, not XRay's. I was dragged in to help flush him out, wasn't I? What is she to you—your moll, I mean?"

Alligator laughed. "Why, she's my wife, Mr. Valentine."

Samson shook his head. "And how did she know

to contact me? How did she know I had the stone?"

He continued. "When you made off with the stone at the train station, I was informed immediately by the men you managed to outrun, and then later hit on the head with a frying pan of all things."

"He *knew* me?!"

Alligator laughed. "You really are a drunken mess, aren't you? You didn't even recognise them, did you? Not even the one who fell under the train?"

Samson's mouth formed an O. "No…"

Alligator shook his head. "I can't believe how well my plan worked—the two men you foiled were put behind bars by you some ten years ago. Back then, they were working for a thug in Cardiff, before they came into my employment. When we found out all there was to know about you, we allowed you to run rampant and cause as much trouble as you could."

"So let me see if I've managed to connect all the dots, just out of curiosity."

"By all means. It's really not that difficult."

"The spun lies throughout this whole thing I can deal with. I mean, after all, I'm just a broken fool. I'm guessing you found out who Mr. Barnes was around a year, year and a half ago, and decided to put your wife into place to try and sucker the poor bastard in, but things didn't quite work out as you'd planned, did they? No, because Barnes got wise to who he'd 'married' and tried having her rubbed out. How am I doing so far?"

"Impressive, Mr. Valentine."

"I'm also assuming you set her up with the house and money to make it look convincing?" He turned to 'Mrs. Barnes', "you haven't got two pennies to rub together, have you? It was all a smoke screen, right down to the hoity-toity accent."

Mrs. Barnes smiled. "Admittedly, it's Alligator's money...

"I *almost* saw through it, but I guess I'm a sucker for a dame with a tear in her eye—especially one waving money under my nose. And, as you've all pointed out, I'm a drunk. You played me well, but any idiot can make a fool out of a broken man. Shame on you. You must have been rubbing your hands together with glee when you found out I had the stone."

"Very good, Mr. Valentine. I was, especially after I knew about your problems."

"But why wait? Why place your wife in Mr. Barnes' care for so long? Why not just kill him?"

"*Information*, Mr. Valentine. I was hoping Tracy could pump him for as much as she could, but he kept tight-lipped, and by the time I was about to use brute force, the man had gone into hiding."

"How long into the marriage?"

"A mere six months."

"And then I happened along."

"And the rest is history, as they say."

"Now that we're going to be working for the same side, hopefully we can all be friends?" Tracy asked.

Samson scoffed. "Aye, if you want."

"Good." Alligator slapped Samson's knee as he got out of his chair. "Release him."

Now that her hands were free, Roxie rubbed her wrists and scowled at the men. With a quick flick of his head, he motioned for her to come to him.

"One other thing, Andrew?" said Samson. "Well, two actually. What's so important about that stone?"

"Don't you watch the news, Mr. Valentine?"

"Not lately."

Andrew smiled. "So, you had no idea you were carrying the codes around?" He laughed. "Hilarious."

"Say again? I don't get you."

He ignored the question. "What else do you have on your mind, Sam?"

Samson let the first question drop. "Why did you send your chopper squad over to Mrs. Barnes' house to gun me down if you wanted me to aid you in flushing out Mr. Barnes?"

Alligator's brow furrowed. "I beg your pardon? I am not sure what you mean."

Samson clicked his tongue as he mulled this over. If Alligator hadn't sent the hit squad, then that ruled out everyone but D.I. Davis. "Bastard," he said under his breath.

"What did you say?"

Samson looked up and made eye contact with Alligator. "Come closer, and I'll tell you."

As Alligator bent down, Samson pounced out of his chair and wrapped his rope around his neck before anyone knew what was happening. Samson pulled on it as tight as he could, pinning the crime boss to his chest.

"Drop your weapons or I'll pop his head off like a bottle cap! Roxie, get the door. *Now*!"

Alligator coughed, spluttered and gasped as he tried to get his fingers under the rope and pull it from his throat.

The hatchet-men threw their guns to the ground and watched helplessly as Samson backed up to the door.

"Roxie, get outside."

As Samson stepped into the afternoon sun, someone yelled from behind him.

"*Freeze*!"

He turned, seeing sunlight glint off metal.

"Down!" Samson yelled, shoving Andrew out in front of him. The sudden movement got the better of the thugs' trigger fingers. Before they were sure of what had happened, they had unloaded a short burst of gunfire that tore through the crime boss, sending him to the turf as a blood-spattered mess.

Samson dove to the side, taking Roxie with him.

"The Jeep!" he yelled over the gunfire. When he looked back, he saw Andrew's men in the barn's doorway—they returned fire, too busy to notice Samson and Roxie's mad dash to the vehicle.

He only hoped the keys had been left inside.

"Shit, shit, shit!" Samson yelled as he ran towards the Jeep with Roxie just ahead. "Get in!"

When he got behind the steering wheel he immediately noticed the keys dangling from the ignition. Not wasting a second, Samson kicked the engine to life, reversed and then U-turned into the direction he guessed was the exit.

As they whizzed by Andrew's corpse, Samson saw the three gunmen attacking the barn—they were kitted out in black, right down to their balaclavas and tactical gear.

One of them took a few pot shots at them, but turned their attention back to the men in the metal barn. When he looked in the rear-view mirror, Samson saw Dan, Gary, and Mrs. Barnes go down in a hail of bullets, blood and screams. He felt no remorse.

They got what they had coming to 'em!

Chapter 22

They were ten miles clear of the barn by the time Samson was positive they weren't being followed. He pulled onto the motorway's hard shoulder and killed the engine.

Neither of them had spoken a word since leaving the O.K. Corral.

"What the hell happened back there?!" He turned to Roxie. "I have a funny feeling you're behind that slaughter, doll face."

She lowered her head. "Yeah, you're right, but I had no idea it would go down like *that*."

"Je... *sus*! If we'd been any slower in getting out of there, we would have been smoked with the rest of 'em. Again, what the *hell* did you do?"

"I'm *sorry*! I didn't think anyone would get hurt, I promise."

"Tell me how you did it. I knew you were up to something." Samson's face flushed, his hands curled into fists. He shook his head and stared at her. She had tears streaming down her face.

"I thought I was doing the right thing, Sam." Her lower lip trembled.

"It's okay. *We're* okay, and I guess there's no real harm done."

"I used this." Roxie handed Samson a device that resembled a mobile phone, but it was missing a keypad and screen. All it had was a single button. "Mike gave one of these to each of us girls—it's sort of like a rape alarm, and when that button's been pressed, it sends a distress call back to Mike and his goons."

"It must have a sort of satellite navigation system built into it if they managed to pinpoint your exact location. Why send a death squad after one of their girls who's supposedly getting attacked?"

"Probably because I'm miles out of the area, Sam—us girls *never* venture further than Mike's property or the city's limits. Not only that, they know whose alarm is whose—we're tagged."

"Yes, of course, and they know *I'm* in your company. I'm guessing they were watching us, waiting to see what would happen. I bet they knew all about Mrs. Barnes."

"You think they were following us, and that my alarm did nothing?"

"Yes. But they managed to lose us somehow, as they were slow in reacting. XRay is going to be pretty mad when he finds out Barnes is dead."

"If they *were* following us, then they probably wanted to wipe us out too. Stupid! I should never have alerted them—they wouldn't have found us otherwise."

"Hey, you weren't to know. Besides, we made it out alive. They must have been laughing their heads off when they saw you and me get captured by Alligator and his thugs."

"Do you think they would have spared us?"

"I doubt it, although I believe Alligator was their main target. All they really want from me is the stone." He frowned.

"What's wrong, Sam?"

"Roxie, I believe I know who the mysterious XRay is."

"Oh?"

"I'm not going to part with it yet, just in case. *Damn*! I should have picked up the stone. I'm going to need—" A sparkle from her direction drew his gaze. Roxie held the diamond out for him to see.

"*How*?" he stammered.

She then produced the money Mrs. Barnes had taken from him. "In all the confusion I managed to snatch both from Mrs. Barnes' bag. You see, before I was a whore in Mike's stable, I was a thief—a pickpocket, to be precise, but that's not all I'm good at. Lifting this lot from that stupid bitch was easy."

Samson made a move for the stone, but she snatched it out of his reach.

"Not so fast, Sam. I'll make you a deal, right here, right now."

"*God*! I'm a little fed up with these games—people are dying, for Christ's sake. I need to put an end to XRay and his army before there's nobody left to give a damn about it."

"The deal is simple. I get to keep the money, you take the stone. Sound fair?"

"Tell you what, give me a little bit of that cash to cover my expenses and to book us into a hotel for the night, and you're on."

She smiled and handed the stone to him which he pocketed.

"Can you drive? Do you have a licence?"

She nodded.

"Great," he went on, "then get us to the first roadside hotel you can find. We need to lay low for a few hours. Plus, I feel like hell."

They got out of the Jeep and switched sides. Samson got into the passenger's seat and reclined it until he was horizontal, making himself comfortable by removing his coat, rolling it up and placing it under his head like a pillow.

"That's it, get some sleep," she said. "I can take care of the rest, Sam."

"Great, because I'm far too old for this nonsense, sugar."

Roxie put the Jeep into gear and pulled out of the lay-by.

Samson drifted off into a deep, dreamless sleep, though he didn't sleep for long.

After what felt like mere moments, someone shook him roughly by the shoulder whilst calling his name, but he didn't know who. As he opened his eyes, Samson realised it was Roxie. Everything came back to him.

"*Jesus*! How long have I been out?"

"About thirty-five, maybe forty minutes, I guess. Come on, I've found us a hotel. It's a classy-looking place," she sniggered.

Samson forced himself into a sitting position and all his bones screamed at once. "It sounds as if there's a heavy metal band playing a concert inside my head."

"*Gig*," she corrected.

"Gig—" His mouth swung open. "My, *God*! That's not a hotel, it's a cesspool."

"Well, you didn't say you wanted the Ritz, Sam. Come on, it's only for the night, isn't it?"

"*Ugh!*" He grabbed his coat and slid out of the Jeep. His legs felt like jelly. When he looked around, stretching his back, Samson noticed a small shop and petrol station adjoining the hotel; most of the letters were missing from its neon sign. A few windows on the upper level were broken, with slates missing from the roof.

"What a joint! You go right ahead, Roxie, and book us in. I'm going to the shop to get a few supplies. I'll meet you in reception."

"Yeah, got it," she called over her shoulder.

Samson hobbled over to the shop and entered. He picked up milk, teabags and coffee, along with a couple of tins of cigarillos, a first aid kit and some tablets for his pounding head. After paying, he made his way to Roxie.

"I managed to get us a room with single beds, Sam."

"Yeah, that's perfect. Once I've taken a shower and sorted myself out, I'll be heading out the door. I've got a few things I need to straighten out."

"You're not taking me with you?"

"Definitely not. You'll be safer here, and I don't want an argument about it. Do XRay's goons know where your daughter is?"

Her eyes flickered. "Yeah. Maybe. I don't know. Why? You don't think they'd go after her, do you?"

"I hope not, but it might be a good idea to get her out from under the stone she's hiding beneath, before someone comes along and kicks it over."

"Oh God, my baby."

"Let's get inside first. There's no reason to panic yet, I was only thinking outside the box to make sure all avenues are covered."

They took the stairs to the fourth floor. The inside of their room looked far better than its outside: the furniture seemed new and the walls freshly painted.

"I guess you really *shouldn't* judge a book by its cover," Samson quipped.

He was also surprised to find a working shower, with hot and cold settings and a healthy pressure. Everything within the room was modern, right down to the bed sheets.

"I'm not sure why you're acting so shocked, Sam—this is the twenty-first century," she laughed.

"I know, but you saw the outside."

"Like you said, don't judge a book…"

"True." Samson placed his bag of goodies on one of the bedside tables and removed the box of Paracetamol. He popped four into his mouth and dry-swallowed them. "Maybe the palooka that runs this place blew his annual budget on maintaining the interior?" Before she could respond, he spoke again. "I'm going to take a shower and get gone. Do you want me to pick up your daughter and bring her back here before I do what I need to do?"

She looked sick with nervousness. "Please, Sam, if you don't mind."

"Right, whilst I'm sorting myself out, ring whoever she's with and ask them to get her ready. I'll be about an hour getting there. She's in Cardiff, right?"

"Newport."

"Okay. I'll get the address from you as soon as I'm ready to go." With that, Samson removed a small bottle of whisky he'd bought and headed into the bathroom. He engaged the bolt and ripped the seal and cap off the drink before stripping, and then took the alcohol into the shower with him. He sat in the bathtub and let the shower pelt him as he swigged from the bottle.

"I can't keep this up, Angie—the whole tough guy routine is getting as old and stale as the clothes and character I'm playing."

"Stop that! You're not playing anything. You are that guy, Samson, and anyone who'd been through what you have in the last few days would be feeling the same way."

"So many lives lost—people I should have been able to protect, like Ms. Peters." He shook his head and took a few more large swallows of whisky. "Now I have Roxie and her little girl seeking my protection. I don't think I can guarantee it, Angie."

"Pull yourself together, man! And leave the devil's juice alone. You need to kick the alcohol once and for all. Come on, you've come this far, and you've managed to protect Roxie from some pretty stern stuff. Just push a little harder, a little further, and you'll have one of the biggest cases cracked. It will help you return to glory, Sam."

"I know. I just need a few minutes to myself, and a drink. My last drink ever! I need to gather myself before going into the breach once more."

There was a faint knock at the bathroom door. "Sam, are you okay?"

He could just about hear Roxie over the shower spray and closed curtain. "Yeah, just having a stern word with myself."

"Oh, okay... Listen, I've spoken with my friend—Charlie will be set to go. I told my friend to expect you, a private detective, and described what you look like."

"A dashing chap in a trench coat and fedora, eh?"

"I didn't quite catch that?"

"It's okay, I'll be out soon. Scribble your friend's address down on a piece of paper for me."

When she went quiet, Samson let the curtain go and placed the bottle of whisky down by the bathtub's side. He then got to his feet and opened the small packet of soap the hotel had provided.

Thirty minutes later, dressed and ready to blow town, Samson pocketed the address he needed for Charlie and made sure the stone was in his coat pocket.

"Are you going to be okay driving with your eye?"

"Yeah, it's just a scratch. Remember, keep the door locked and don't answer the phone. If I need to call I'll let it ring three times, hang up, and call back. Got it?"

She nodded. "Yeah, got it."

"Good. Right, it's seven o'clock now, so give me until nine to get back here with Charlie."

"Okay. And for Christ's sake, be careful."

"Careful's my middle name, Roxie," he said with a wink. "Charlie will be here with you in no time. Trust me." After kissing her on the forehead, he grabbed the keys and left.

Before hitting the open road, Samson filled the Jeep's petrol tank. As he pulled off the hotel's premises, he turned things over in his head.

I've got to get Charlie the hell out of Dodge and into the safety of her mother's arms before I go and see that snake Davis, who'll be the best person to barter with, considering the things I know about him.

"*Maybe ring him, Sam?*"

"Yeah, might be a better idea, Angie. When? Before or after picking up the child?"

"*I'd say go for Charlie first—her life could be in peril.*"

"I agree. And once she's in my care, knowing she's safe, I'll be able to settle down. Besides, there's hours to kill before I need to be at the docks."

"*True, Sam.*"

"If I can get Davis to play ball, then this whole thing should be wrapped up before the night's through—I may not even have to go to the docks."

"*Agreed.*"

"I still feel meeting him face to face would be better. Maybe I can try and pull that off? Perhaps I can fool him into walking away and leaving matters where they are."

"*Or, fool him like you did Alligator?*"

"Not sure he'd buy me turning stoolie, but it's

worth a shot. I'll see."

He turned his attention to the radio—it was still set to jazz FM. The music helped ease him as he drove down the motorway at breakneck speed.

Then the news kicked in.

"The government's efforts to retrieve the stolen warhead codes have gone unresolved…"

Samson slowed his speed and turned the radio's volume up.

"…Military experts have reassured those concerned that the bombs cannot be armed or controlled by the outside forces who have seized ownership of the pass codes…"

Samson's grip tightened on the steering wheel.

"What do XRay and his ilk plan to do? Nuke the Russians? Or maybe the Yanks, and make it look like a Russian attack?" He shook his head. "Not on my watch."

When he reached Newport's apple, Samson had to ask multiple people for directions to the address Roxie had given him. Eventually, he found the house he was looking for in the very guts of the city.

Samson pulled up outside and got out. After knocking on the door three times, he stepped back to give the person some room when they answered. The twitch of a curtain drew Samson to turn his head in the direction of the front window, but he was too slow to catch who'd peeked out at him.

"Who's there?" a voice demanded from behind the closed door.

"It's Mr. Valentine. Samson Valentine. I believe

you're expecting me—I'm Roxie's friend."

The door was opened a crack and a face appeared. The person inside gave him the once-over, then closed the door in Samson's his face. He was about to protest, when Samson heard the safety chain rattle and the locks clack. It was pulled open again.

He was greeted by a short, rotund woman of around forty. She had a rolling pin in her left hand and rollers the size of dustbins in her hair. She stepped forward and narrowed her eyes. "So, I'm s'pposed to let Charlie go with you, Mr. Policeman?"

Samson wasn't going to argue the point that he *wasn't* a police officer. "That's correct. I'm taking her to her mother."

"Yeah, Rox told me on da phone. Where she stayin'? How do I knows you don't have her tied up somewhere? I knows the kind of people she's mixed up with."

"I assure you, I have nothing but Charlie's and Roxie's best interests at heart." And that's when Samson first laid eyes on Roxie's daughter—she appeared at the entrance of a room behind the human barricade guarding the front. She wore torn jeans, heavy black and purple make-up, and a T-shirt with Iron Maiden written across it.

"Charlie?" Samson asked the girl, ducking his head to one side.

The big woman turned her head. "I'm not sure 'bout's this, child. We don't know this fella."

"It's okay, Cynthia. If my mum sent him to get

me, then we have nothing to worry about. She'd rather die than put me in danger."

The girl walked towards Samson.

"Once we get moving we'll give your mum a ring, okay? Let her know we're on our way."

"I think we should do that *before* you leave my sight, mister!" Cynthia said.

"That works for me," Samson said. "You need to let it ring three times, hang up and then call again, or she won't answer."

"Come in here, child. Let's call your mamma first."

"Hey wait!" Samson moved to enter but the door was slammed in his face. Grumbling, he looked at his watch, resolving to give them five minutes before trying again.

Chapter 23

Charlie wasn't much for conversation as Samson drove them out of the apple. She slouched in the front seat, in typical teenage defiance. "Listen, kid, before we get back onto the big roads I need to stop and make an important phone call, that okay with you?"

"Yeah, it's cool." She didn't take her eyes off her mobile phone as she spoke.

Samson could tell he wasn't going to get much out of her, so he gave up trying. *She's safe, that's the important thing. Now all I need to do is find a phone.*

He pulled into a service station and parked in one of the bays close to the shop. "Okay," he said, killing the engine, "give me ten minutes."

Samson got out of the car but didn't bother to lock it. As he walked towards the shop, he removed his wallet and checked he had some spare change. After that, he sought out the D.I.'s number and entered the shop. A bell rang to announce his presence.

"You couldn't have used the girl's mobile, Sam?"

No, Angie. The D.I. might try and trace the call—I don't want that slime having her number.

He walked around the aisles and found the payphone at the rear, next to the cash points. Samson placed his money and the card with the

D.I.'s number on the shelf provided before lifting the handset and pumping two one-pound coins into the money slot.

On the fifth ring, the D.I. answered.

"Hello, Davis here."

"It's me, Samson."

"Well, what a nice surprise. How can I help you?"

"Let's not play stupid. Take this number down and call me back. We need to talk." Samson relayed the number for the payphone and hung up; one of his coins was ejected in the change pouch. By the time he'd retrieved it, the phone was jangling. Samson snatched the receiver out of its cradle. "Samson," he snapped down the line.

"So, what have *we* got to talk about, Sam? Where are you, by the way?"

"Don't play dumb—you know I'm on to you, palooka, and that I've got your cards well and truly marked."

"*Whoa*! What do you *think* you know, Sam?"

"That you're running with the XRay gang and that you're some form of bloody mule for them. What are they paying you, Davis? Hmm?! Come on, spill! Must be a handsome sum for you to turn your back on the oath you took the day you joined the force."

"Sam, I have no…"

"Cut the crap, pal—I have photographic and audio evidence of your involvement." The line went quiet, giving Samson a chance to reflect. *Maybe I should lay off the strong talk.*

"Is that so, Sam?"

"Yes, it's so, and I'm willing to do you a trade."

"Listen, I can't talk on this phone—the line isn't secure. What say I come out to wherever you are for a private chat?"

"You want me to stay put so you can send a couple of heavies my way? No dice, that's already happened once today, but you know that."

"Fine, if you don't trust me, why don't you come by my office later this evening? Once you've done your drop at the docks, that is…"

"*You—*" The line went dead and the dial tone followed. "Son of a bitch!" Samson slammed the phone into its cradle and stormed out of the shop. He didn't waste any time in getting behind the wheel and speeding out of the petrol station, much to Charlie's fright, as they hurtled along the road.

The bastard will trace me. God only knows how many good ole' boys he's got in his pocket. Doesn't matter—I'll be long gone before anyone gets out here.

He looked over at Charlie, who'd gone back to texting, playing games, or whatever it was youngsters did on their phones these days. Samson faced front and continued to turn things over in his mind.

By the time he got back to the hotel it was a shade after nine; the sun had long since gone down and the place was lit up like a neon Christmas tree. With the traffic on the motorway slackening, the stillness surrounding the place was enough to unsettle Samson.

"Right, come on—let's get you inside, young lady." They got out of the Jeep and met at the vehicle's front. "Do me a favour and give your mum's room a call? Let it ring three times and hang up—that way she'll know it's us."

"Okay."

Samson gave her the room's telephone number.

When Charlie hung up and gave him a nod, he led her into the hotel and up to Roxie's room. On approaching the door, Samson's heart sank—it stood ajar.

"Oh, hell…"

"What is it?" Charlie asked, stopping behind Samson and then moving to his side to look. "I don't understand? What are we seeing?"

"The door—it's *open*."

"Mum probably did it. She's expecting us, remember?" The girl pushed by him and put her hand to the door handle. But before she could enter, Samson grabbed her and pushed her behind him. "Hey, *oaf*!"

"Let me go in first, okay? I'll let you know if the coast is clear." She gave him a condescending look and scoffed. "I'm just keeping my promise to your mum, Charlie."

Samson turned to the door and put his hand to it. All the lights were on and there was no sign a disturbance had taken place. "Roxie? Are you in the bath…?" On the bed he spotted a note. His first thought was that she had run out on him and her daughter.

Samson poked his head out the door. "Wait there

a sec, would you, kid? I need to check something."

He closed the door to a crack and had a quick look around the room to make sure he was alone. Then, once he was sure the room was safe, he went to the note, picked it up and read it.

We have the girl. If you want her back in one piece, we suggest you make it to the docks tonight. Someone will be waiting for you outside the whorehouse. Be there. Midnight.

"*Damn!*" he shouted, crumpled the paper and tossed it to one side. "I was going to go anyway. Why all this cat and mouse?" Samson gave the dresser a hard kick, making the mirror on top of it wobble.

"Hey, what's going on? *Who* has my mum?" Charlie had tears in her eyes. Her bottom lip quivered.

"Damn it. I didn't foresee this. How did they know where to find her? There was nobody following us. Maybe it was that gadget she'd been carrying? I knew I should have destroyed it."

"*Her rape alarm*," Angie said.

"Yeah, they must have traced her with that. But how? I thought she had to activate it?"

"*Someone could still be hanging around here to take you out, Sam.*"

"Hey, who are you talking to?" asked Charlie. "Answer me, man. You're starting to freak me out."

Samson snapped out of it and looked at the girl. "We have to get out of here. Now." He grabbed her arm and dragged her towards the door, but she struggled against him and Samson stumbled. The stone fell from his pocket and rolled along the floor, coming to a halt when it hit the wardrobe hard. It cracked into two perfect halves. "Oh, no!"

He rushed to the precious diamond and picked it up.

"What's that?"

"This was the thing that was going to save your mum's—" his words tapered off. There was something protruding from one of the diamond's halves. "What's this?"

"*Save* my mum? What have *you* fucking done to my mother?" Charlie ran up to Samson and pummelled his back with her fists. "I'll kill you!"

"Calm down." He turned around, grabbed her wrists and forced her to sit on the bed. "I haven't done *anything* to your mother. People have her–people who aren't very nice, who she works for... or used to, I should say."

"Let me up! You're hurting me."

"Fine. But you have to trust me, Charlie. Please."

"Yeah, whatever. Just take me to my mum, dude."

"I plan to." He let go of her hands and plucked the piece of paper from the stone and unfolded it. It was A4 in size and had a bunch of numbers written on it.

The codes for the warheads? Surely not. Then again, it would explain why they want this thing so bad. He shook his head, folded the paper, and then placed it back inside the stone. To his surprise, the precious-looking diamond *clicked* back together. "Nothing but a fake. It's the numbers—that's the real treasure."

"Are we bloody well going?" Charlie stamped her foot.

"Yes." He pocketed the stone and closed the door behind him. On his way out to the car, Samson checked the time, relieved to see it wasn't quite ten o'clock. "It's going to be a tight squeeze getting to the docks in time, so I guess I'll have to stand Davis up. He'll keep."

Samson got into the Jeep and waited for Charlie to fasten her seatbelt. She opted for the back seat this time and glared at Samson in the rear-view.

***

Samson pulled onto the docks at precisely eleven-thirty, having floored it all the way down the motorway. The place was deserted.

Debris blew about in the breeze. Samson had his window rolled down a smidgen and could hear voices nearby. Dogs barked, ship horns blared. *The dock is an eerie place at night,* he thought. There was little light, just the odd streetlamp few and far between.

In the shadows, Samson saw pro skirts lurking. Two had punters in their company, and he could hear their sounds of satisfaction. He kept the Jeep moving at a crawl as homeless people staggered out of the darkness and cut across his path. They looked dead behind their eyes.

Samson shook his head.

In the distance, Jim's pro skirt house loomed. It

was lit up like a welcome beacon. A few goons hung about outside. Even though they were mixed in with punters and working girls, Samson could tell who was who; he didn't need a degree in criminal law to spot a no-good punk when he saw one.

"There's nothing quite like a welcoming committee," he grumbled. "What do I do now, go in?" He smiled. "Yes, I think I should."

He noticed the clock on the dashboard was slowly creeping towards midnight.

Some of the hatchet-men spotted his vehicle and one pointed, whilst another went inside.

Samson killed the engine and got out. He then turned and poked his head back inside. "I'm going in. As soon as your mother gets here, tell her to drive off. Do *not* wait for me." He gave Charlie the keys to the Jeep and his flat. "Tell your mum to go to my place. Got it?"

The young girl had tears in her eyes. "I'm scared!" she whispered.

"There's no need to be. Nobody's looking to hurt you or your mum—it's me they're after." He managed a weak smile and reached a hand over the passenger's seat to wipe the tears from her cheeks. "Your mum will be here before you know it."

Samson shut the door and walked toward the heavies awaiting him. He knew there would be no pleasantries. He stepped off the pavement, meandered across the road to the other side and dug his cigarillo tin out of his breast pocket. Samson popped one into his mouth.

He found himself standing before five brunos

varying in shape, size, hair length and how many times they'd had their beezers smashed. *Like walking into a den of Mike Tyson's!* he thought, blowing smoke into their faces.

"Evening," he smiled. "And which one of you pretty little muffins do I check in with?"

"Get a hold of this prick!" one of them said. Samson felt rough hands on him all at once, grabbing his arms and holding him tight. "Not so tough now, are you, Action Man?" He slugged Samson in the guts.

Samson doubled over, clutching at his middle. Groaning, he straightened up, took a drag on his cigarillo and blew smoke into the man's face. "Is that all you've got, princess?"

Not so sure I could take another off him, he mused. *Guy's built like a brick shit house.*

"Get this fuck out of my sight!"

"*Charming*," said Samson as he was dragged away, flanked by the four bruisers, leaving the fifth to stand guard. "So, where are you wise guys taking me?" His question fell on deaf ears. "Is there a need to drag me? I'm capable of walking."

Someone punched him in the small of his back. His legs buckled, and he dropped his cigarillo. Samson winced through the pain that travelled through him and settled in his guts. "Oh, you snake," he said between gritted teeth.

"Shut the fuck up! Or there'll be more where that came from, mate."

Palooka! he thought. *They're tough in a crowd.*

Somewhere close by a door clicked open. "Bring

him in here," a voice called.

Samson recognised where he was being dragged to—it had been the same door he'd been standing outside of the last time he'd been here, where he had managed to get all the juicy information with his recorder.

The thugs rushed him inside and hustled him into a chair. Pain radiated through the bones in Samson's arse, but he didn't complain, just smiled.

"You boys can leave the room."

The Anthill Mob rushed out the door and closed it behind them. When Samson looked up, he noticed the voice was coming from behind a chair that had its back to him. "You've been quite the pest, Mr. Valentine."

Samson was sat round a large oak table with three other people. To his left was Slots, to his right, Big O. At the far end sat Roxie. She didn't appear tied, but she looked terrified. Tears were streaming down her face. She trembled like a leaf.

"What is this?" Samson said. "More bullshit scare tactics? I've got your goddamn number-stuffed-diamond, palooka, so why don't you take the bloody thing and stop this game of Tic, Tac, Toe. This isn't Gangster's Paradise, and you're not some Al Capone of Cardiff. You're just another smartass who thinks he's some tough nut. I've seen your type many times."

"I admire your gumption, Mr. Valentine, and that's why I'm prepared to let you and the girl walk. As it happens, you've managed to serve me rather well."

"Yeah? Good. I'm so thrilled to hear that. So, why don't you take Laurel and Hardy here," he said, indicating Slots and Big O, "and crawl back under the rock you've been hiding under, *X*."

"Why are you being so obtuse and bull-headed, Mr. Valentine? I've just told you I'm prepared to let you go. *Both* of you. There is no fight here, sir; you've helped me achieve what I wanted. My superior, too."

"*Huh*?! You're not...?"

"I'm afraid not, sir." The man in the chair turned to face Samson. "Like the fine gentlemen at your sides I, too, am just a cog in XRay's machine."

From behind him, Jim stepped out of the shadows. "You've killed quite a few of our men, but we're willing to forgive and forget. Just give us the stone and we'll allow you to go. It's that simple."

"And what about poor ole' Steve? You battered the living hell out of him and threatened to torch his bar. Where's his sorry? *Huh*?!" Samson slammed his hands down on the table. "What about the girl found dead in Vampire's apartment? You sons of bitches."

Big O and Slots grabbed Samson's hands and pinned them to the table.

"Calm down, Mr. Valentine. We realise that the dead whore in Vampire's flat was a friend of yours. Her family has been compensated. We're not animals, Mr. Valentine, we're businessmen, and when errors are made we correct them. Steve, your friend, will also be remunerated. We just want our property back."

"How did your apes make such a mistake by getting my sorry arse dragged into this mess?"

Jim went to speak, but the unknown man in the chair slowly stood up. "It was no mistake, Mr. Valentine. You were chosen."

"*What?*"

"We sought a man like you—a highly skilled individual with a proven track record. Our intentions at first were to send Vampire to the station, but we knew he would have been out-muscled by the thugs who tackled you there."

"Are you *serious*? Why not send help along with Vampire? You do realise Alligator's thugs knew me? What a coincidence, eh? It really is a small world, and never have I been so sought after."

The man shook his head, smiling. "We could have sent him with help, but it would have been too conspicuous. Not only that, the item you have in your possession is extremely hot property—it's being hunted down as we speak."

"How come? Alligator's dead. I'm sure his organisation's down the pan."

"Come, Mr. Valentine. His organisation has taken a slight blow, that's all. He has high-ranking officers who are capable of taking over, but we hope to have that under control by the end of next week. Not only that, but there are others out there who know about the stone."

"A seek and destroy mission, eh?"

The man smiled. "Something like that, yes. It shouldn't take much to mop up his men—most can be bought, I dare say."

"I—" Samson tried to speak, but was cut off.

"Just give us the stone, sir. If we have to take it from you by force, then I will have my men cut you, the girl and the child stashed in your car into tiny pieces and fed to the pigs in the basement. Please, don't let it come to that."

"How could I refuse such a pretty offer? I have it right here in my pocket. Now, if your goons—"

Big O and Slots removed their hands from Samson, allowing him to dig the stone out of his pocket. He held it up for them to see.

"Before I hand this over," he went on, "I want to know if the numbers inside are the missing warhead codes."

The men exchanged nervous glances. "What's it to you, Mr. Valentine?"

"I want to know *what* I'm handing over. If they're merely the codes to the locks on your travel luggage, then take it, but I'm assuming they're not, and that they are indeed the warhead codes. If so, then I'm afraid…"

"Afraid what? Why don't you enlighten us, sir? Because one way or the other, we're taking that stone."

"If they are, then I *can't* let you have them. God only knows what you're capable of."

"It's none of your concern, sir."

"My worry is this: I think you're planning to jumpstart World War Three. Who do you plan to nuke? The Russians? Chinese? Americans? After all, there's a lot of profit to be made in war, isn't there? Or do you bastards plan on selling them to the highest bidder? The only thing I can't understand is how. Don't you have to have codes sent to you by another individual to activate the arsenal? Can't the army change them? Then again, you probably have someone on the inside there, too. Please, stop me if I'm wrong."

The man smiled. "Very good, Mr. Valentine—and they told me you'd be a waste of time; that your whisky-soaked brain would be too slow in thinking. I guess you were underestimated, which may be your downfall. I mean, can we really let you out of here knowing what you do? The girl, too."

"I just say it as I see it, boob, and I'm willing to make a trade with you for the girl's life and mine." Samson knew full well he had them by the balls, that their operation would be sunk come tomorrow night. The only thing he was worried about was that it would be too late by then—that the codes would have changed hands. How deep did the river of shit run? Who else was involved? Members of parliament? High-ranking military officers? Was there even a way of stopping it? He had to try.

Before they could answer, Samson spoke again. "You have the army in your pocket?"

"Yes. Well, certain individuals, Mr. Valentine. Getting a hold of further information required to detonate the nukes will not be a problem. This thing runs far deeper than you could expect, sir. It's way over *our* heads. And call me Harris, since we're doing business, such as it is."

"Yeah, you're just a number on a payroll, I get it. Now, what say you let me and the girl go, Harris?

You've got what you want. Your competition is also on its knees thanks to me."

"Let me think—"

"Then let her go. I'll stay."

"Sam, no!" Roxie blurted, tears streaming down her face.

"Hmm, interesting, but why would you want to die for a whore, Mr. Valentine? Surely you should be pitching me the idea of wasting her and you working for us?"

Here we go again! he thought. *You palookas never learn.* "Let her go and I'll be your little lapdog. I'll feed you inside information, informants, the lot… I'm prepared to bend over and take it in the glory hole if you spare Roxie. She has a young daughter, for Christ's sake. I'm not going anywhere. Have me. That was going to be my deal, anyway."

Harris rubbed his chin as he thought it over. "Okay, release her."

"But Harris, shouldn't we discuss it with X first?" Jim said, placing a hand to the man's shoulder.

"No, it'll be fine. We're not going to let this one out of our sight. Go on, Roxie. You're free to go."

Tentatively, she pushed her chair back and got up to walk away. Samson smiled and nodded at her. "Charlie's in the Jeep across the street. She knows what to do. I'll be fine."

All she could do was sniffle in response.

"Give her a phone," Samson demanded. "I want Roxie to ring here once she's pulled away and is safe. And don't you bastards tail her. Got it? Or I'm out. No deal."

"Jim," Harris said, "sort her out."

Jim did as he was instructed and gave her his phone. "You'll find Harris' number in the speed dial. If it was my choice, you'd both be dead."

"Sam..." she blubbered.

"Get outta here, kid. Go! Charlie needs you."

"How touching," Harris said.

Samson glared at the man. "Keep flapping, jug head."

Roxie walked out the door and closed it behind her. Samson heard her rushing footfalls as she ran down the hall.

"You know full well we can't let her live, Samson. When we're done here, we'll hunt her down and kill her. That's the way it has to be. Sorry. No hard feelings, yeah?" Harris nodded. Big O and Slots got up and walked over to the door, blocking any chance at escape. "We'll allow her to think she's safe for the next day or two before pouncing."

"You cold-hearted monsters!" Samson clenched his jaw until it clicked.

"And if you think you're going to prevent this, or dig your heels in and not cooperate, then you're wrong, my friend. I have nasty ways of breaking people, of bending them until they think my way." Harris smirked.

"Think you're pretty damn clever, don't you?" Samson growled.

"The stone, Samson."

"Take the bloody thing!" He shoved it into the

man's hand. "Now, with that out of the way, mind if I stand up and stretch my legs?"

"By all means," Harris said.

Samson's heartbeat kicked up a few notches. He balled his hands into fists and prepared himself for something he knew was going to hurt like hell.

If I'm going down I'm taking at least one of these bastards with me!

The phone on the table rang.

As Jim picked the phone up to speak, Samson bull-charged Harris. He grabbed him by his expensive suit jacket and propelled him backwards and out the window.

The drop to the floor outside the window was longer than Samson had anticipated. He cushioned the fall by landing atop Harris, but the shock was hell on his legs, which radiated dull hurt from his ankles to his hips.

Harris did not take the fall quite as well. He had landed wrong, the crown of his head hitting the ground first. It caused his neck to bend at an extreme angle and snap under the force of their impact. Blood fanned out of the mess of twisted bone and sinew that was once the man's neck.

"Get him, fuckers!" Jim shouted from the room above.

Samson was slow getting to his feet. He hobbled in a bent-over posture and scooped up the stone in mid-stride, limping away as fast as his throbbing legs could carry him.

Chapter 24

Still reeling from the fall, Samson staggered down the alley. The shock of that last blow had left his head spinning and his legs wobbly. He ducked into the shadows around the dock area and heaved his guts up. But despite how banged up it had left him, his gambit had paid off: the stone was safe in his pocket once again.

I need to get to Roxie!

Samson heard men shouting in the distance. He pushed off the wall he was leaning against and ran into the night.

Out on the main street, Samson put a brick through a window of a four-by-four that had a decorative bull bar. It was an old model with no alarm system.

After opening the door and hopping inside, he tore the panel from underneath the steering column and hot-wired the vehicle. Once the engine growled to life, Samson threw the gear into reverse and floored it, smashing the back end of his vehicle into a car behind him. He wrestled the Jeep out of the tight space and punched the gas, headed for his flat.

He whizzed through speed cameras but slowed when he saw good ole' boys parked at the side of the road—he couldn't afford to be stopped now; there wasn't time for explanations.

When his street came into view, he noticed a Land Rover pulling up outside his building, its windows blacked out. A goon exited, confirming Samson's fears.

Roxie might *not be here yet. What if she's gone elsewhere?*

The goon walked around to the back of the Jeep, and that's when Samson saw Roxie's vehicle moving up the street towards the hatchet-man.

Without thinking, Samson put his foot down on the accelerator, ploughing into the back of the goon's four-by-four, crushing the man who'd been standing between both vehicles. His screams were cut short as blood splashed onto Samson's windshield.

Samson got out and ran toward Roxie, waving his hands over his head. As he passed the vehicle he'd ploughed into, Samson saw the driver hanging out the windscreen.

"Jesus…"

"Get in!" Roxie screamed.

He threw himself into the passenger's seat, and Roxie tore off into the night.

"What was that all about?" she asked. "Where did you come from?"

"They were sent here to kill you, Roxie—they had no intention of letting you go." He produced the stone from his pocket and showed her. "We've got to go to the hospital."

"What? Why?"

"We need to get Steve out of there. Step on it, Roxie, a man's life's in danger. I'm sure they'll try and eliminate everyone close to me."

"And then what? We can't keep running."

Samson removed a phone from his pocket. "They never searched me. I have the whole conversation recorded. I plan to ring my friend later and get this whole thing shut down. They're finished. Dead in the water. We just need to get Steve and lay low."

"Any ideas where we can go, Sam?"

"Yes, Steve has a holiday home somewhere."

Their conversation turned to tense silence as Roxie concentrated on driving. Samson settled in his seat. In the back, Charlie was curled into a ball, sleeping—she'd missed the whole episode outside Samson's apartment complex.

All the better for her, Samson thought.

Twenty minutes later, they were outside Cardiff hospital.

"Keep the engine running. If you see someone or something suspicious, get the hell out of here. Don't wait for me. If we do get separated, I'll meet you back at that hotel we checked into, got it?"

Roxie nodded.

Samson got out and walked into the hospital.

The receptionist eyeballed him as he approached.

"Hi, I'm here to see a Mr. Steve Jackson—it's a matter of urgency," said Samson.

"Sir, visiting hours are between—"

"I'm with the police, ma'am." He flashed her his badge, not giving the nurse a good enough chance to see it. "As I said, this is a matter of urgency. Where is Mr. Jackson?"

"But..."

"Please, Miss!" he pressed her. "Where?"

"Second floor, fourth corridor along," she

answered, consulting with the computer on her desk. "Room 209."

"Thanks."

Causally, he walked over to the elevators and took one to the second floor. When he got out, he noticed the hallway was clear—not a nurse, doctor or patient in sight.

He took the fourth corridor as instructed then searched for the room he needed, which was towards the end. The door was closed, so Samson grabbed the handle and plunged it downwards as quietly as he could.

The door didn't as much squeak when he pushed it inwards. The lights in Steve's room were out, making it a good sign. For a few seconds, Samson stood and listened. He could hear a fan whirring, but nothing else. In the corner of the room, he could see a red light blinking, which he took to be the TV.

"Steve?" he whispered. The further he walked into the blackness, the louder his friend's rhythmic breathing became. His hand searched the wall, finding a light switch. "Sorry, good buddy."

"*Huh*! Hey! Who's there?!" Steve gasped, sitting up in bed. His face was looking better, despite still being terribly smashed up.

"Steve, calm down. It's me. Samson."

"*Jesus*!"

"I'm here to get you out, friend."

"Are you mad? Look at me!"

"I'm not planning on entering you in a bloody beauty contest. This is a matter of life and death, palooka." Samson went to the wardrobe and removed Steve's clothes. "Get dressed, you have five minutes. There could be brunos outside as we speak."

"What on Earth have you…?"

"Get dressed! I'll fill you in on our way to your holiday home. It's the only place I can think of where we can be safe. Now *move*! I'll wait outside the door."

Samson left the room, looked at his watch and tapped his foot. "Come on, come on." He started to pace the corridor, keeping his ears pricked for the slightest sound of trouble. Nothing moved.

Steve appeared at his door in short order. He was hunched over, and unable to move fast. In his hand, he held a carrier bag.

"What have you got there? A packed lunch?" asked Samson.

"*No!* You know something? I wouldn't be looking like this if you hadn't fucked with—"

"Pipe down! We've got to get moving. Take my arm."

Steve didn't argue, instead he grabbed Samson as roughly as he could.

"Good. Now, let's go."

He led his friend towards the elevators and rode one to the bottom floor. When the lady at reception saw them approach, she left her post to try and stop them.

"Keep walking," Samson whispered to Steve.

"*Hey!* You can't take him out of here, sir. *Sir?*"

"Sorry, Miss," he answered her, "but this is a police matter."

The young woman didn't bother getting in Samson's way. Instead, she ran back behind her desk and picked up the phone. "Security!"

That was all Samson heard her say, as they were outside and approaching their ride.

"Get in!" Roxie said.

Samson helped Steve into the backseat next to Charlie, and then got in the front. "Drive, Roxie."

She pulled off as his door slammed closed.

There had been little in the way of discussion as Roxie drove. It consisted mostly of Samson telling the others how it was going to go down.

Steve's holiday home would serve them well. It was an out of the way place, nestled in the middle of Canaston Woods, west Wales—quite literally a cabin in the armpit of nowhere. They made a quick stop at Steve's place to pick up the keys to the cabin, then continued on their way, hurtling down the M4 corridor towards Pembrokeshire.

"When we get there, Sam, what are we going to do?" Roxie looked over her shoulder and saw Charlie and Steve were sleeping.

"I told you, I'll ring my friend. He might be out of the force, but he's still got a lot of pull. He'll take it beyond the top."

"What's that supposed to mean, 'beyond the top'?"

"He knows people in much higher places. People he trusts. You see, he's like me—he only wants what's best for our city, and hates crime, especially when it's organised. Everything will be fine, you'll see."

"I trust you, Sam. You've kept me and Charlie safe so far."

He put his hand out and rested it on top of hers, which was on the gear stick. "Let's get there first—we can work the details out tomorrow."

"Agreed, Sam."

"Are you okay if I close my eyes until we arrive? I'm not going to be any good to anyone if I'm half dead on my feet."

"Not at all. You go right ahead."

Samson pulled his hat over his eyes, slipped down in his seat and turned to rest his head against the window. Within seconds, he was fast asleep.

Some while later he awoke to the sound of Steve and Roxie talking—he seemed to be giving her directions. The Jeep was rocking violently, suggesting they'd left the motorway and were headed down a rough trail. Samson peeled his face off the glass and looked up.

"We close?" Samson croaked.

"We're at the woods, Samson," Steve told him. "Roxie, you want your next left, but take it easy—there are a lot of potholes around this part." As he spoke, the Jeep shook with tremendous force. "If we get bogged down there's no getting out. We'll have to abandon ship."

"How do you own a place out here, Steve? I thought they were cutting most of this place down?" Samson asked.

"They are, but I was here first, so there's not much they can do. A few years ago, some hotshot businessman tried buying me out, but I wouldn't budge. He even offered me property elsewhere, but I didn't want it. This cabin has been in my family for generations, there was no way I was giving it up, and so they had no option but to tear the woods down around it."

"Surprised the palookas didn't just knock it down by 'accident.'"

"If that should happen, then I'll sue them for everything they've got, and they know that. Next left, Roxie. Once you get to the end, take the right and then your fourth right."

Roxie did as instructed. Soon, a large log cabin crossed the Jeep's headlights. For a structure that had been standing for as long as Steve said it had, it looked in good shape.

"Is there a phone inside?" Samson asked.

"No," Steve said.

"Doesn't matter, Sam—I have my mobile," Roxie answered.

"Seeing as I have the keys, I'll go and open up, Steve. I'll come back for Charlie and carry her in." Samson stepped out and slowly walked over to the cabin. He stayed within the Jeep's headlights, so he could see where he was treading. *The last thing I need right now is to twist my ankle!*

When he got to the door, he stood to one side of it and dug the keys out. He pushed the door wide and stepped over the threshold. It smelt a little musty inside, but that was to be expected.

The light from behind him illuminated parts of the inside. Samson found a light switch to his right and flipped it up. A warm, welcoming milky glow drenched the room, giving Samson a much better view. It was clean and tidy—nothing seemed out of place.

He turned around on the porch and signalled for them to sit tight. Then he then went in and gave the one-level property a thorough search. Whilst he was at it, Samson lit a fire. He then went back to the Jeep for Charlie.

He opened the back door and gently cradled the teen in his arms.

"What was wrong inside?" Roxie asked.

"Nothing, I just wanted to check it out before you came in. Steve, can you manage, or do you want me to come back and help you?"

"A little help—"

"I can manage with Steve, Sam. Just get my girl inside."

Samson nodded, turned and walked over to the cabin as quickly as he could. Once indoors, he placed the girl on the fleece-covered sofa, removed his coat and draped it over her.

As he straightened, Roxie was helping Steve inside, so he went to them and closed the door behind them.

"Put me in the chair," Steve said between clenched teeth. "Jesus, my ribs are killing me."

"Do you have painkillers here, Steve?" Samson asked.

"There should be some in the cupboard above the sink. Mind getting me a glass of water while you're at it, Samson?"

"Of course. Get yourself settled."

Samson went to the kitchen and returned with a tumbler of water and tablets. "Roxie, you may need to make a run to a shop in the morning to get some supplies. Cupboards are bare."

"I've not been up here in months," Steve admitted. The pain he was in was evident on his face. Samson watched as the man rooted through his bag and removed a couple of boxes of tablets. Samson handed him the water. "Thanks." He popped pills into his mouth and washed them down.

"I think the best thing you and Steve can do, Roxie, is get some shut eye. I'm going to make that phone call, see if I can get this mess straightened out so we can go on living our lives," Samson said. "Can I borrow your phone?"

Roxie handed it to him. Samson rang the ex-chief of police, pacing the room as he waited for him to answer.

"Adam?" Samson spoke into the phone before the man even had time to announce himself. "It's Valentine. Listen, I'm in deeper since we last spoke, friend, and I need your help more than ever. Did you receive my mail?"

"Yes, of course," the ex-chief replied, but was cut short just as quickly.

"Great!" Samson spoke over him. "I had all kinds of worry going on. Look, I don't have much time. I'm laying low at the moment, but I've got more evidence I need to send your way. I need to meet you at the Sarn service station out on the M4."

"Out in Bridgend?"

"Yeah. Midday. See you then." Samson ended

the call and offered the phone back to Roxie.

"No," she said, waving his hand away. "You keep it for now. Sounds like you're going to need it."

Samson pocketed the mobile and flopped into a chair opposite the sofa.

"Everything fine, Sam?" she asked.

"Yes. Adam's a good man, and he's concerned about our wellbeing. Also, he's on the phone to his people as we speak. Now, try and get some sleep. This will be all over soon."

Chapter 25

"The *swines*!" Samson stood up and slapped his thigh as he watched the morning news. The images on the TV showed the Jazz Hole ablaze. A few minutes before that, the broadcast had been talking about Samson's apartment complex, and how that had suffered the same fate as Steve's bar. According to the news, there'd been a so-called 'rash of fires' across the city.

"What's going on?" Steve croaked. Before Samson had time to change the channel, Steve clapped eyes on the broadcast. "Oh, Jesus! Is that my bar?"

Samson hung his head. "I'm sorry, Steve. I truly am."

"My..." Steve clutched his side and crumpled in his seat. "*Argh*! My ribs. *Fuck*!"

"Take it easy, Steve, we'll sort it out."

"That's my livelihood going up in smoke, Samson! I told you not to mess with them. Didn't I?"

"We can't allow ourselves to be pushed around by hoodlums. They're not above the law. And if we continue to allow them to do so, then the problem is only going to intensify. We have them by the balls, and they're going down. This is their way of lashing out in frustration—we've disappeared into the night with a pile of evidence that'll rip their organisation down to the ground."

"Don't start giving me that 'one good cop in a bad town' crap! They own Cardiff, the government and the police force, Sam. Wake up, man."

"Steve, cool it. Please. I've been in this game a long time, and I know what's what."

Steve's cold expression melted somewhat as Samson's words sank in. He had known the gumshoe long enough to recognize that he spoke the truth. What's more, he knew Samson was a poor loser—if the criminals eventually won, it would not be for Samson's lack of effort.

"Morning, boys," Roxie chirped as she stretched and got up from the sofa. The news had changed topics. "Did I miss something?"

"No," Samson answered. He and Steve exchanged furtive glances.

"Well, all right," she said, heading for the kitchen. A few moments later, she called out, "I've found some coffee and dried milk. Anyone interested?"

"Aye, I'll have one," Samson said.

"Me, too," Steve answered.

"Have you got another vehicle here, Steve?"

He shook his head. "Why, what are you thinking?"

"I could be gone a few days, and you're going to need some supplies."

"Ach." Steve waved his hands. "There's a shop a couple of miles from here. We'll be fine. Just go and do what you have to, and get us out of this bloody fuck-up."

"Yeah..." Samson got up and went out to the

kitchen. He helped Roxie with the cuppas, taking his into the bathroom. He stripped to the waist and gave himself a once-over whilst taking sips from his mug. His body was bruised and bloody all over.

I'm too old for this shit, he thought. Once he was finished, Samson headed back into the kitchen and placed his empty cup in the sink. He bade Roxie and Steve farewell, and told them to keep hidden, that he'd be back as soon as everything was under control. Roxie kissed him, thanking him once again for everything he had done for them.

"Thank me when it's all said and done," Samson said. "Take care of yourselves." He walked out, got into the Jeep and pulled away.

As he drove, he suddenly started to worry. Did someone know where he'd stashed them? Was there anyone else involved? Panic got the better of him, causing Samson to pull over and consider driving back to the cabin to make sure everything was okay.

But he managed to calm himself, along with his raging thoughts. *It would be impossible for anyone to know anything. Nobody followed us, and I made sure to ditch Roxie's tracking device. And why would Steve be in on it? That's stupid talk.*

"They burned his bar down, Sam," Angie chimed in. *"If Steve was leaking information to them, then why would they do that to him?"*

True, Angie, unless they were proving a point. But no, I doubt it—they gave the man a beating of a lifetime. I couldn't see Steve siding with thugs who did that to him. And Roxie? No, she was playing everything straight. Definitely. I know things about people. The drive to the Sarn service station took less than two hours, which was pretty good for that time of morning. At nine o'clock, Samson had expected to hit a pile of work traffic, but it was light, and he was thankful.

He arrived at eleven-thirty, which gave him enough time to pop inside for a piss, and grab a coffee and bacon roll. He then headed over to the section of the car park the truckers used.

When he got there, Samson saw a car parked between two rigs towards the far end. Its headlights flashed. That was the signal he'd been expecting. Samson rolled his vehicle up beside Adam's and cranked his window down.

"*Samson!*" said the ex-chief, smiling. "So good to see you after all these years, lad. You've been keeping yourself *in* trouble, I see?" Time had turned the man's head of hair completely silver and wrinkled his face like old leather, but despite this, Samson could still see that spark of mischief in his eyes.

"Always, sir. How's Eileen?"

His smile faltered. "The Lord saw fit to take her from me two summers ago, Samson. Heart attack."

"I'm sorry to hear that."

"Don't be. She was a good woman. The *best*. She did right by me, and I was there with her at the end."

"Just like my Angie." He shook his head.

"I'm glad you reached out, Samson."

"Oh?"

The glint in Adam's eye became strong, tangible,

almost. "You think I'm happy spending my days twiddling my thumbs? I've missed active duty and the chance to tangle with death and danger, and by the looks of your face, you've seen a fair bit of it lately. Well, I want in. I'm ready for one last hoorah."

Samson smiled. "This will be one *big* hoorah, sir. We have the chance to do something special."

"Yeah, we have the chance to dismantle the whole corrupt fucking department!"

The man's vehemence caught Samson by surprise—not once had he heard Adam curse, let alone say a bad word against the force. But he guessed everyone had their limits.

"What's the plan?" Samson asked.

"We'll start with this new information you have. Where is it?"

Samson dug the camera out of his pocket, sought out the video recording he was after and played it for Adam.

"Oh, we have this lot by the short and curlies, Samson, my boy. Do you remember Frank Bowman? Used to work with the firearms unit? He was around your age."

"Yeah, but didn't he get out of the game?"

"No, they moved him to a special branch. He became a Captain. Like us, he's clean, and will help take this lot down. Frank will be able to rally a weapons unit to assist us at the docks tonight—he's already been informed."

"Won't he need authorisation?"

Adam shook his head. "No, the man runs the

show. Also, I've gone over the new chief of police's head and taken the stuff you sent me to a member of parliament. He's an influential man at Scotland Yard. Turns out, they've known about Davis for some time, but haven't been able to catch him with his drawers down. This is our moment, Samson."

"So, how do we play it?"

"The good ole'-fashioned way—we're going to crash their party with a bang."

Samson smiled. "Nobody likes an unexpected guest."

Both men laughed.

"I'm glad to see you still have that sense of humour of yours," added Samson.

"Waiting in the wings for the grim reaper will never dampen my spirits, lad. Now, follow me."

"Where are we going?"

"Back to my place. Frank is waiting. We're going to map out a plan for tonight. The bastards won't see us coming."

***

Adam lived on a well-respected street on the outskirts of Cardiff, where the houses went for an arm and a leg. His home came with a driveway, massive front garden and a two-car garage.

When they pulled onto the driveway, Samson noticed a car parked there. A man was leaning casually against it. Samson recognized him immediately, though it had been many years since he'd seen him—Frank Bowman. He was a squat man, with wide shoulders and a bull-like neck. The years hadn't changed him at all.

Samson, Frank and Adam exchanged brief pleasantries before heading into Adam's home for an in-depth discussion about what Samson had managed to uncover.

Once inside, Samson played the recording for Frank, who then informed Samson and Adam that he had two units on stand-by in preparation for this evening.

"My men have been hand-picked for this," Frank said. "There are no bad apples, I can assure you of that. I can get them into position an hour before we swoop in."

"Do you have a sniper in your unit?" Samson asked.

"Two, why?"

"We may need them. Will your men be on the ground?"

"Yes, with some of them blending in as tramps or worker-types. XRay's thugs won't know a thing."

"Excellent," Samson said. "I want feathers well and truly ruffled, so when word gets out, the rest of the palookas on our streets will know Samson Valentine is back to his best. I need to make sure I arrest XRay, along with Davis and the rest of the goons."

"But nobody knows who XRay is," Adam said.

"If this deal's as big as I think it is, then I'm sure he'll be there, along with his senior soldiers. The thing is they're not going to expect me to turn up, not after what's happened, so it will throw them completely off-kilter."

"You don't think they expect this move?" Adam asked.

"Definitely not! They think I'm a washed-up booze hound who's good for nothing."

"What if things turn ugly?" Frank asked.

"Then you and your men step in. Quash the whole thing."

"I think you should go in as the deal is being done, Sam," Adam said. "That way we'll have 'em dead to rights."

"I agree," Samson said. "We need to make sure we do it right." The others nodded. "Let's go over it again." Samson looked down at the map of the dockyard Adam had spread across the kitchen table. As they went through their plan for a second time, Adam broke out the whisky and cigars.

The rest of the day was spent organising their tactics and sipping booze, especially Samson, who had more than one too many. By ten o'clock it was time for them to leave, with Samson feeling a tipsy.

When they arrived at a street close to the docks, it was just past ten-thirty. A few seconds later, a couple of unmarked Transit vans pulled up alongside them filled with Frank's men.

The back doors to the vans opened and out popped a dozen or so blokes from each—some were wearing high-visibility jackets, boots and work helmets, whilst others wore tattered clothes and fingerless gloves. Frank briefed his men, then ordered them to take up positions.

Samson and Adam got out of the car and joined Frank. On the other side of the houses, they could hear the thump of cranes and rumble of heavy trucks.

"Right, I'm getting myself over there," Samson heard himself slur, the whisky kicking in like never before. Frank and Adam appeared not to notice. "You pair, keep your distance—I don't want either of you getting hurt. Frank, on my signal, get your team to pounce. If there's any sign of guns, you know what to do."

Frank nodded. "I'm going to take up a position as close to the shipyard as possible."

"I'm coming with you, Samson," Adam said.

Frank gave them a stiff nod and left.

"Come on then, let's get this over with," Samson said.

***

The night was dry and mild, but the rain from earlier had left its damp mark, with puddles of water dotted along the roads and pavements. As they neared the dockyard, Samson could sense a buzz of activity—forklift trucks were lined up near a ship that had docked, and lorries with their back doors open were waiting to be loaded.

Nobody noticed Samson and Adam. The workers were too busy, too distracted to care, allowing the pair to move deeper into the lion's den until they were close enough to see a group of men standing by the ship that was now being unloaded.

The pair took cover behind crates and peeked out.

"I *know* that man on the far left!" Adam whispered. "It's Popov Smyrnoi—the biggest arms dealer in the world. God, if we can net him…"

"Look, there's Davis and a couple of XRay's goons," said Samson.

"Who are they?"

"They go by the names of Big O, Slots and Jim. However, I'm not sure who the other two are."

"You can bet your bottom buck they aren't unloading vodka, Sam. This is some nice work. They never should have kicked you off the force, heavy-handed or not."

"Do you have that walkie-talkie Frank gave you?"

Adam fished the small radio out of his pocket and gave it to Samson. "Frank, do you copy me? The palookas are unloading down here and a huge sum of cash has just traded hands—the deal's been made. On my signal, get your men into position, over."

"Copy that!" Frank responded.

"Right, here goes…"

Samson felt the cool metal of a muzzle against his temple.

"Get up!" someone instructed. "You too, old man!"

Samson was grabbed roughly by his coat and pulled to his feet. "*Move!*" The muzzle was rammed into his back. Alongside him, Adam stood with his arms raised in surrender as a gunman ordered him out of his hiding place.

Samson looked over his shoulder, his vision slanting, and noticed there were four men with Tommy guns—their faces hidden beneath trilby hats and shadows.

What's going on? Is this real? I've been off the booze—I've sobered up! Angie, are you with me?

No reply.

Wait. The booze at Adam's...

"Take it easy, bruno, we're moving," Samson said to his captors.

Once Samson was forced out of hiding by the chopper squad, he found the dock had changed: gone were the ships, modern day forklift trucks, lorries and workers dressed in twenty-first century clothing. All he could see were gangsters in tailored suits, well-polished, two-toned shoes and trilby hats; they were well-armed, toting shotguns, Tommy guns and .38 snub-nosed revolvers.

"What's going on, Adam?" Samson said, turning to his friend. But there were only thugs around him.

"Get fucking moving!" one of the hop-heads barked, shoving him in the back.

It was obvious where he was being frog-marched to. As soon as he got within feet of Davis and the rest of the dapper jug heads, they turned to look at him.

"*Samson*! How nice of you to drop by," Davis smiled. "I take it you didn't bring the stone with you?"

Samson shook his head.

"That's such a shame, because now I'm going to

have to kill the girl and Steve," he said, smiling. "That stone, as you know, contains sensitive information. I was going to hand it over to my Russian friend here as partial payment for lots of lovely guns."

"Best of luck, palooka! I've stashed them."

"Yeah, Canaston woods, right? I sent a team over there earlier today." The D.I. grinned wider, causing Samson to clench his teeth. "Never took you as the trusting kind, Sam. Surely you must have known Steve would break? Once we'd told him about his bar going up flames, and that he'd be sleeping with the fishes real soon, he cried like a little girl. People are easy to scare."

"You paid him a visit at the hospital?"

The D.I. crossed his arms and gave him a smug look.

"You don't have to kill them; I can get you your property. Call your dogs off, *XRay*!"

Davis laughed at Samson, his men too. "Wrong again, Samson…"

"Oh, knock it off. I've known for the last couple of days—you're the man pulling the strings. The whole errand boy mask isn't working, pal. And what's with the 40s get-up? Trying to muddle my mind further? Ain't going to work."

"Huh?" Davis said, looking perplexed, and then shook his head. "So, what was the grand plan? Come down here and arrest us?"

His men laughed.

"Think you're so damn smart, don't you?" Samson bared his teeth.

"Such a shame what's become of you—I hate to tell you this, but there's no such person as XRay. I don't know how you've got it into your head, but…"

"Oh, cut the crap! We both know he exists."

"I suppose you really think you were taken to a man's farm and watched as Mr. Barnes was force-fed to an Alligator?" Davis and his men laughed. "I'm behind it all, Sam. Me. There never was a Mr. and Mrs. Barnes, Alligator or anyone or anything else you cooked up in your head. You've spent the last few days evading my capture by hiding in the fucking woods! Do you know how hard it's been to find you?"

"*No!*" Samson roared, spittle flying from his lips. "Stop messing with my mind!"

"You belong in a straitjacket, pal."

"You're lying!"

"I haven't any time for your nonsense, Samson. In less than an hour, I'm going to have millions in my bank account, and there's not a damned thing you can do to stop me. You've been outgunned, outwitted and fooled the entire time—and you did it to yourself, Sam, a sorry state of affairs."

"Millions, huh? You make me sick. Swapping nuke codes for hardware and selling your country up the river in the process."

"It doesn't matter about the codes for now—my money will have to be good enough." Davis looked at his watch. "Maybe I should check in with my team at your hideout in the woods, Samson, see how it's going?"

"You—" Samson stepped forward, fists raised, but he was dragged back by Davis' goons.

"See, it's that hot-headed temper of yours that got you kicked…" His phone rang, and he snatched it up to answer the call. "Simmons, is that you? You have the codes? *Excellent.* Bring the woman, child and Steve here with you—Samson can watch them die." Davis hung up. "At least you'll get to see them beg, cry and go out at your feet."

"You're lower than a sewer rat!" Samson had all but given up hope, then he placed his hands in his pocket and felt the radio Frank had given him. *So, this bastard is messing with my head! But where's Adam? Never mind that now.* He pushed the button on the side of the radio, causing it to crackle.

"What was that?" Davis demanded.

"You must think I'm an idiot. I know exactly what's been going on, and you won't fool me by dressing as 40s gangsters. *I'm* the one who's one step ahead, Davis, and I've been off the booze for days."

Frank's men popped out from all the dark spaces around them, weapons drawn and yelling, 'This is the police—put down your guns, you're under arrest!' At that moment, the world seemed to shift before Samson's eyes. No longer were the goons wearing pinstripes and trilbies—they were dressed like run of the mill thugs in T-shirts, tattoos, and jeans.

"Fuck this!" Big O said, drawing his gun. His men scrambled for cover behind shipping crates and opened fire.

"Get me out of here!" the Russian screamed in broken English.

Before Davis could make a break for it, Samson dove on him and pummelled the man's ribs. "I'm taking you in, *pal*!" He yanked Davis' hands behind his back and cuffed him.

All around him, gunfire erupted—men hit the deck as hot lead peppered their bodies. Over his shoulder, Samson was relieved when he saw Adam, who took the Russian to the ground. For an older man, Samson was impressed with the strength he still possessed. The Russian's men tried to aid him, but they were gunned down where they stood by Frank's snipers.

The stench of gun smoke and oil stung Samson's eyes, making it difficult to see what was going on. However, he could see Davis' boys well enough. They laid down their arms and surrendered as Frank's men swarmed to arrest them.

"You son of a bitch!" Davis yelled, his face pressed into the ground from the weight of Samson's body atop him. "You'll burn for this, for what you've done."

"Ah, shut up, palooka," Samson said, giving the man a right hook to his jaw. He lit a cigarillo as he waited for the cavalry to arrive.

"So, there was no XRay after all!"

Angie! You're back. And no, it would appear not.

Samson smiled. *Now that it's all over and I'm off the booze, I can start rebuilding my life and finally move forward.*

"I'm happy to hear you say that, Sam, and for

you to do so, I think I need to say goodbye, my love."

He found it hard to say the word, but knew letting go was the only way forward.

Goodbye, Angie. Know that I'll always love you...

Epilogue

An hour after the gunfight and arrests on the docks, the car carrying Steve, Charlie and Roxie down the M4 had been stopped, their kidnappers apprehended. Thankfully, the police had caught them in time, and Samson's friends had not been harmed. The stone, which had been in the driver's pocket, had been retrieved and the codes handed over to the police, along with the rest of the evidence Adam, Frank and Samson had in their possession.

It took several weeks, but Steve eventually made a full recovery. He sunk his life savings into rebuilding the Jazz Hole, and decided to take an extended holiday while construction was underway. He felt he'd deserved it.

Even though the dank joint would never be quite the same ever again, Samson was glad it was being pieced back together. After all, it was a home away from home, not that he would be dependent on it, or the whisky, ever again.

Once his head was clear, Samson began sorting out the facts from the fantasies his addled mind had generated. The whisky had caused several holes to form in his memory. In time, he knew it would all come back to him. But for the time being, he was happy to let it lie, not wanting to ask too many questions in case it made him look crazy.

"The ole' whisky-addled brain will work itself

out," he'd told himself. "Just got to give it time."

Work picked up for Samson, thanks to him cracking the biggest case of his life. When it had finally gone to court, Davis, along with a few others, had been put behind bars for life, with the D.I. confessing to running the whole operation.

With Davis' gang finally inside a cell, it was time to say goodbye to Roxie and Charlie, who he'd kept safe until things were over. With the money she'd kept, she and her daughter were able to disappear and start their lives anew, away from the criminal element. She'd wanted to tell him where they'd eventually settle, but he'd told her not to say.

"It's safer this way," he'd said. "Go and start your new life."

"I'll never forget you, Sam," had been her parting words as her train pulled out of the station.

"Nor I you, kid," he'd whispered, pulling his coat collar up and turning to leave the platform.

Now, as he walked the streets of Cardiff at two a.m., Samson suddenly had a hankering for pie and coffee, knowing just the place to visit.

"Hi, Alice!" he said, entering the small coffee shop.

She scowled at him.

"I'm sorry about the last time I was in here—I didn't mean to cause so much trouble. Could I grab some elderberry pie and a cup of coffee?" He winked.

"After what you did? Running around the place, half out of your mind and yelling about gangsters? I should throw you out!"

"I am sorry... I was..." He decided to leave it there. "Sorry."

"I don't think my dad would be pleased to see you..."

"Here," Samson said, removing a fifty-pound note from his wallet. "Take this for any damages I may have caused that night. I'm sorry about the frying pan—I had every intention of bringing it back, but some fool burned my flat down."

Somewhat shocked, she took the note from him. "Frying pan? Oh, I—we couldn't accept..."

"Take it," Samson said, balling her hand around it and pushing it away from him. "Now, how about some pie and coffee?" He turned from her and sat at a booth.

"Of course. Sam, is it?"

He nodded. As she walked off he looked out the window—late night people seemed to stroll with casual ease, now that the streets were cleaner. It wasn't perfect out there, but it was getting to where it needed to be. No longer did Samson hear sirens in the background every five seconds. Nor did he hear the screams of people being attacked.

"I *am* the night," he said, smiling.

Alice put his pie and coffee on the table. "No charge, sir. You've paid more than enough."

"Why, thanks, Alice. Now that I'm back on the streets again, you'll be seeing a lot more of me."

"*Great!*" She smiled. "I can't wait. It's always so boring around here at night."

After Samson finished his snack, he took to the streets again, headed towards his new home. He wasn't working a case at the moment, having decided he'd take some time off, and was enjoying his freedom.

With Roxie, Charlie and Angie gone, it's going to get pretty lonely, he thought, walking into the night.

When he got back to his new flat, he went inside and poured himself a glass of lemonade which he took to his new easy chair. He then lit a cigarillo.

"It's about time I had some..." His words trailed off when he saw an envelope poking through his letterbox. His heart raced.

He ripped it open and removed the piece of paper from inside.

"Dear Samson," he read aloud. "You played your part well. Even though you've won the battle, you've *not* won the war. I'm still running my organisation from another location. One day, I shall return to Cardiff, my friend. Until then, be safe.

XRay."

Samson let the note flutter to the floor.

The game had just begun.

The End

Also from Red Cape Publishing

Anthologies:

Elements of Horror Book One: Earth
Elements of Horror Book Two: Air
Elements of Horror Book Three: Fire
Elements of Horror Book Four: Water
A is for Aliens: A to Z of Horror Book One
B is for Beasts: A to Z of Horror Book Two
C is for Cannibals: A to Z of Horror Book Three
D is for Demons: A to Z of Horror Book Four
E is for Exorcism: A to Z of Horror Book Five
F is for Fear: A to Z of Horror Book Six
G is for Genies: A to Z of Horror Book Seven
H is for Hell: A to Z of Horror Book Eight
I is for Internet: A to Z of Horror Book Nine
J is for Jack-o'-Lantern: A-Z of Horror Book Ten
It Came from the Darkness: A Charity Anthology
Castle Heights: 18 Storeys, 18 Stories

Short Story Collections:

Embrace the Darkness by P.J. Blakey-Novis
Tunnels by P.J. Blakey-Novis
The Artist by P.J. Blakey-Novis
Karma by P.J. Blakey-Novis
The Place Between Worlds by P.J. Blakey-Novis
Home by P.J. Blakey-Novis
Short Horror Stories by P.J. Blakey-Novis
Short Horror Stories Vol.2 by P.J. Blakey-Novis
Keep It Inside & Other Weird Tales by Mark Anthony Smith
Everything's Annoying by J.C. Michael
Six! By Mark Cassell

Novelettes:

The Ivory Tower by Antoinette Corvo

Novellas:

Four by P.J. Blakey-Novis
Dirges in the Dark by Antoinette Corvo
The Cat That Caught The Canary by Antoinette Corvo
Bow-Legged Buccaneers from Outer Space by David Owain Hughes
Spiffing by Tim Mendees

Novels:

Madman Across the Water by Caroline Angel
The Curse Awakens by Caroline Angel
Less by Caroline Angel
Where Shadows Move by Caroline Angel
Origin of Evil by Caroline Angel
The Vegas Rift by David F. Gray
The Broken Doll by P.J. Blakey-Novis
The Broken Doll: Shattered Pieces by P.J. Blakey-Novis
South by Southwest Wales by David Owain Hughes

Art Books:

Demons Never Die by David Paul Harris & P.J. Blakey-Novis

Children's Books:

The Little Bat That Could by Gemma Paul
The Mummy Walks at Midnight by Gemma Paul
A Very Zombie Christmas by Gemma Paul
Grace & Bobo: The Trip to the Future by Peter Blakey-Novis
My Sister's from the Moon by Peter Blakey-Novis
Elvis the Elephant by Peter Blakey-Novis

Follow Red Cape Publishing

www.redcapepublishing.com
www.facebook.com/redcapepublishing
www.twitter.com/redcapepublish
www.instagram.com/redcapepublishing
www.pinterest.co.uk/redcapepublishing
www.patreon.com/redcapepublishing
www.ko-fi.com/redcape
www.buymeacoffee.com/redcape